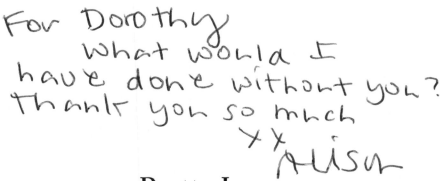

For Dorothy
What would I
have done without you?
Thank you so much
xx
Alison

# Pretty Is
# As Pretty Does

*by Alison Clement*

# Pretty Is
# As Pretty Does

*by Alison Clement*

MacAdam/Cage Publishing

San Francisco ◆ Denver

MacAdam/Cage Publishing
155 Sansome Street, Suite 620
San Francisco, CA 94104
www.macadamcage.com

Library of Congress Cataloging-in-Publication Data

Clement, Alison, 1953 —
    Pretty is as pretty does / Alison Clement.
       p.   cm.
    ISBN: 0-9673701-9-1 (alk. paper)
    1. Beauty contestants — Fiction. 2. Farmers' spouses — Fiction.
    3. Young women — Fiction. 4. Illinois — Fiction. I. Title.

PS3603.L46 P7 2001
813'.6 — dc21                                        2001026695

Manufactured in the United States of America.

10 9 8 7 6 5 4 3 2 1

Cover painting by Mike Young.
Book design by Dorothy Carico Smith.

Author's Note: Even though the town in my story is called Palmyra, Illinois, it doesn't take place in the actual town of that name. It doesn't even take place in Pike County but rather somewhere between Brown and Schuyler Counties. I took liberties with place names using them as I saw fit, based often on the way they sound rather than where they lay on the map.

Publisher's Note: This is a work of fiction. Names, characters, places, and incidents either are the product of the author's imagination or are used fictitiously. Any resemblance to actual events, locales, or persons, living or dead, is entirely coincidental.

Chapter 14 of *Pretty Is As Pretty Does* first appeared as a short story titled "Salt Lick" in *The Alaska Quarterly Review*, 2000.

Chapter 25 first appeared as a short story titled *Trudy Deere Goes to Heaven* in *The Sun* in March 1988.

*For Chuck Willer, my sweetheart,*
*and our kids Charlotte and William*

*Chapter 1*

I knew as soon as I laid eyes on Billy Lee here comes trouble, that's what I said to myself. Here it comes. I was twenty-two and I had just got married, see, and everything was set to go like it should.

Billy's working at Aunt Babe's Cafe. I come in to meet Bob for lunch, but he isn't here yet. It's only me and Virgil in the whole place. I'm sitting at the counter thinking how Bob never was late before but, now that we're married, maybe he thinks he can start right out disappointing me.

So I'm sitting here and I look up but instead of Aunt Babe there's this fellow behind the counter. He doesn't look like anybody you see in Palmyra, Illinois. I tap my fingernails on the countertop, telling him I ain't got all day.

"What can I do for you?" he says, but he says it like he isn't talking about maybe he can pour me a cup of coffee or maybe he can give me a chocolate shake. He leans on the counter. He doesn't even have his little pad to write something down and he's looking me straight in the eye.

"Can I help you?" he says, but he doesn't say it like Aunt Babe does. He says it like it's the nastiest thing you ever heard, but he smiles the whole time, daring you to say a word about it.

I don't answer. I tap my fingernails. I look away. Maybe I forgot he's there. I turn and look at Virgil, over by the window, and then I swing back around finally, and ask, "What's the soup du jour?" But he laughs, like I just proved something about myself that he knew all along, and he says it back, "Du Jour," copying my French accent, and I look at the clock and think where the heck is Bob Bybee. If he thinks I'm the kind of girl he can keep waiting, he's got another thing coming.

Finally I say, "Give me a burger with fries," and he goes over to the little window that looks into the kitchen and he yells, "Burger and fries!" real loud, even though Aunt Babe's is smaller than my own living room and you could about whisper and be heard anywhere.

He starts making coffee, pretending to ignore me, while I forget all about him, but sit sipping my glass of tap water and wishing I'd thought to order a cherry coke like I usually do.

He starts working his way down the counter with a rag but I'm not watching him. He can tell by looking that I'm not just someone who wandered in off the street. And when I leave, Virgil will tell him about my beauty awards. He can see for himself what I look like, but still it's good to have everyone else say it too, for proof.

I pick up the menu and start reading it. I read all through the breakfast menu. Mostly Aunt Babe sells eggs for breakfast. Eggs with toast. Eggs with biscuits. Eggs with biscuits and gravy. Eggs in the snow and eggs in a nest. You can get your eggs any way you want them.

That's what Aunt Babe's menu says. Scrambled, poached, fried, over easy, over hard. Aunt Babe has listed all the possibilities right there on her menu, in case you can't think of them yourself.

There's a breakfast announcement in the menu, clipped in where you can put special things. Usually it'll say blueberry pancakes, but today it says Cowboy Eggs. Usually, like I say, it's blueberry pancakes or sometimes strawberry pancakes and two times it's been Dutch Babies. I haven't never heard of Cowboy Eggs and I sit, trying to imagine what it might mean. It has a wild sound to it and I know it has something to do with this new fellow. I lean over the counter to see does he have cowboy boots or not, but they're just regular brown shoes like anybody from Palmyra might wear.

I turn around on my stool to look out the window at the parking lot, but Virgil's sitting over there eating a bowl of soup and he thinks I'm looking at him. "How's the soup, Virgil?" I call out, to say something, and then I remember I'm not supposed to mention the soup and I take a drink of water and think that if Aunt Babe was working at least I could have a cherry coke.

And then, to prove how much he isn't a gentleman, this new guy says, "And how do you like the soup du jour?" to which Virgil says that he likes it very much. And I turn back and say, "Can't a girl get a cherry coke around here?"

I sit drinking my cherry coke until the food comes. I hear Aunt Babe's voice from the kitchen, "Billy!" so I know that's his name. It's Billy which means William, but he's not a William, he's a Billy, like what she said. Billy slides the food to me and walks away like I'm just one more thing he has to do and now he's done it.

He's doing this on purpose, I can tell. When I leave, Virgil will explain how I'm married and I can just see his face. In other words out of the running. And then he'll hear that I'm married to the richest family in the county, if you don't count the Winklejohns, and that my husband, his family anyway, they about own Aunt Babe's, which is something to do with the way banks work and I don't get it, but that's what I've heard. And he'll think on top of everything else, rich. But what does he expect?

When I'm finished, I push my plate away and he comes over to stand in front of me. He's not tall. He's only a little taller than I am. And he doesn't have a face like the face of Glenn Pinshaw or Teddy Runels or any of the other boys we call handsome. It's a different kind of face, broad and smooth and golden colored. His eyes are black and they hold very still. He doesn't move them around, but just points them where he's looking and they stay there. He has long fingers and big square hands. He moves quietly. He doesn't bang things around the way Babe does.

I think he'll ask me to the picture show over in Beardstown, or to meet him at the swimming pool tomorrow, but instead he pulls out a little notebook and starts writing things down.

"What kind of pie does Aunt Babe have today?" I say.

"She's got rhubarb."

I say, "Make it a la mode," and then I say, "Ice cream," thinking about the problem we had with the soup du jour.

I eat the pie one little bite at a time. Aunt Babe grows her own rhubarb from right out back of her kitchen window. I like the way rhubarb looks when it's growing, long and purple and smooth. You see it growing and you want to stuff your mouth with it, it's so pretty, but before cooking and before adding a ton of sugar, it's about the most bitter tasting thing imaginable. You can't see how anybody tasting rhubarb would have stuck with it long enough to figure out how to make it into pie.

It occurs to me that I'm waiting for my husband. I've only been married for two weeks and I'm not used to thinking of Bob Bybee as my husband, but he is. I think I'll mention that to Billy when he comes to my end of the counter. I'll say, "I'm waiting for my husband."

Billy starts loading the napkin holders. He starts at one end of the counter and he works his way down towards me, humming to himself, and watching me from the corner of his eye. I expect he'll ask for my phone number. I think I should tell him I'm waiting for my husband so he doesn't have to embarrass himself, but then I remember about the soup du jour and I think Let him go ahead.

But before he has time to go ahead, Bob Bybee comes rushing through the door. He's red in the face and sweating — he's been out in the fields all morning — and he sits down beside me, breathing hard, like he's run all the way to Aunt Babe's, instead of took the car. His arms are red and freckled from being out in the sun. His hands don't hold still but move nervously across his face and to his neck and over his lap and across the counter. I watch them, pink nervous hands with thick fingers and small flat thumbs.

Bob's in a hurry to order his food. "Two double cheeseburgers, double fries, and a cup of coffee." Just like every day. Billy leans over the counter and says, "The soup du jour is creme of tomato," and Bob says, "Don't Aunt Babe know how to make any other kind of soup?" and Billy says, "Guess not."

Bob sets his hand on my leg and gives it a little squeeze which is the kind of thing he can do now, whenever he wants to. "How's my little wife?" he says.

When Bob eats his food he bends way down to the plate like he expects the food to escape, so he'd better get down there before that happens. And when it gets close to his mouth, he sucks at it, and before he's got it chewed up and swallowed, he shovels another bite in, like he's somebody who sat at the dinner table all his life without nobody ever once saying, "Eat with your mouth shut and don't slurp your food." And his being one of the best families in the county and almost as rich as the Winklejohns.

I call Billy over and ask him to bring me a chocolate shake, thinking at least I ought to have some reward for having to sit here.

Bob says, "But, Lucy, you've already had a piece of pie." Thinking to himself, she's going to wind up like her mother, I just know it.

And I say, "If I feel like a chocolate shake, I guess I can have me a chocolate shake."

I lean on the counter now, with my fingers pressed over my ears to block out the sound of Bob's chewing. Bob's chewing is like the sound beavers make, if you've ever heard a beaver. That's what Bob's chewing is like, only about a million times louder. How I never noticed the way Bob eats before, I can't imagine. And I wonder how many other things I'll find out now that we're man and wife.

Billy sets my chocolate shake on the counter and he refills Bob's coffee. The coffee cup says "The Chatty Corner" on it because Babe she got her cups from over in Ava when The Chatty Corner closed down. "You must be Aunt Babe's nephew," says Bob.

"That's right. My name is Billy Lee."

"You must be from over to Pearl."

Billy says that he's from lots of places. I don't know what he means by that, but I'm not speaking to anybody right now, so I just go on wondering.

Bob he stuffs half a cheeseburger in his mouth and the grease from it is running all down his chin and before he even starts chewing, he says, "Welcome to town, Billy, my name is Bob Bybee and this here's my wife, Lucy. The former Lucy Fooshee."

"Fooshee?"

"That's right," I say, even though I'm not speaking. "F-o-o-s-h-e-e. Fooshee. Now some people they see the name spelled out and they call it foo-shee, like if it was Chinese. But you say it foo-shay. It's a French name and that's how they talk."

And then Bob has to go and say how we were only married two weeks ago, so Billy stands there looking at us, thinking he knows what we're doing every chance we get. I pretend I don't know what he's thinking. I pick up the menu and read it again, like I haven't already seen it a million times, at least, and then finally he turns back to Bob, "Aren't you a lucky man."

*Chapter 2*

After that lunch I tell myself Billy Lee is one person I'm going to avoid, but you know how that is. I don't know where was before, but now Billy Lee is everywhere at once.

I'm coming around the corner and I run right smack into him. We both scare the living daylights out of each other. Then I stand there looking at him and he stands there looking at me. Neither of us say a word, just stand froze on the corner of Second and Main, across from the launderette, looking into each other's faces.

I stop at the Texaco and guess who's at the next pump. I roll up my window and turn on the radio and look straight ahead of me. Billy, he comes over, ignoring the fact that I'm ignoring him, and he taps on the window but I don't hardly notice him standing there. When I roll it down he says, "Hello there, Mrs. Bybee." He says the Missus part real loud like it's a big joke and I say, "Hello yourself."

He says, "You're the daughter of Mrs. Elton Fooshee, isn't that right?"

I turn down the radio and say, "Yes, that's right, sure enough." I don't know what he's getting at, so I reach into my handbag and get my lipstick out. I look in the rear view mirror and start putting it on, like maybe I forgot he's standing there. Or, at least, I have more important things to think of.

"Mrs. Elton Fooshee, that's right," I say, but I'm not looking at him. I'm getting the lipstick on just perfect. I have full lips. My sisters have narrow lips like our mother's people but I have Fooshee lips.

Ralph Egree is washing my windows and I watch him. Ralph is a skinny boy just out of high school and he has himself plastered over my windshield. His shirt is riding up and I'm looking at his belly, which is flat and muscular and has a little ridge of black hair around the navel and moving on down. I watch his hips thumping against my car for about as long as I can take it and then I get out my pocketbook again and start going through it, like I just remembered I had to find something.

Billy says, "Your Mama hired me to do some work around her place."

"What kind of work?"

He tells me she's hired him to shore up the north wall and to work on the floor and to split some firewood and rebuild the chimney and lay some linoleum in the kitchen. He has a list so long that I think Billy is going to be at my mother's house permanently, until she dies and then on into the next generation, before he can finish all those things.

I say, "But my brother Jimbo always cuts the firewood."

And all this time there are Ralph's hips in my face.

I say, "What's wrong with Jimbo cutting the wood?

That's the way we always done it before." I say, "My sister Evaline can split wood too, there's nothing wrong with her."

He bends down then and says, "Evaline splits fire-wood, does she?"

"Yes, Evaline splits firewood," I say, and I tap my fingers on the steering wheel. "She's built like a horse, if you haven't noticed."

"No, I didn't notice that. No."

"Well, she is."

And instead of just trusting me on this, Billy scratches his chin and thinks it over and he's shaking his head the whole time, like he can remember my sister better than me who's known her my whole life and had plenty of chance to notice. "That's not how she struck me."

If Billy Lee thinks I'm going to sit at the Texaco and argue with him over the size of my sister's body, he's got another thing coming. "Anyway," I say, "she's as strong as a cow."

And I think to myself that Ralph ought to be finished with the darned windshield by now.

Then there's the Buy-More incident. Here I am, all the way over in Jacksonville. Jacksonville is a city, not like Palmyra where you walk down the street and you see about everybody there in the first five minutes. You can get lost in Jacksonville. You can go a week and not see everybody there is to see, or half of them, in all that time. You can go to Jacksonville all your life and walk down the street and not one person will say hey the whole time because that's how big it is. What I'm trying to say is that if I'm in Jacksonville and you're in Jacksonville, then it'll be about a miracle if we run into each other.

I'm over here because I had a beauty appointment and

then, afterwards, I stopped by the big supermarket, Buy-More it's called, to get a few things.

I've got my cart loaded up and I'm looking for just the right cashier. I've got two giant-size boxes of Kotex and you want to get the right cashier when you have a situation like that. Not some manager filling in for one of the girls who's sick. Not some teenager who'll make a big fuss over it and not some nitwit who will leave the boxes sitting out for everybody to see and then load them last of all. You want to pick an older woman, but not so old she's going to be slow. Not so old she won't be able to get the boxes in a paper bag. You want a woman with her head on her shoulders. You don't want her shouting over to the next cashier what button does she push for the Kotex. Well, I've looked over the whole row of cashiers and I've found just the right one. She's at the last counter on the end. But I've been so intent on looking at the women behind the registers and congratulating myself for being smart, I haven't noticed Billy. He's standing in line right in front of me.

"Well, well. Are you following me, Mrs. Bybee?"

I about jump out of my skin when I see him. "I should say not!" I exclaim, but then he laughs so I know he's making a joke. "I had myself a beauty appointment," I say, to make sure he understands I have a reason to be here.

Mother Bybee says a beauty appointment all the way over to Jacksonville is just another example of Bob spoiling me rotten. There's a beauty operator in Palmyra, she says, and that's good enough for her.

"You come all the way over here for a beauty appointment?" says Billy, but I've already been through this before with Mother Bybee and I don't say anything back.

I look in my shopping cart like I have to make sure I've remembered everything.

He's still watching me. He's watching me a long time past when he should have stopped and now I feel myself blush, when it's not me doing anything, but him.

"You look like your sister," he says.

"Like Flora." Flora is my baby sister.

"No, I mean Evaline. You've got her same wide face and her same smile."

I don't point out that I'm not smiling, but I say, "No, Evaline she's got a mouth like my Mama's people," I'm not going to say Hogg, "but I have got a Fooshee mouth. As a matter of fact."

Now his eyes slip down to my mouth. I put my finger on my lips and trace their outline. "See, I've got full lips, same as the Fooshees, but Evaline she's got lips like the other side of the family. So does Betty, my other sister, and so does Flora. All them girls but me have got lips like the other side." The other side, we always call it. You don't want to mention how you're a Hogg, if you can help it. "Poor things."

I expect he'll want to argue with me, same as that day at the Texaco, and I'm ready for him, but he doesn't say a word.

"My sister Flora and me, we're built like our Daddy," I tell him. "Thin, like he was. Our Mama's people — you've met her — well, they're big, and that's the side my brother, Jimbo, and my sisters, Evaline and Betty, take after, the big side. Flora and me, we're like the Fooshees, slender. The Fooshees never do get fat. Even the old ones, they just stay nice and thin, all their lives. They can eat whatever they want. Not like some people."

Every time I see Billy something embarrassing happens and it's always through no fault of my own. Can I help it the way my husband eats a cheeseburger with the grease running all down his face? Is it my fault a teenage boy is grinding his hips six inches from my face at the Texaco? And now I've got a cart full of Kotex and I'm looking into my cart to see if you can read the Kotex word. I've covered it up with a bag of potatoes and cans of pork 'n beans, cartons of eggs, and loaves of bread. You can't see anything you shouldn't from where he's standing, I'm sure of it.

"I'll be by your Mama's house in a day or two to start in on that north wall."

"Is that a fact?" I slide my hands down my hips, straightening out my skirt and he looks at my hands and then away. "Sure is hot," I say, and he says, "Sure is."

I can just imagine how he must feel, arriving only two weeks past the wedding date and now being out of the running entirely.

"Where you from?" I'm smiling now, my Fooshee smile, and relaxing too, now that my problem with the Kotex word is over. "You aren't from around here, I knew that soon as I laid eyes on you."

He's smiling back, not speaking.

"That day at Aunt Babe's," I remind him.

"I'm from all over the place."

"You aren't from nowhere?"

He laughs then. "That's one way to say it."

There's silence for a long time now. I can see that Billy isn't too good when it comes to keeping the conversation going. Now Bob, he don't have that problem. One thing leads to another with Bob and on and on, like how they say numbers never end because there's always one more after that one. Same way with Bob and conversation.

The Buy-More store has got a big display of laundry soap right where you wait in line, in case you forgot your laundry soap before. There's a special of some kind and the boxes are stacked up in a pyramid. I feel sorry for Billy that he doesn't know how to talk to a pretty girl and now I pretend to think about the soap, to let him off the hook.

I'm about to help him out with the conversation. I might ask what kind of laundry soap does Aunt Babe use or did he notice this big sale here. Anything can be used as a conversation starter. But then it occurs to me to won-der if Billy will buy his groceries and say good-bye and walk on out the door, or if he'll think of excuses so he can stand around and watch me unload the Kotex.

There's only one person in line in front of Billy and then it's his turn. I'm reading one of the boxes of laundry soap when I feel his finger tap me on the shoulder. "You go on ahead."

"What's that?"

"You go first."

"But it's your turn."

"Ladies first."

"I said, no!"

Billy unloads his groceries and pays, but then instead of going on out, he sticks around. His groceries are in a bag on the counter and now he pulls my cart forward and starts unloading it for me, like I don't have two good hands myself.

"I don't need your help," I say. "I got two good hands."

"My pleasure," he says, like I'm only worried about inconveniencing him.

He reaches into my cart and pulls out the pork 'n beans. He sets them on the counter.

"Maybe I'm not ready yet!" I say.

He unloads the peanut butter and mayonnaise and the cashier, the one I picked special, she just goes on and rings them up like he's the boss of my cart and not me and that's just too much for me. I jerk my shopping cart back, away from him and turn it. Maybe I forgot something. I pull it out of the aisle and turn but it clips the edge of the laundry soap display and I watch in horror as all the boxes of laundry soap topple over and then crash onto the floor.

Everywhere in the store, people stop and look. All it is is a laundry soap display for crying out loud but these people got nothing better to get excited about.

"You have gone and done it now!" I say. "You have!"

"I'm sorry," Billy says, but the checkout lady takes his side.

"She rammed right into it," she tells him.

"Like it's your business," I say to her.

I think to myself it doesn't matter how careful you are sometimes. It doesn't matter how smart you are. I start to cry, right here in the Buy-More Store in front of the mean checkout lady and everything.

Meanwhile Billy is unloading my cart for me. He picks up the boxes of Kotex like it's nothing to him and then he unloads the potatoes and then the bags of frozen corn and peas and then on top, the bread so it doesn't get smashed. And I think to myself all that worry and he doesn't even know what a Kotex box is in the first place.

*Chapter 3*

I know how to cook a few things. I make a nice ham gumbo and I can whip up ground beef on toast without even looking at a recipe book, but most nights we'll go over to my family's house. We'll go there for dinner, to keep Mama and Evaline and Flora company. It's the least we could do, is what I always say to Bob.

We're over there and I'm doing the mending before dinner. Evaline is making pork chops and, for dessert, Calumet Gold Cake. I can smell the cake baking. I see that I have to pick up a spool of orange thread and some buttons. So I walk to the five and dime, which is where I had a job before I married Bob and I stood on my feet all day. Evaline has a little dog, name of Foxie, and I've got her with me.

I don't know what other people think about, but I like to plan things. When I was a girl, I'd think about my husband. First, I thought he'd be Glenn Pinshaw because Glenn is such a nice looking boy and me and Glenn, *Don't we look fine together?* Everyone said so. And then, later, I thought it'd be Hammer Johnson, but it wasn't him neither. I could have married the Winklejohn boy but he was one year behind me in school and, besides, there's the name. Winkle-john. So he's marrying my little sister, Flora, instead and if she isn't going to worry about burdening her children with a name like that, then I won't trouble myself about it neither.

When I realized my husband was going to be Lyle Bybee's son, then what I liked to think about was our furniture. Of course, we'd move into the house Lyle's daddy built and I liked to plan what furniture I'd put where and what color I'd have everything.

And then, lately, what I think about is the children I'll have and the addition we'll put on the house, for a playroom. I'm going to name my first child Elton, that's after my father, and my second one I'll name Patsy, which is my favorite little girl's name. And I'll buy Patsy so many little dresses and put bows in her hair and everything. I expect she'll look pretty much exactly like Shirley Temple what with the Bybee curly red hair and my looks combined. That's what I'm thinking about as I walk to the five and dime.

As soon as I go in, I know who's there. I can tell without looking, like how you can feel somebody staring at the back of your head and you turn around and there they are. I can feel the heart beating in my chest, kaplunk, kaplunk, kaplunk. Has my heart always sounded this way and I just never noticed it before? OK, I think to myself, you came in to buy a spool of thread. Spool of thread, spool of thread. I'm more nervous than what I was on the wedding day with half the county hanging on my every move.

I'll just go over and pick up my thread and go to the cashier and give her my money and walk outside and say, "Here, Foxie!" and then I'll go on about my business. Just like usual. This is Palmyra, the town I lived in all my life. Same store I worked in, every day. Same aisles I walked down. Everything's just the same. At home Evaline is making a Calumet Gold Cake, I remind myself, and it's my favorite.

I go over to the sewing section and I keep my eyes down. I'm hunting for a certain shade of orange thread and I'm thinking don't look up, don't look up, don't look up. What do I have to be upset over? I'm just going about my business, like every other day. We're going to build an addition to our house, me and Bob, for when we start a family, which could be any minute now. And hadn't I just walked down Main Street thinking twelve by fifteen or fifteen by fifteen? Bob thinks twelve by fifteen is big enough, but I'm not sure. Bob's someone who thinks small, is what I had found out. So I'd been trying to figure out if he was right about the twelve by fifteen, or if this was just another example of how he doesn't think big enough.

In Palmyra, things only come in a couple colors. You got your brown and blue and green. You can hardly even get red which is a main color, because it's too excitable for Palmyra. My favorite color is orange but not like a pumpkin. You can find Halloween orange in Palmyra but you can't find the orange I like, so what you do in Palmyra is you make a compromise. You take brown, instead of orange. You buy blue instead of teal. You take green and not turquoise. You take something else, instead of what you want.

I find a spool of dark brown thread and I'm so relieved to have made a decision that, for a second, I forget about holding myself in and, in that second, my eyes fly up, all on their own, and land right at the back of Billy Lee's

head. He's down at the end of the aisle. He feels me looking and swings around and as far as he can tell I've been
staring at him the whole time, which, like I explained, I
haven't.

"I was hunting for thread," I call out.

"Mrs. Bybee," he says, and he nods his head.

"I was just doing some sewing. For my husband, Bob,
you remember."

"Oh, sure, I remember your husband," he says, but he
says it like he's making fun of me, like with the soup du jour.

I'm thinking of some way to put him in his place,
when he says, "Aren't you too young to be married?"

"I've only been married for three weeks," I say, and
then I remember how that makes everybody think of
things. Three weeks, don't they know what you're doing
now, every chance you get. I know I should change the
subject, but I don't. I just stand looking at him and he just
stands looking at me and we're both thinking the same
thing.

We look away, finally, down the dusty aisles of the five
and dime, and I say, "I've only come in for some thread,"
and I hold the spool up, for proof.

I walk right over to the cashier, Glenn's sister, Sadie
Pinshaw, and I pay for my thread, looking down the
whole time. And then, just as I walk away, I turn around.
I can't stop myself. I look back into the store and Billy is
standing in aisle three, the one with screws and light
bulbs, and he looks at me and I look at him and then I
walk outside and call out, "Here, Foxie!"

The next night, we're back at Mama's for dinner. All
my sisters are there too, Evaline and Flora, because they
live there, and Betty, who's visiting from Buckhorn with
her husband, Larry Bodell. We go early, so I can help with

the baking. I'm baking three loaves of bread today — hot as it is — and biscuits, along with two pies, a berry pie, for tomorrow, and a butterscotch meringue pie, for after dinner this evening. Evaline is cooking dinner — fried chicken, like always, and mashed potatoes with gravy, creamed corn — which she creams herself when you can buy a can already done for you and it tastes just the same — and peas from the garden.

I've just set the butterscotch pie in the window to cool when I hear the sound of the axe.

Whack, whack, whack. I stand at the kitchen window. Whack, whack, whack.

Evaline and Mama are behind me, fussing around. I hear their voices but they're far away. I hear them moving about, opening the ice box, getting out silverware, opening and shutting drawers.

The first thing I did when I got here was set my bread to rise and I already punched it down once and now it's ready for kneading. I dump it from the bowl it's in, onto the countertop. I split it in half, because all of it at once is too big for my hands, and I start kneading it.

Mama always says you've got to knead each piece 300 times and so that's 600 in all. The dough is soft like the butt of a baby, is what Mama says every time, but today it's more like a thigh, I think, moving it back and forth. It's soft and smooth and it moves under my hands, like a thing that's alive, which it is. Bread is alive until you cook it and today I can feel that about the bread, feel how my rubbing it and pulling it and folding it into itself is what wakes it up to the fact of its own life.

I'm moving the dough back and forth and outside I can hear the sound of Billy Lee. Whack, whack, whack.

I've only made it to 195, but I stop. I think, has somebody gone and left the oven on? Because it's so hot in this kitchen, must be a hundred. I feel the sweat dripping down my sides and on the back of my neck and on my forehead and my legs. I go over to the sink and put cold water on my face. My hair is pinned up, off my neck, and now I adjust it. I'm not even half finished and already this bread has got the best of me. I start in again, not letting myself think about the other half, waiting for me once this one is ready. Anyway, maybe I'll freeze that one for later. Emma Swank, she freezes hers and you can't tell the difference. And I knead again. 207, 208, 209. When you first start kneading the dough, it's sticky. It gets on your hands and between your fingers. Outside, I can hear the rhythm of the axe. Whack, whack, whack.

I like the smell of it, damp and alive. Not like other food that's already done, it's living by the time it comes to you. I'm only on 273 when my hands suddenly fold it over, tuck the ends in, and throw it in the pan. Where Mama came up with 300, I don't know. I put a washcloth over it and set it on top of the cupboard, where it's even hotter than down here. I don't even look at the dough that's left.

"You're not done, are you?" asks Mama, but I don't answer.

"Where are the biscuits? Are they ready to go in?" says Evaline, but I don't say.

I take my apron off and lay it on the counter. I wash my hands. I run them over my hair, which is pinned up for the heat. I smooth my skirt down over my hips and bend forward, looking at my reflection in the metal toaster, and I pinch my cheeks — but they're already pink — and I lick my lips and they're pink too and shiny and big, Fooshee lips. I get in the refrigerator and pour a big glass of cold lemonade. I press the glass to my face. I stand in the kitchen, looking out the window into the yard where Billy is bent over the firewood. Whack, whack, whack.

"I'm baking these biscuits, if you aren't," says Evaline, and she gets my bowl of biscuit dough from the cupboard, sighing.

"I thought you come to help," adds Mama.

I move the glass down my neck and down to my chest, where my blouse opened up, and I hold it there. I'm watching him the whole time, how he bends back and then forward and how his hips move back and then thrust out with the movement of the axe, and I take a drink of the lemonade myself.

"She ain't even preheated the oven," says Evaline, just to prove how bad I am, but I don't defend myself.

I run my tongue along the rim of the glass, in a circle, and then I go outside. I hear the sound of the screen door shut behind me and I walk to where Billy is working and stand a little ways off until he looks up and sees me.

He's looking hard at me, at my eyes and my mouth and my face and everything else, from the top to the bottom. He stands looking at me like that and I stand letting him do it. We're under the tree in plain view of Mama or Evaline or our neighbor, Mrs. Leland Hobbes, if she's looking out her window.

But I've only come out to give him a drink of lemonade and now I hand him the glass and he takes it. He puts his mouth against the rim where my tongue has been and I watch while he drinks it all down with one long drink and his Adam's apple moves up and down and finally he looks back at me.

"I don't think it's ever been this hot before," I say, and I laugh a little, nervous sounding laugh and then, to cover it up, I pull my hair away from my face and back off my neck where it wants to fall.

He doesn't want to comment about the weather, I can see that. He looks at the axe but I catch his eye, "I'm making pie for dinner. Are you staying? I'm making butterscotch meringue pie."

My eyes go down to his shirt, where it's wet from his sweat and sticking to his chest, and then I look away again, at the axe and at the ground, at the empty glass in his hand, at the sky.

"Meringue, you ever had it?"

He moves closer to me. "What's that?" He reaches out to give me the empty glass.

"It's my grandma's recipe, and it takes four eggs. Or the whites of four eggs, I mean. You've got to do them just right. People don't know that. Say you get them started and then the phone rings — you can't answer that phone. You've got to keep on going, once you start, but people don't pay attention to that rule. It tells you in all the recipe books. You can't be half-hearted about it, that's what my grandma said."

"It sounds like a lot of work."

"Oh, but it's worth it!" I exclaim. "It's so good. There's nothing like it."

He's looking at my mouth and I'm watching his. "You can't be in a hurry neither." It's like we're two people who can't hear but have to watch what the other is saying. "You start out slow." I can see the tip of his pink tongue. "Gradually you increase the speed. Once you start, you can't let nothing stop you."

"Lucille!" Evaline shouts, like I'm halfway across town instead of just out the back door. Evaline stands at the door with a dishrag in her hand, scowling. "Lucille!"

she shouts again, like I'm not staring right at her. "Get us some radishes out of the garden." And instead of moving away, Evaline stands there looking at me with her hands on her hips like I'm a child who has to be watched.

The garden is in the backyard. It's June and the radishes are coming up, and the peas and strawberries. We have lettuce and greens, too. The earliest flowers are blooming and the plum tree is just loaded with fruit. Every year my roses get a blue ribbon at the county fair but it's too early for my roses yet.

I go over and start collecting radishes. Evaline likes to set out a plate of radishes, with salt to dip them in. She likes radishes and salt and so does everybody but I just like the way they look on the plate. There's something cheerful about radishes. I hear the screen door slam shut and I know she's gone back inside, but I don't look up.

Bob says I ought to plant my garden at my own house now, meaning his house, and I say I will next year. I say, *Oh, won't that be nice* and then Bob shuts up and forgets all about it.

I make a little pile of radishes on the ground and then I sit down next to them while Billy watches me. I can feel his eyes on me same as I feel the sun. I can feel everywhere his eyes touch.

We have a big yard. There's a maple tree, must be over a hundred years old, spreading out its shade in the yard. There's a Burr Oak tree, named after somebody, Aaron Burr, maybe. We got a Rome Beauty apple tree, planted by my great grandmother. And there's still room enough for the clothesline, which goes from one end of the yard to the other. We grow about all the vegetables we eat. We grow lettuce and potatoes and spinach, greens, okra, zucchini, and peppers. Bell peppers, red peppers, and hot chili peppers. We grow two rows of Beefsteak tomatoes.

So anyway, I sit down in the yard. I sit out in the sunshine. I have a skirt on and it's pulled back around my legs. I watch Billy work and he acts like he doesn't know I'm watching. He takes off his shirt.

Billy looks over at me. I think he might be looking up my skirt, the way it's spread out there and the way his eyes point, but I don't feel like fixing it. I watch him and he wipes his forehead with the back of his arm.

"Nice garden," he calls out and he raises his eyebrows to tell me it isn't the garden he's talking about.

*Chapter 4*

At dinner that night, Mama has Billy seated next to Evaline, who's an old maid, almost thirty now and no prospects whatsoever. It's because of her long, narrow face and her thin, cold-looking lips. One of those things might have been overlooked, the lips or the face, but not both. Besides, Evaline has a worried, fussy way about her which makes me think she was born to be an old maid, born to it, nothing anybody could do about that. But Mama, ever hopeful, has got Billy next to her and just as soon as we sit down, before we can say a word, Mama says that Evaline has made this entire dinner herself. "She's some cook," says Mama. She's hard of hearing and she says it too loud.

And Bob says, "Yes ma'am, she's some cook."

My little sister Flora is at the dinner table too, along with our married sister, Betty Bodell, and her worthless husband, Larry. Bob sits across from me, same as always, with Billy on his right so I can look at both of them at once. Evaline has a dress on and she has her hair brushed and lipstick on her little Hogg's lips, even though it's only dinner at Mama's house and nobody has dressed up for that before.

Not long ago I sat at this very table and planned my wedding. Now that wedding day has come and gone and here I am. But I'd never planned past that day, like if my life was a story and after the wedding part I'd shut the book and go do something else.

They think I belong to them. When they look at me all they see is the Fooshee face, the mouth and the chin and the hair of the Fooshees, the long fingers, the blue eyes. They think all I am is the best parts of the Fooshees all put in the same place. They can't see how all those parts got put together and came up with something new. They can't see how I'm different than them. It's like the fairy tale, Snow White, and Snow White ends up with the dwarfs and pretty soon they think she belongs there. But even the dwarfs face facts, once the prince shows up. It isn't like they can say how they found her first.

But then I think, I'm forgetting who I am. I am Lucy Fooshee Bybee. I'm the best looking girl in Pike County, that's what everybody says, and I can have whoever I want, that's what they say. And who I have got is Bob Bybee, the son of Lyle, and the biggest farmer in the county, next to the Winklejohns. Isn't everybody dying with envy, too. I look across the table and I remind myself Billy Lee is my Mama's handyman. He works behind the counter of a cafe, making milkshakes.

What I like to do is make a list. You know, put one thing on top of the paper on one side and another thing on top of the paper on the other side and then you make a list of the good things. If you put the good things about being married to Billy Lee in one column and the good things about being married to Bob Bybee in the other, like how I done with Bob and Hammer Johnson, Billy wouldn't have a chance. Even with Bob's table manners and such, it doesn't take a genius to know who'd come out in front. I don't even need a piece of paper for it, I could do it in my head.

"I don't know why Jimbo isn't putting up Mama's firewood anymore," I say, but nobody answers me. I think Bob or Larry Bodell will jump in about now and offer to help. Larry is about seven feet tall and he isn't skinny neither. Larry is one of the strongest men in the county, everybody says, but what good it does I can't tell. "There's plenty of men in this family to take care of you," I say to Mama, and I kick my sister, Betty, under the table.

"That Jimbo never was good for anything," says Betty, and she kicks me back, hard.

"Jimbo has got himself a job," says Mama, like we should be thrilled, but before she can say anything else, Evaline interrupts.

"Billy fixed that back wall today, didn't you, Billy."

Billy says that yes he did. Billy says, "The floor on the north side has dry rot."

"I knew that," Bob says.

Billy says, "You've got carpenter ants."

I'm thinking that I should have pulled that meat loaf out of the freezer at home and stayed there tonight with Bob. Bob and me have our own house now and we don't have to come to Mama's every night. I can cook a few things.

"Carpenter ants will destroy a house," says Bob, and he sticks a chicken leg in his mouth.

I say, "Evaline makes the best fried chicken, doesn't she."

But that's the wrong thing to say. Everybody agrees

and, instead of leaving it at that, they start ranting and raving about just how good it is. "Delicious!" they say. "The best ever!" they exclaim. "Nothing else like it!" And then Billy says he hasn't never seen anybody who can cook like Evaline. He says Evaline is about the best cook he has ever run into. He says Evaline is one woman who sure knows how to cook. I just look at him across the table. I start to mention how he's getting carried away. I could point out how one chicken dinner isn't hardly enough to go on, but I don't say anything.

Billy looks at me and says, "That's some garden you've got, Mrs. Fooshee." Everybody keeps eating, putting food in their mouths, swallowing, wiping their hands, drinking milk. He isn't talking about the garden, but I pretend I don't know that.

"I'm glad you like it."

I pick up a drumstick and raise my eyes to his eyes. As I take a bite, my eyes shut. The skin is brittle, from being fried, but Evaline doesn't batter it. It's just the skin of the chicken, smooth and warm. And as I bite into it and feel the juice in my mouth, I open my eyes and look at Billy, sitting there, and he's looking back.

I swallow and pat my mouth with my napkin, put the napkin back on my lap, straighten the edges out, and lean forward, looking at him, "Not too many men take a interest in gardening."

"That's not true, Lucy. I love your roses. You know I do," Bob says.

"Men claim to have a interest," I say.

"Lucy's got the best roses in the county," Bob tells Billy.

"Althea Runels took number one at the fair, you remember," puts in Betty.

"That doesn't mean a thing," says Evaline.

"Lucy thinks her garden is the most important thing in the world," says Flora.

"Remind me sometime, I'll show you the rest of it," I say. "You only seen a little bit."

"I can hardly wait," Billy says.

"It's not the gardening she likes," says Betty, "it's the hope of winning a prize."

"The hope?" I say.

"Althea took number one, you remember," says Betty, patting her little mouth with a napkin, and before I can refresh her memory about all the other times, when I came out number one, she adds, "I don't take to gardening, myself."

"Isn't that a shame," says Billy, and he takes the napkin from his lap and coughs into it, to hide his laugh.

"Betty doesn't like to get all dirty," I say. But then I bust out laughing and have to say, "Excuse me. I'm sorry."

I can see my sisters looking sidelong at me. They're thinking *Lucy forgot how to conduct herself around a young man, poor thing.* That just makes me laugh harder.

My sisters start to talk about their weddings. They talk about their bridesmaids and they talk about their dresses. Flora tells Billy about the wedding dress she found over to Springfield.

I'm the prettiest sister and then, after me, is Flora. Flora has fair skin that you can about see through and she has rosy cheeks and little pink lips. In a few years you'll look at Flora and what you'll see is all the blue veins in her cheeks and along her temple. Her skin, soon as it gets a little wear, will start pulling loose and hanging down, way before it should. White skin like hers, it doesn't last. But she'll make a pretty bride, anyway, and that's all the further Pete Winklejohn is thinking.

"What color are they again?" I say, knowing full well they're babydoll pink, but getting ready for Mama to throw her two cents in about how my bridesmaids' dresses were peach colored, to match my complexion, a point my mother never failed to make before. But I look over at her and she's stuffing green beans in her mouth and, before you know it, the opportunity is gone because Flora is telling me not only the color, which I already know, but the style too, which I also know. She's telling Billy about the flower girls and about the ring bearer and about all the flowers she's going to order and about the music she picked out. She's asking doesn't he think the Baptist Church is the prettiest place you can ask to have a wedding in and Billy isn't saying anything, but he's smiling.

I start to mention my honeymoon in St. Louis but before I can, Billy says to Flora, "Aren't you too young to be getting married?" Which is the same thing he said to me, but he doesn't seem to recall that.

Flora says to Billy that Pete Winklejohn and his daddy have the biggest farm in Pike County and he says, "Is that so? Whoee."

I know he's making fun of her but when I look around at everybody else, I can tell I'm the only one who has figured that out. I think it's like the soup du jour, like Billy has little jokes he tells to himself and everybody else is left out. The Winklejohn farm is over a thousand acres and nobody ever laughed at that before. At least I realize it's a joke, even if it's a joke I don't get. I look over at Billy and I can see he's enjoying himself very much, sitting at the dinner table telling private jokes at my family's expense, and him just the hired man and shouldn't even have a seat at the table in the first place.

"Mama, Jimbo and Bob here can cut your firewood.

You don't have to go hiring somebody else to do it," I say again.

My Mama says, "Jimbo is living clear over in Pittsfield now."

Like I don't know where my own brother is living. I say, "Pittsfield ain't that far." I say, "He's not walking, you know." I say, "Bob here could do it."

But instead of jumping in, Bob says, "My back has been acting up again, Lucy."

He says again like it's happened before, instead of this being a new development, one more way Bob Bybee is falling apart just as soon as he turns into my husband. I look at him and wonder, is this like buying a car? As soon as you pull out of the lot, things start going wrong.

I say, "Bob, you haven't never had back trouble before," but I say it sweet. I don't say it like I'm discovering the small writing at the bottom of our contract.

I'm watching Bob and I'm thinking, when did he start looking like this? Bob looks more like his daddy than he does himself and I'm wondering when did that happen. Bob is reaching for another helping of potatoes and gravy and I say, "Bob, you've had two helpings of gravy, don't you think that's enough."

I know what Flora is thinking. Flora is thinking how Pete Winklejohn would never let her talk to him like that and she's thinking that, anyway, she'd never want to in the first place.

Billy says, "I don't mind cutting wood for Mrs. Fooshee."

"That's not the point," I say.

"The point is getting the wood cut, Lucy," says Bob.

But I look at him like he's crazy. If the danged firewood was the point then that would sure be easy enough now, wouldn't it.

Billy says, "Cutting firewood suits me just fine. I won't even charge you extra, Mrs. Fooshee. All the work I'm doing around here. I'll just throw cutting the firewood in." He looks over at me and winks. "I could use the exercise."

I look down at Billy's arms resting on the table. It doesn't look to me like he needs exercise. It looks to me like he gets just plenty of exercise.

"Men can die from too much exercise," says Betty. "They can go out to cut firewood or do chores and next thing you know, they're dead. Look at Mr. Howell. Here one minute, gone the next."

"Mr. Howell? It wasn't exercise that killed him," says Evaline. But Betty is only interested in working the pig story into the conversation some way.

Betty leans towards Billy now and lowers her voice like she's telling a secret. "Lemuel — Lemuel Howell — he had a heart attack in the pig pen one night, is what they figure."

"The Howells, they were pig farmers," says Flora. "And one night Mr. Howell goes out to feed the pigs —"

"And he never come back," finishes Betty.

Evaline frowns at our sisters. "Girls, we're eating."

"We're trying to have a nice dinner," adds Mama.

"Last thing that man ever did was to feed those hogs," Betty goes on.

Flora adds, "He loved his hogs, Mr. Howell did."

"Oh, and his hogs loved him too!" says Betty, giggling, but Mama gives her a look.

Flora shouts out, "They ate him up!"

Everyone is watching Billy, to see what he'll do, and now he looks at us and sets down his fork. "The hogs did?"

he asks Flora.

But it's Betty's story and she says, "All but his feet!"

Billy makes a face.

"And his boots!" throws in Flora.

Billy looks down at his plate, thinking of those feet out in the pigpen, but we've all heard the story a hundred times and we don't mind it.

Betty pours gravy on her potatoes. "Our brother, Jimbo, he went out and found them, Lemuel's feet, still in his boots, just as perfect as could be, not a scratch on them anywhere."

"On the boots, you mean?" asks Billy. He looks like he doesn't believe his own ears.

"Lemuel and Jimbo, they wore the same size, always did," says Flora.

## Chapter 5

After dinner, we go out on the porch and I sit on the top step, with Billy on one side of me and Bob on the other, and I think about the night Bob asked me to marry him. We were sitting right here, same as now. I felt like somebody had just handed me a million dollars. I felt like a big door opened up and on the other side was a happy life. And all I wanted was Bob for the rest of my life and I couldn't even think of it being different than that.

Is it finished and all those feelings are gone? Or is this a little slump and then they'll come back? I don't know the answer. And I think, what's a feeling anyhow? You can think about the things you want to think about and you can do the things you want to do, but why can't you feel what you want to feel?

I look at Bob and I make a promise, I'll feel the way I did before, when you were the happy ending of my story, when you were my crowning glory. I'll feel like that again. But the next second, I'm not so sure of it. The next second, it occurs to me that maybe Bob doesn't deserve this. Maybe he didn't even know it when it was there and he won't miss it now that it's gone. I look at him and I don't feel a thing, just bewilderment.

After a while, somebody goes in the house and somebody else goes off the other way, and then, for about five minutes, it's just the two of us, Billy and me. "Anybody ever tell you you look like Elizabeth Taylor?" he says.

"My hair's not black."

He says, "Out in California, if you just walked down the street, somebody would come up to you and make you a movie star."

"Oh, go on," I say.

But he says, "I really mean it. You're hiding your beauty under a basket out here."

That makes me think of my beauty like if it was a rose bush. And I have a basket, a bushel basket like the ones we put apples in, and I've got that basket stuck right on top of my roses. The basket is the town of Palmyra, Illinois.

And then to show me this isn't just him making an observation like anybody could make, like commenting on the sunset or such, he reaches over and slides his hand next to mine, where it's sitting on the porch. And we sit like that, looking at our hands lying side by side, on the porch at my Mama's house. It's a June night and still hot, late as it is. Usually a breeze will come up but there's no breeze tonight. I look at his hand and he looks at mine. For a moment I think I might pick his hand up and put it on my leg. I think I might put that hand of Billy Lee's just under where my skirt is or I might stick it up under my shirt. I might put it in my mouth. But before I do any of those things, Mama comes back out, and Bob and all the rest of them, and me and Billy look up then to see the moon, coming up over Palmyra.

## Chapter 6

The next morning, when I open my eyes, everything's different. I lay in bed and I'm all alone. Bob has got up early and gone down to his folks' house where his mother's cooking up a big breakfast for him and his daddy to eat, before they go out in the field. She cooks up ham and eggs and biscuits and bacon and gravy and all kinds of things. All they're going to do is ride their big Allis Chalmers tractor around, but she cooks them up a breakfast like they're expecting to go out there with plows tied on their own shoulders and turn over those fields like that.

The sun is shining in my window. I can hear the birds outside.

I should get out of bed. It's Friday and Friday I wash the windows. It's ironing day, too, and Mother Bybee says nobody ever must have taught me how to dust, but I don't want to do that neither.

I look at myself lying there. I look at my nightgown, which is soft and white, and I notice how it lies across my belly, and how it hugs itself on my hips, which are just possibly my best feature. I look at my breasts and how they press themselves to the nightie and I just about die at how nice they look. I think what a shame nobody else is here to see all this. Like when you make a perfect flip off the diving board, but everybody's looking the other way. I think that, well, anyway, it'll still be here tonight and tonight Bob'll be home. But that idea doesn't make me feel better.

I think what a shame that it's just Bob, Bob, Bob forever and that makes me think of the Bible verse pearls before swine. I think how I'm a pearl and Bob is a swine, but that seems like a very bad thing to think and I make myself stop.

I take my hand and run it over the top of my body to see what it feels like from the outside. I think, *Does Bob know what he's got?* And then I stop thinking about Bob.

I think maybe I'll go to town and visit my mother and my sisters. I think maybe Billy is up on the roof fixing the chimney today and maybe later he'll split some of that firewood for my Mama. I think I'll sit out on the porch and drink lemonade with my sister, Evaline.

But, downstairs, I find a note from my husband and it says he loves me and he's so happy I'm his wife and he's lucky too and he knows it. The note says he'll be home at lunch time and he's really looking forward to that! He put in an exclamation point at the end just to show me how much he means it. I'm not as irritated as you might think. In the first place, it's over a mile to town and to my Mama's house, so I'm thinking after lunch Bob'll give me a ride in the car.

I fold the note over and set it down and then I go outside to sit on the porch. It's past my breakfast time but, the way I feel, I'll never eat another bite of food again as long as I live. I sit on the porch in the hot sun and, instead of feeling closed off, my skin feels like it's an open thing. It feels like in the night somebody peeled it back so all the nerves inside are laid open on the skin. I sit like that for I don't know how long. It's like I'm someone who has no mind anymore to notice the passing of time. It's like all of who I am has got pressed into the body I've got and I'm alive like a animal is alive with just its skin and its legs and its face. I look out across from me and I can see the Dunavans' horses. The Dunavans, they've got six horses. I think I'm alive like those horses, with just the sun on their skin and the air blowing their manes around.

It's hours later when Bob pulls into the driveway. I watch his car come toward me but I don't think how this is Bob, my husband, coming home for lunch. I'm just sitting, feeling the pressure of the porch swing on my legs and the softness of the morning breeze across the prairie, on my skin. Feeling my hair lift up on the back of my neck.

When Bob pulls in and sees me there, first thing he thinks is I'm waiting for him. He comes rushing up smiling, like it's Christmas morning and I'm about ready to hand him a big Christmas present. He stands there, breathless, looking at me, and then he says, "What's for lunch?"

What I'm picturing is a prairie from a long time ago, before you looked out and saw the fences between everybody's land and before you saw telephone poles and electric wires and all the rest. I'm picturing a wild horse standing there in that flat land that goes on forever and you can see all of it. Lunch. It's a hard, mean-sounding word.

"Lunch," Bob says again, like I didn't hear it the first time. "What's for lunch?"

"There's no lunch," I say, and he looks at me, puzzled and cocking his head to the side, and then he starts smiling again, because he's understood that I'm having a strong feeling, and he thinks everything I feel winds up pointing back to him.

He says, "Let's go upstairs," and he winks at me.

People say someone is good or they're bad — in bed I mean — and after Hammer Johnson, not that we done it a lot, but after him, Bob seemed like he was probably one of the good ones, but now I'm wondering. Maybe Hammer Johnson isn't much of a yardstick to go on.

After Bob gets done, he dresses, but I'm still laying in bed. I'm feeling the softness of the sheets against my skin. I'm watching the outline of my body under those sheets. I'm thinking I could stay here all day.

Bob says, "Let's have some lunch."

I just lay there, laughing. Bob smiling the whole time like isn't he clever. "There's nothing here to eat," I say, finally. "But how about we go over to Aunt Babe's and have us some of her soup du jour?" I giggle when I say that. "I could really go for one of Aunt Babe's cheeseburgers."

Bob says he's got a better idea. Bob says, "Let's go over to the Tic Tac for some steak sandwiches."

I say, "But the Tic Tac is clear to Jacksonville." I say, "But I just was over in Jacksonville a few days ago." I say, "But don't you have to get back to work."

Bob winks at me again and he says he guesses he can take a Friday afternoon off to be with his bride.

"What will Daddy Lyle say?" I'm thinking how this is very unusual, Bob coming up with an idea like going to the Tic Tac when he's supposed to be out in the field with Mr. Lyle Bybee, and I'm wondering how many more surprises are waiting for me.

Just then Bob says, "It was Daddy Lyle's idea."

"What?"

"That's right. You heard me. Why don't you take the afternoon off, Bob, my father said, and spend it with that new wife of yours?" And then Bob moves over to where I'm laying and he sets his hand down on my belly, smiling, patting it. I can see how he's hoping he has put something in there and how all of them are hoping for the same thing. It makes me think of when men will put the bull in with the cow, when they put the pigs together, the dogs. Sometimes they'll hold the female still and sometimes they won't. If they need to, then they will.

We drive to Jacksonville and I have the window rolled down so the air's blowing over me. I say, "I guess later I'll go to my Mama's house and help out."

"Help out?" Bob says. He's thinking what about the mess in my own house. He's thinking isn't this Friday, window washing day, and what about all the knickknacks that need dusting, according to Mother Bybee, but he doesn't say that. He says, "You're messing your hair up."

At the Tic Tac, the waitress sits us at a small table near the front door. There's an aquarium beside us for people to look at while they wait for their seats. Usually there are all different colors of fish, pink and blue and silver, but today there are only three silver ones. They're so flat it's like someone has rolled them out with a rolling pin, and they've got fins that go up and loop around. Those fish come from the other side of the world where it's warm all the time, so the tank has to be kept heated. I don't know if somebody caught them and brought them here or if they got bred in a tank someplace and sold. You can't tell by looking.

I'm watching the fish and they're watching me back. I tap on the glass next to them but they don't flinch.

We order steak sandwiches today because this is a special day and cheeseburgers won't do.

"Eat your food," Bob says, but I ignore him. "It's good," he says. I can't eat a thing. The food sets on my plate getting cold. I sip my cherry coke and look at Bob.

Bob's sitting there and he's fat, I tell you. Not stocky or thickset, like I used to tell myself, but fat. He has fat hands and a fat head and he has a fat neck. Now Billy, he doesn't have a neck like that. His neck looks like something you want to put your fingers on, it looks like something you want to taste with your tongue. Which is something I oughtn't say, but I guess I can have my own thoughts anyway. I sit in the Tic Tac looking at my husband, Bob, and thinking about Billy Lee's neck and I feel like I'm a little deer and his neck is a big salt lick. It's standing out in the woods, just calling to me.

Bob says this is going to be a good year for soybeans. He tells me about the new tractor again and he tells me other things too, but I've stopped listening. I'm wondering did he always talk to me like this or is this the way a farmer talks after he marries you. And I can't remember.

I get a funny feeling, like I'm not who I was before but someone different. Like I'm an alien from another planet, like my sister Flora is always reading about. I've been given Lucy Fooshee's body and I've read about her life and seen pictures and been told all about her, but every now and then something comes at me that nobody thought to mention. I finish my cherry coke and order another one.

I think how I'm being silly and I'm not usually silly. Flora is the silly one. I think maybe this is because I haven't eaten a thing all day, only two cherry cokes, and maybe if I forced some food down my throat I'd start thinking like I usually do. Maybe if I stuffed that steak sandwich in my mouth I'd go back to being the way I was before, but I look at the steak sandwich and I think, *What's so good about that?*

Bob never fails to notice if I order a chocolate malt when I've already had myself a piece of rhubarb pie, but when I'm starving myself to death before his very eyes, he doesn't see a thing. He looks over at my plate then and says, "Let me finish up what you haven't ate, Lucy."

I don't point out that what he's referring to is an entire steak sandwich lunch that I haven't even touched. I just push the plate over to him and drink my cherry coke.

I'm watching the girl at the next table who's eating lunch with her boyfriend. I'm noticing she has on a skirt that's a little bit short and she forgot to wear her nylons and the skirt is riding up on her legs. I'm especially notic-ing how she flaps her legs together while that boyfriend of hers is talking. I just bet he ain't talking about soybeans neither. She's flapping her legs back and forth, like she's trying to cool something off. And then that boyfriend, he takes a ice cube out of his soda, holds it in his fingers, and runs that ice cube all around her neck, like he thinks he better cool her off before she goes and ignites right here in the Tic Tac. As soon as the waitress walks by, he calls her over and I hear him ask for a doggy bag because they just remembered they have an important appointment. I think to myself, important appointment, I'll say.

About this time, Bob has finished up my food and done everything but licked the plate. Bob's daddy, Mr. Lyle Bybee, is a big fat man and it's dawning on me that

Bob is looking more and more like him. Bob calls the waitress over and he says, "Kiddo, what've you got for dessert today?"

And Kiddo says, "We've got pineapple upside down cake today, Mr. Bybee, and I know that's your favorite."

Bob puffs out his mouth and pretends he's thinking, *Do I want my favorite dessert or not?* But really, he's so pleased with her knowing his name and with her knowing what he likes — he's so pleased with all this that Bob is stretching the moment out, so it can last as long as possible. Just when it's getting to be too long, he says, "Give me some of that pineapple upside down cake then, Sweetheart. Lucky I saved room."

She's smiling as big as her lips will go and I can just about hear her thinking what a charming man this is. *I wish I could have me a man like this, whooee*, she's thinking. She has never seen Mr. Lyle Bybee and so she can have a thought like that. She's so happy with my husband that she forgets to ask if I want dessert. She skips away with her ponytail swinging back and forth and my husband watching her.

"What a nice kid," he says.

"Your favorite dessert is cream pie," I say.

"I sure am glad I took the day off, Lucy," he says and he's thinking of upstairs in our room earlier, but I'm not.

"Why'd you pretend pineapple upside down cake is your favorite dessert when you know it's not?"

Bob asks me how did my beauty appointment go the other day, like he can't see with his own eyes." Bob doesn't have much finesse when it comes to changing the subject. He says, "Mama doesn't see why you don't go to the girls in town." Which means Tammy and Lottie Lois, in Palmyra.

"I already told your Mama those girls don't like me and you don't want a enemy cutting on your hair. I already told your Mama that."

The waitress puts Bob's dessert in front of him and says she hopes he enjoys it and if she can do anything else, just ask. I think, *anything else*, that's a big category. Anything else, that opens up lots of possibilities. And because my mind is the way it is today, I think of the waitress on her knees under our table with her ponytail bobbing back and forth.

And it's like she can read my mind because then that waitress, Misty her name tag says, wouldn't you know it, she looks right at me and smirks and I stick out my chin and bat my eyes at her.

She's only put one fork on the plate, which tells me if I want a bite of pineapple upside down cake, well, that's my problem. Bob doesn't notice any of this because he's digging in. When he's got about half the pineapple upside down cake in his mouth Bob says, "I think we need to talk, Lucy."

Bob stuffs the other half of the cake in his mouth, on top of the first half, and now he's got the whole danged thing in there and he's mushing it all around. His mouth's so full he can't get his teeth together to chew.

I wonder if it's too late to get our marriage annulled. Mavel Runel's aunt from over to Pekin, she got annulled. I think at least then I wouldn't have to watch Bob's table manners no more.

I'd have to let everybody know it was my own idea, and not Bob's. First, I'd tell Sadie Pinshaw down at the five and dime because everybody comes in there all day long and she talks to them all. I'd say to Sadie that Bob is a very nice man. I'd tell her that I don't have a bad word to say about him. That's the kind of person I am. But then I'd say, in a low voice, how me and Bob aren't compatible and she could just wonder what I meant by that. Sexually, that is what they'd say at the five and dime. He just isn't man enough for her, they'd say. She's some woman, the men would say, and the women wouldn't say it out loud but that's what they'd think too, despite themselves.

I sip my drink and wonder where I'd go after this. I know where I wouldn't go and that's back to the five and dime where you stand on your feet all day and get varicose veins so you can't even wear a swimsuit no more. I've moved on past the five and dime. The five and dime is for girls like Sadie Pinshaw who've got nothing better to do than stand on their feet all day long and anyway never could wear a swimsuit in the first place.

I think how my sister, Betty, is married and living over in Buckhorn and I could go and stay with her, but I don't want to. Eliza March is taking a leave of absence at the Palmyra Lumber and Grain Company and I could take her job, but I don't want to do that neither.

Bob says to me, "It's time for us to start looking ahead."

Bob can never just say a thing outright. He has to hem and haw and beat around every bush he can find first. So Bob sits there saying a lot of things. They'd be the introduction, if this was a book. You know how some books they have an introduction that takes fifty pages before they even start, that's the way Bob is.

I set my hands on either side of the plate and stretch my fingers out. My hands are dark against the pale blue tablecloth and my fingers are long. I have my wedding ring on, of course. Bob's ring with a big diamond. I stretch my fingers out against the pale blueness of the tablecloth, and I move them.

I think about what happened upstairs in my bedroom this morning, when I was alone, and then later when I was with Bob, and I think to myself if I'd known the way married relations could interest me, then I'd have been more careful about who it was I got married to.

Just one month ago Bob Bybee seemed like the perfect husband for me but look how much things have changed in that one month. And what if my whole life ended up being that way, so every time I turned around I realized what a big fool I'd been, but now I had changed.

In the back of my mind, a little voice says, what about the pretty house you just moved into and the addition you're fixing to build? What about your furniture and the clothes Bob bought you? That little voice says, if you got annulled you wouldn't be a rich farmer's wife no more. You'd have to scrimp like your sister, Evaline, and you'll be an old maid like her, too.

I turn in my chair so my legs are out to the side and I cross them. I look down at my legs and they're tan, from me lying out in the sun, and they're slender. I stretch them out and point my toes and I think how I don't care about the house or the furniture. And anyway, I can keep the clothes, I guess.

The whole time, I'm stretching my legs out thinking how lucky I am to have nice, smooth legs, thin legs but not skinny. The girls in my family, we all have nice legs.

But then Bob's voice sums up all that he's been leading to and what he says is, "I just can't wait for us to start our own family."

I don't say nothing for a long time. Bob has two married sisters but so far they've only had girls, ugly little redheaded things with tiny eyes and skin that blisters as soon as the sun hits it. Girls that cry and kick up a fuss over everything, which is the way the Bybees are, everybody knows it.

Bob adds, "No reason to wait around."

I just look at him. My sister Flora told me once about a girl who wanted to go to a party but her father wouldn't let her. And she wanted to go so bad that when she laid down on her bed, her spirit broke away and got dressed up and went to that party and everybody who was there saw her and she danced all night. But when her father looked in her room, it looked just like she was sleeping. And that's the way I am.

The girl who's here in my place says, "I'm not getting any younger," and that makes me giggle.

Well, anyhow, I think to myself, I don't have to move out of the house anymore. I don't have to find me a job.

"We got everything going for us," Bob says, and he winks.

Bob Bybee is living with an idea of somebody and that idea is stronger than me. Who would have thought it? You can live side by side with someone and, at the same time, you're in your very own world that they don't know nothing about. This gives you some privacy anyway, I think. And I feel like I did the first time everybody in my family went away for the day and left me alone. Like I could run through the house saying, "Goddamn it, goddamn it," and nobody would know.

"No reason to wait around sitting on our hands," Bob says again. "That's what Daddy said."

"Oh, Daddy said that, did he?" And I think about me and Bob upstairs and the way I picture it Daddy Lyle is standing there, off to the side watching, the way the men do with their animals.

"A Bybee," Bob says and he means the name. A boy with that name.

I think to myself, I'd better be careful. Something I remember hearing many times over the years, she wasn't careful, if she ain't careful, she better be careful, that's what she gets for not being careful. People act like being careful is something you could do by sheer force of will, like running with scissors facing out instead of in, but I don't see how that could be true.

Bob says, "I want to name him after my daddy."

That means Lyle, I think. And I picture Daddy Lyle Bybee and I can just imagine a little boy looking just like him, busting out of his bib overalls and all bloated up, like a hog dead too long without being buried, and red in the face and yelling.

Just the other day, I was walking through town, saying baby names out loud to myself, and picturing what a little baby of mine would look like. Daddy Lyle never once came up. I walked all over town with my sister Evaline's dog Foxie thinking of how fine it would be to have my very own baby that looked just like me and everywhere we went people would say, "Don't you look alike!" and when she was older they'd say, "You look just like sisters!"

*Chapter 7*

Every Fourth of July the Bybees throw a big party at their house. They spit roast a whole hog and everybody comes from town and, from the whole county, the best families show up.

Everybody brings plenty to eat. They bring barbecued chicken, potato salad, baked beans, pig's feet, corn on the cob, coleslaw, sweet potato pie, deviled eggs, and home cooked biscuits and rolls. They bring their own preserves and they bring bread 'n butter pickles they've put up themselves. They bring all kinds of cakes and pies and desserts. Lemon pies, chiffon and apple and pear and banana creme pies. And cakes, too. German chocolate and caramel and checkerboard cake, pineapple upside down cake, spice cake and sponge cake, seven-minute lemon cake and, of course, angel food cake. And there's the hog too, like I said.

Some people come and some people don't. We don't say who, folks just know. If you have to wonder about it, then stay home, is the way it works. Of course, the Fooshees, they come. My Mama and my sisters. But the

Hoggs, they don't. The Gertlers and the Runels and the Dunavans, the Marches, and the Pinshaws, they all come. Mrs. Gertler brings the best cherry cobbler. But Aunt Babe Lee doesn't come. Frank and Lloyd Garber do, but the Mossers and the Egrees, the Blanches, and the Quiggs don't.

Everybody who doesn't come, they act like they have better things to do anyway. If you see them before, they might even say how they wished they could come but they're afraid they have company coming, "You know how it is," they say, like not being welcome is the least of their concerns. But you don't point that out. You say, "Oh. Uh huh. Of course."

Aunt Babe she never comes to the Fourth of July party but Billy Lee, he came. Invited special, at my suggestion.

Billy said I could walk down the street in California and somebody would make me a movie star. At first I had liked the idea and I'd go about my day pretending somebody was making a movie out of me and where I came from. Like somebody was following me around shooting a movie all the time.

I'd be at the kitchen sink and there'd be a voice, "Lucy Fooshee" — using my maiden name — "came from humble beginnings." I'd be hanging my clothes on the line and that voice would be talking, "Lucy Fooshee was married to the richest family in Pike County, except for the Winklejohns, but she risked everything for the man she loved." Sort of like what happened to Grace Kelly, but the other way around.

But then it started to work on me. I started thinking how living out in Pike County and spending my time with people who knew me all my life and are just used to how I look and think nothing of it, take it for granted, it's like having a child who's a genius and then never letting them go to school. It's like being Liberace and not having a piano.

I thought how I was already twenty-two years old and how I had had my looks for seven years and I was somewhere close on to the middle of how long they would last. Time is running out. Every second I'm getting older. Every day is one day less of being like I am.

The people in Palmyra have known me all my life. I'm like the sun setting over the prairie to them. First time somebody sees it, they stop everything to look and point. Maybe they buy a picture postcard of it and send it home. But people from here, they don't even look up. They seen it all their life. And that's how I am. Elton Fooshee's girl.

But when Billy is around, I'm America just being discovered by Christopher Columbus. That's what I am. I am something nobody's seen before. I've been invisible and now somebody sees.

When I'm in the vicinity of Billy Lee, it's like I'm on television. Like his eyes are cameras and they're pointing at me and my picture is going all over the world for everybody to look at. That's how I feel when I'm with Billy Lee, even when I'm standing over by the house in the shade and he's clear across the yard by the pig that's being roasted whole, with its head on and everything, and he's drinking a beer, talking to my sister, Evaline. Even before he spotted me, even before he turned my way, it's still like there's a camera pointed at me and it's coming from him. Everybody can see it, all over the world. I can just picture them, sitting in front of their television sets.

I think to myself this is better than Miss Corn Festival

where you ride in Bobby Blanche's red Corvette Stingray convertible and wave your hand, while everybody waves back and takes pictures and points to you saying *look!*

I'm standing off with the women but I'm also watching myself, like if I'm in my own living room watching a movie of myself on the TV set. Everything I do, even just standing here holding a paper cup with beer in it, pushing the hair from my face, sighing, licking my lips, everything I do, is bigger than it ever has been before. Like the director is saying, *Get in close now! Slow it down!*

I don't say a word to Billy all day long. Even when I'm right next to him, it's like I'm so busy with everybody else I forgot who he is. Like he's no more to me than the man down at the Texaco. Like if somebody asked his name, I'd have to think about it a little while.

I'm working it all out, standing in the Bybee yard drinking my beer from a paper cup and saying to everybody how it's so hot and how I just can't wait to eat and did they see Eliza March's new baby and isn't he a doll.

The Bybees aren't drinking people but on the Fourth of July they buy two kegs of beer and everybody drinks. They eat and drink and they talk. The men stand on one side and what they talk about is farming. They talk corn and soybeans and fertilizer and farm equipment and they might talk a little baseball too and such. And the women, they stand on the other side. They talk about their diets and their recipes and who has done what and who is mad at who. All the time the kids are running everywhere and nobody cares.

By the time it's dark, everybody is about half drunk and it's time to set off the fireworks. Bob, he's a big one for that. Buster March has a cousin from over to Peoria who's a truck driver and he brings in all kinds of fireworks from Missouri, where he drives, and from the south — Alabama and Mississippi. Things we can't get around here. The men are all out in the middle of the yard, setting them up, and there's confusion and running around with parents finding their kids and people setting up lawn chairs and putting down blankets. Mother Bybee she goes inside to make sure all the lights are shut off and it's dark.

I'm off to one side, back behind Billy and Sadie Pinshaw, Mavel Runels (who I hate), my sister, and the Marches, Betsy and Eliza, along with their babies. I've been waiting all this time, thinking it through. I know a chance will come. Like when I went hunting with my brother, Jimbo, one time for deer. You set up a blind and you wait. You put out a salt lick and the deer they come up to lick it and then you shoot them. Deer got to have salt just like anybody else. You wait all day sometimes, twiddling your thumbs. It's like what Jimbo said to me, you wait long enough, something is sure to come by. And that's what I've been doing with Billy Lee. Not like other guys, you have to beat them off with a stick.

Eliza March has a blanket but we don't all fit on it. I hear Billy say he has a blanket back in his truck. He thinks he'll get his blanket out for Evaline and the rest of them to spread out on. When I hear that, I know it's my chance. I've been watching, like I said, and I know his truck is parked way down the highway. It's about last in line. But then Evaline she sits down right on the grass and says to him to come on and sit down. She says she doesn't need anything. Which is just like her. She says, "You don't want to miss the fireworks."

Betsy March lays her baby girl down and Billy sits next to it, beside Evaline. The Marches are big breeders. All the March girls have babies and they're always showing them off like this is something special about them, how they can churn out copies of themselves and aren't they just dolls!

I sit down now, next to Betsy's little girl, and I say, "What a sweetheart!" I say, "Doesn't she have the cutest little pouty mouth!"

"It looks like somebody is ready for a baby," says Sadie Pinshaw, and they all turn to look at me, Sadie, Billy, Evaline, Betsy, Eliza and Mavel.

"Oh, let me hold her!" I say, and I pick the baby up and make noises at her but she only sticks her lip out further.

"Don't they look sweet!" exclaims Betsy. Now that she has her own baby, Betsy is always pushing other people to have them too, like she's in a club but there aren't enough members yet.

But Eliza doesn't like Betsy's baby getting all the attention and it makes her mean. She says, "Babies take a lot of work. You've got to think of someone else first all the time, when you have a baby. You have got to sacrifice." And she looks at me, doubtful.

"They say having a baby will teach you those things, if you don't already know them," says Betsy, frowning at her sister.

"Lucy will make a good mother," throws in Evaline, like I have to be rescued and now here she is doing it. Billy shoots her a look to say, aren't you nice, and it about makes me sick.

"At least she's married," murmurs Mavel, looking at Eliza who had her baby too soon after the wedding. I giggle and Eliza scowls at me like I'm the one who said it, instead of Mavel.

Now the baby's whole mouth begins to quiver and its

face gets all pinched together and it starts screaming its head off. I hand it over to Betsy, who fumbles around sticking a bottle in the baby's mouth.

We all sit, waiting until it quiets down and then I lean towards Evaline. "Watch out for your clothes, Evaline. This grass is wet."

"Wet? How can it be wet? It's July, Lucy, and this grass is as dry as straw."

"Watch you don't sit on food. The kids was over here and they smashed everything into the grass," I tell her. "Somebody must have a blanket for you to sit on."

"I have a blanket in my truck," says Billy, and he starts to get up but she stops him. A bottle rocket has gone up and she grabs at him in the dark. "Look! It's starting already."

"You know how they warm up first." I look over at Evaline. "Evaline, watch you don't get anything smashed onto your new dress all light-colored like it is. You know how it'll spot."

Just then Buster sets off a firework that explodes over us, shooting out red and orange colors and everybody looks up and, while it's going up, they say, "Ohhh," and, when it explodes, they say, "Aaah," and I lean over into Billy's ear and whisper, "You better hurry."

I sit there for a little while after he's gone and then I say to nobody in particular, but loud enough for Evaline and Mavel and Sadie and the rest of them to hear, I say, "Oh, look there is Glenn Pinshaw!" And I jump up and slip away. I turn back to look at them once and they're sitting with their heads back and their mouths wide open.

So I hightail it through the yard, running smack into one of them folding tables loaded up with bowls and trays of leftover food. It turns over, upside down, but I leave it

there, with all the food spilled out, Jell-O salad and baked
beans and deviled eggs and what have you, laying out on
the ground waiting for the dogs to find it. I climb through
the shrubs and over the fence and out onto the highway.
Only one car passes and it's nobody I recognize. I make
my way to Billy's truck and I'm laughing so hard the
whole time, I'm bent over double. I'm talking out loud to
myself, imitating Jimbo's voice, "You wait long enough,
something is bound to come by." I think that's about the
funniest thing I ever heard.

By the time I get to Billy's truck, I've got a hold of
myself. It's a blue truck, an old Ford pickup, and I put my
hand on the hood to see if I can feel the heat from the
engine. I want to feel it on my hand, right now, the heat
from the motor, coming through the metal. I want to sit
on the hood and feel the heat on my legs and on my rear
end. I want to pull my skirt up and feel it on my skin. I
want to lay back and rest my head on the windshield of
Billy Lee's truck while the heat from his engine comes
into my whole body. That's what I want. But the engine
is cold, so instead I just stand there, leaning against the
bumper, squinting down the road until I make out the
shape of Billy, coming towards me. He's staggering a little, drunk like everybody. I can see his outline coming my
way. I can see his legs and his arms and his head and his
whole shape.

Horses have one kind of rhythm when they move.
You can sing to a horse and it'll run right along with your
rhythm, that's what I hear. You can sing row-row-row-
your-boat to them. I don't know why I'm thinking of that
now, watching the shape of Billy coming towards me.
Horses have one kind of rhythm and men have another.
Drunks have a third kind and that's the rhythm Billy has

right now. I start singing under my breath.

*Row row row your boat*

*Gently down the stream*

And it seems to me like Billy is moving in time with my song.

*Merrily, merrily, merrily, merrily*

Here he lurches to one side and that seems about right, too.

*Life is but a dream.*

Billy doesn't see me until he's right there, on top of me. So to speak.

"Hi, Billy," I say, and he stops, leans forward, squints. "Lucy?"

I run my hands over my skirt, smoothing it down, and Billy's eyes follow the motion of my hands, moving along my hips and then they come back up, looking into my face. "Is that you?" I just stand there looking at him and he looks at me. I don't think I have to answer that question.

"Why aren't you watching the fireworks?" he says, and just then a big one goes off, pink and red and blue. He leans back to watch it but I'm looking at him, at how the colors light up his face.

"Are you looking for a blanket? I've got one right here." Billy goes around to the back of his pickup and gets a blanket. It's full of hay, looks like, and he shakes it out.

I ignore him. I slide up on the hood of the truck. It's cool to the touch but I sit there anyway, watching the fireworks in the sky, my skirt pulled up on my legs. Maybe I'm just waiting for him to leave, he can't tell.

He comes over. "Is something the matter?" He leans forward to look at my eyes, have they been crying or not. "Are you okay?"

"Do I look okay to you?"

Billy goes over to his truck and opens the door, fumbles around inside until he finds a cigarette, and then he lights it and comes back to where I sit. I take the cigarette from his fingers and put it in my mouth, put my lips around it and inhale. I stop myself from coughing my head off. I blow the smoke out in his direction, playful, and hand the cigarette back. All this time, Billy still has a hold of that blanket. It's an Indian blanket, I can see, with zigzag designs, red and black. In a minute he'll notice the weight of it in his hand and that will make him think of my sister and the rest of them, up in the yard.

"Ain't it a hot night," I say, and he says that yes, it sure is. It's about as hot as it has ever been and, where Billy stands across from me, it's like someone has opened the oven door and all the heat is pouring out. You can feel the hair on your arms starting to curl up, that's how hot it is.

"You're going to miss the fireworks, Lucy."

Billy hasn't ever been to one of our fireworks parties, so he doesn't know just how many fireworks there are. We've got fireworks to last all night long.

"I know a good spot for fireworks," I say, and I giggle.

I'm sitting on the hood of the truck and he stands facing me and now I slide my knees apart. "Come here," I say.

Billy is dazed. He can't believe what's happening. I didn't hardly look at him the whole day and here I am like a movie star, which are his words, you remember, and not something I made up on my own.

"Your sister is waiting for me."

"Which one?" I say.

He looks down at the blanket, like he's looking for a clue. He notices the hay all stuck to it and gives it a shake. He's too surprised to know what to do.

I lean forward and take him by the waist and pull him in, close to me. I feel my legs on either side of his hips. He's dropped the blanket but he doesn't notice that. And when a firework goes off and the sky lights up red and yellow, he doesn't notice that either. He puts his hands on my back and pulls me forward. He puts his hands on my throat, my neck, my face, on the back of my hand, whatever skin is bare, he puts his hands there. My skirt has got pushed up around the tops of my legs. I find his zipper and begin to pull it open but then there are headlights coming at us down the road.

We pull back from each other but we don't move away. We stand there like we're froze in their beam, like what you see deers do, and then finally I see that it's my sister Flora and the Winklejohn boy, showing up late and hoping nobody will notice.

They pull their car up beside us. I slide off the hood of Billy's pickup and we walk over to where they've stopped. Flora sits looking straight ahead with her hands folded in her lap. She has got gum in her mouth and she's working it.

"What are you doing?" yells Pete Winklejohn, leaning around her. "You're gonna miss the fireworks!" He's looking from me to Billy, confused. Pete isn't a big one for putting two and two together.

"Where's Bob?" asks Flora. "Where is your husband, Bob?"

I lean down on the window, beside Flora. "Mama has been looking all over for you! Oh, and you have got your hair all mussed up, Flora! Where have you two been?"

Flora knows how to pop her gum and now she's doing it. Pop, pop, pop.

"You ought to watch fireworks with your husband, is

all I'm saying." She won't look at me.

"We've got fireworks all the way from Alabama," Pete shouts, and just then a big one goes off in the yard and Flora and Pete they look up at it and their faces light up, red and purple. "See. See there, what did I tell you." His voice is high with excitement.

The sky goes black again and Pete turns back to us. "These are some fireworks! You don't want to miss them," he exclaims and Flora, beside him, sighs and crosses her arms over her chest. "What are you doing out here?" he asks, leaning over Flora again to look at us. "What are you doing?"

Billy holds up the blanket. "We needed a blanket," he says, "to sit on."

"Oh, to sit on," says Flora.

## Chapter 8

The next day I'm sick as a dog. I can't get up for the next three days and every time I move, I throw up in the big pan Bob put by the side of the bed. I'm so sick, I bust all the blood vessels around my eyes, throwing up. I'm so sick I wish I could die. You hear people say that and you think it's just an expression, but now I know what they mean.

After three days, I sort of come out of it, like how it happens in the Bible. Like I've been Jesus in the tomb and now I'm getting ready to come back out again. That's when Evaline stops over.

"So you're sick, I hear." She's in the doorway with a bowl of something, must be chicken soup, I'm thinking. "Is it the flu, honey?"

I don't say a word. I can smell that chicken soup now and it smells good. Lots of pepper, the way Evaline makes it.

She says, "You been married six weeks now." I shut my eyes to show her that I'm not up to a big discussion. Maybe she has forgot what she's here for, how I'm sick and everything. "Six weeks is long enough."

I turn my head away from her, facing the wall.

"That's what everybody is saying, how six weeks is plenty long."

"Long enough for what?" I say, and I'm surprised by the strength of my voice.

"You know the Fooshee women always spend the first three months in bed throwing up. That's what Mama says."

"First three months of what?"

Evaline looks away from me now, at the floor. "Maybe you're in the family way, Lucy."

"Family way?"

"You know."

"Family way. Who said anything about the family way? Did Bob say that?"

I can just see Bob now. I can see all them Bybees and how they'd be so happy, like there aren't enough of them already. And all the Bybee women would shriek and grab my arms and pat my stomach, like this is a big present from me to the Bybee family and they can't wait to open it. And then they'd tell me about when all their babies was born and what that was like, forgetting I know all the details by now as good as the back of my own hand.

Then Bob would take me over to the Tic Tac for lunch, to celebrate. I can just hear him, telling the waitress his big news. I can just see her looking me over. She'd look me up and down, and it would be like I was wounded, like an animal with one leg missing. She'd say that she'd better go get some of Bob Bybee's favorite pineapple upside down cake so he could celebrate. Then she'd wiggle away, in her little black uniform skirt, with my husband Bob watching the whole time, until the kitchen doors swing closed behind her. Already, just laying in bed, I can feel my body start to swell up.

I can just see Billy Lee now, sitting across from me at the dinner table with my body all swoll up, like something out in the water too long, and throwing up and my nipples leaking and my feet puffed up and varicose veins sticking out on my legs and everything. Elizabeth Taylor wouldn't even enter his mind for a second, no sir.

I think about when Alice Yardley got cancer of the breast and how she must have felt with that thing growing in her and how every time she fed herself or got a drink of water she was feeding it too, and giving it a drink. That thing took over Alice and she couldn't do nothing about it, just sit and watch it happen and drink water and eat food and watch it get stronger while she got weaker and finally had to give up. I wish I had been kinder to Alice Yardley when I saw her at the store, but then she never did like me neither.

Before you get married, you think everything in your life has been leading up to this and it's your crowning glory, those are my own mother's words, it's the culmination of your whole lifetime starting back when you were a little girl. You think getting married is like you've lived on the outside of something all your life and finally one day the big gate opens up and you get to walk through it. You think that when you're inside then you'll be happy and you'll stop wanting things to be different.

Evaline sits down on the bed beside me. I expect she's going to start in talking about babies, but she doesn't. She sits there looking at me like I don't have to say a word because it's all written on my face.

Somewhere out in California there's somebody who would make me a movie star, if I just gave him the chance.

"I don't want to have a baby."

All my life, I wanted a husband like Bob Bybee and a room like the one we're sitting in and a bed like this one and nice clothes to wear. First thing Bob did when we got engaged was take me to Jacksonville and buy me a whole closet full of whatever clothes I wanted. Pocketbooks and shoes, too. Everybody said I was spoiled. And Bob said I deserved to be spoiled. Bob is nice like that. Bob said I needed to be spoiled. Bob said that's what he was there for, to spoil me. Which is nothing like how his family thinks. They don't believe in things like that. Farmers, they're careful people.

My whole life all I talked about was getting married and not having to worry about money. Having a nice house. And here I am. I'm waiting for Evaline to point that out, but she doesn't. She puts her hand on my forehead and she says, "You're burning up with fever."

"I don't want Bob Bybee's baby," I say, and Evaline doesn't bat an eye, just keeps sitting there. "I don't have to have it, if I don't want to."

She has got a wash cloth and now she pours some of my drinking water on it and sets it on my forehead. "Shhh."

"Gloria Quigg, she didn't want her baby neither." Gloria Quigg went up to Chicago and seen somebody. She claimed she went to visit an aunt up there, but everybody knew what she really did. Bobby Blanch, he told everybody and he should know. "You find out from Gloria who she seen."

"Hush now."

"You can't make me have this baby, Evaline. You can't make me and neither can Bob. I'm not having a baby with Bob, I'm just not."

Evaline looks over to the door now, afraid maybe

Bob'll be there listening. "You aren't having a baby," she whispers. She stands up and walks to the door, looks out it, up the hall one way and down the hall the other, and then she shuts it, quietly, and comes back to the bed. She's looking at me with her head tilted to one side, the way she does when she's figuring something out that's hard, but I don't care. I don't care if she can see everything. I don't care if it's written on my face in a red pen. What more can happen to me?

"You find out who Gloria Quigg saw, up in Chicago, and I'll go there myself. I don't need you to take me. I don't need Bob neither."

"Quiet!" Evaline says. "Whoever heard of a baby giving a woman a fever like this? You ever hear of that? You've got the flu, is what you've got." She moves over to the window and opens it wide. She doesn't look at me now but stands watching something outside. You can see the Dunavans' horses from that window. Maybe she's looking at them. "You're never happy with anything," she says, but I ignore that.

"All the Fooshee women they get sick for the first three months, is what Mama always says," I say, watching her. "You remember the way Betty was, that time." Now I've mentioned Betty's child, Little Sal who died, and I'm afraid because none of us mention her. But if I've gone too far, Evaline doesn't notice.

"You don't get a fever," she says, still looking out the window. "Nobody gets a fever, not even the Fooshees."

"You sure?"

"Yes! What you have got is the flu, pure and simple. It's going around."

"Maybe it was Mrs. Runels' potato salad," I say.

Evaline comes to the bed and sits down but she doesn't

want to speculate about the potato salad. She doesn't look at me. One of my blankets is a quilt made by Grandma Hogg and Evaline takes a corner of that quilt in her hand and she traces the design with her finger. She twists the tassels. She sits there for a long time, forgetting how I'm sick and might be worn out now, from all her visiting.

"Flora told me what she seen," she said, at last.

"What she seen?" I ask, sarcastic.

"You and Billy Lee, out at his truck, that night. The Fourth of July," she says.

"Out at his truck?" I sit up now in the bed so I'm as tall as she is.

"By yourselves."

"Oh, by ourselves," I say. "No telling what we were up to, out there all by ourselves. You want to know what we were doing? You want to know? We were getting a blanket, Evaline, for you to sit on. That's what we were doing. You were so worried about your new dress and all. Your new beige dress, remember, and so we got a blanket, Evaline — why do I have to explain myself all the time? And me sick, like I am."

"Well, Flora says —"

But I don't want to know what Flora says. "Only reason Flora is pointing her finger at me is so she can get the jump on me telling everybody how she showed up late, with Pete Winklejohn smiling beside her, and Flora with her face all flushed and her hair mussed up and you know, Evaline, she ain't married yet and if she don't watch out that Pete Winklejohn he'll throw her over, now that he's got what he wants. Can't you see how nasty and low down this is? Her pointing her finger at me when it's herself that's doing wrong?"

I slide down now, pull the cover over my face and lay

there like that. I'm ready for her to leave.

But she sits. She's picking at that quilt, I can feel it. "You know Bob thinks the sun rises and sets with you," she says, like she hasn't heard a word. "You ought to stop and think about that, Lucille. He's a good man and he loves you."

I'm under the blanket, face up, so you can just see my shape, lying there. I kick my feet.

"You've got a lot to lose," she says, and I can tell she's facing me now, the way her voice sounds.

I kick again.

She stands up now and I can hear her moving around the room, fussing, and then she goes out, shutting the door behind her.

My sickness gets everybody thinking.

The first day I'm out of bed, Bob and I drive to Mama's house for dinner. On the way there, he starts in, "Mother Bybee thinks a baby is what you need, honey."

*Need,* I think, *what I need.* I could tell them what I need all right.

"You always did want children." He adds, "A baby would settle you right down, that's what your Mama is predicting."

"Oh, everybody's got an opinion."

"We're concerned about you is all."

We pull in at Mama's house and I look up and down the street, to see if I can find a sign of Billy. It's been four days since I seen him. It's been four days for him to go over in his mind what almost happened at the party. Four days to think about me on the hood of his truck, about my knees opening, about what would have happened if Flora hadn't come up just then and what still might, if I ain't changed my mind. Maybe I was drunk, he's telling himself. Maybe he dreamed it.

"I'm all better now." I scoot around sideways in my seat and hold my arms up, presenting myself, "See? All better."

"You'd be happier if you had a baby is all I'm saying. That's what everybody thinks."

"A little by-bee," I say, making fun of his name.

"It'll calm you, Lucy."

"Is that what Mother Bybee says? How it'll calm me down. I know what she says. She says a baby is what I need to take my mind off myself."

We stop in front of Mama's. Billy's truck isn't there, but Betty's car is. "You didn't tell me about Betty," I say. My sister, Betty, is the last person in the world I want to look at right now.

Billy might have walked. He stays with his Aunt Babe and she doesn't live far from here. You go down Pleasant Street, where my Mama's house is and where I grew up, you go west until you get to Lemar Filson's green house and you make a right-hand turn. You go two blocks and turn left on Elm Street and then you see his truck, if it's there. Aunt Babe lives in the third house then, a white house. If Billy is home, his truck'll be out front.

"I don't want to make you mad, Lucy," Bob is saying. I'm looking down the street, seeing if I'll spot Billy coming on his way to dinner. "Come on, Lucy, smile for me."

I know we've passed some marker, me and Bob, and we'll never get back to where we were but I don't care. It's like we took too many wrong turns, each one moving us further away from where we were going, and now we're lost to each other.

I look at Bob and he looks back, running his hand over his scalp. It's like we were on a road called A Happy

Marriage and then one day we turned off on a little side street and, instead of circling back, we kept turning off more and more roads and pretty soon we're so far away we can't ever get back, even if we wanted to, which I don't. And the thought of us being lost like that, it doesn't make me sad. I only feel irritated that Bob doesn't seem to notice it.

"Do me a favor," Bob says, but I don't answer him. "Lu-cy."

"You want me to smile."

"I want you to go to the doctor. I want you to see if he's got something to calm you down."

"Calm me down?"

"To help you relax."

I look away from him, at Mama's house. I'm trying to see if I can make out Billy in the yard or through the window, but I can't. "I'm just fine."

"You don't seem fine to me, you seem nervous. You know your family. You got a good family and all but bad nerves runs in it." He waits to see if I'll yell at him, and then he adds, "We can't be too careful."

He's thinking of my Mama's crazy aunt Sue, but he doesn't want to say it.

I got other things on my mind though. I haven't seen Billy for four days now and I feel like I can't wait one more second, like when you've skipped breakfast and then you missed lunch and then you go out to eat at a restaurant, but they don't bring you anything for a long time. You're sitting there, smelling the smells of the kitchen, and your mouth is watering and you keep saying to the waitress, "Miss, will you bring us some bread first or something?" but she keeps forgetting. "Crackers, any-thing," you say. Every time she walks by, she doesn't have your bread. She has a big tray full of somebody else's food and it's steaming and giving off a scent trail. You think any minute you'll jump up from your seat and run to the kitchen. You'll pull the food off the stove and stick it right in your mouth.

"Let's go in," I say. "I'm starved half to death!" And I start to open my door but Bob stops me. "Let's go inside, Bob. I haven't ate all day."

But he ignores me. "Everybody's worried, Lucy."

I think about Hammer Johnson and how one day he jumped off the water tower on Third Street.

"I made an appointment for you already, for next week."

When Hammer did that, when he jumped off the water tower like he did, I couldn't imagine what he was thinking. How could he do such a thing? Didn't it occur to him that now he didn't have anything to lose anymore. So now he could do about anything he wanted. If you're ready to jump off the water tower, then can't you do whatever you want first, because you're already going to die? You can walk right up to Mavel Runels and say, "I hate you. I hate you." You can take off your clothes and walk down the street because you're already going to jump off the water tower.

"It's in Springfield."

And I think to myself, if it was me like that, with nothing to lose, then what would I do? It's all fine and dandy to tell everyone you hate that you hate them but then, after that, what do you do?

"I said Springfield, Lucy, are you listening?"

"Springfield? All the way to Springfield? Why not Jacksonville? That's where the nuthouse is."

"He's a nerve specialist, come here from Chicago is what they say."

Could be that Billy is inside right now, waiting for me. "You hear me, Lucy?"

The blinds are open but I can't see anybody inside. "Bob, can we go in now. I'm just about ravished!"

We go inside and I can tell without looking Billy isn't here. Mama is here, of course, and the girls, Flora and Evaline. And Betty is here too, along with her husband, Larry Bodell.

Betty and Larry live over in Buckhorn, like I said, and they don't come to visit too often, but when they do they always stay for dinner. There used to be a little girl, a little baby girl, Sally, who belonged to Betty but then she died.

I take my seat. I don't say a word about Billy. I say, "Bob says the sheep are ready to be wormed this week, isn't that right, Bob?" I say, "Bob just loves his new Allis Chalmers tractor, don't you, Bob?"

Betty, she's somebody who doesn't shut up. She's got to tell you everything that's happening just in case maybe you aren't paying attention. You sit down at the table and Betty says, "Time to eat now," even though we're all taking our places and the food is right there in front of us and everybody already knows it. And then she says, "Looks like we got fried chicken and green beans and apple sauce. Uh huh. Looks like we got cream of corn with little pieces of cracker floating in it." Like we're blind.

And after she's described it all to us, the ice-cold buttermilk, the biscuits and jam, everything she can see, she says, "We had fried chicken on Tuesday night, isn't that right, Larry?" Larry's her husband's name, like I said. "Or was it Monday?"

Nobody says anything, but just keeps eating and passing things back and forth, while she racks her brain.

We're sitting on the edges of our chairs, Betty thinks, wondering which one it was, Monday or Tuesday, but she never does figure it out. "Anyway, we were over to Loretta Howell's for dinner. You know since her husband passed on, she's all alone. Well, you know how big and fat Loretta Howell always was, big and fat. Not like some women they get fat later, Loretta she always was that way, always was." We all keep eating, thinking about Loretta and how big and fat she is. "Some men, I've noticed they like fat women." Betty leans forward and looks at each of us in turn, to make sure we're paying attention. Then she sits back and takes a bite of fried chicken and the grease runs down her chin and she pats it with her napkin and puts the napkin back in her lap and straightens out the edges.

"I've observed that. Fat, fat women. Some men like it. The bigger the better is what they think." She pauses. "You know, Loretta she has a mustache. I can't remember if she always was that way." Betty takes another bite of chicken. She brushes her fingers off daintily on her napkin. "Surely I would have noticed."

"Surely you would have," I agree.

"So we're eating dinner over there, fried chicken like I said, and then Loretta, for dessert, she serves us a maple cake made with real maple syrup, she says. Real maple syrup she bought over in Springfield. I told her, I said, I always use corn syrup myself, and she says how it's a maple syrup cake and you've got to use the maple syrup. It's not a corn syrup cake she tells me and I think she says it in a little bit of a huff, don't you think so, Larry?" Larry starts to say that he does think so, but Betty goes on, "I told her she's poor now. You know she never was rich, even before she was a widow woman, but now she's poor. Poor —

there's no other word for it. And so, I told her, I said, 'You don't know about being poor. You don't know how to be poor. If you're poor, you've got to eat poor. If you're poor, that's what you've got to do.'" Betty continues, "Everything has its price. Some people marry for money and they find out that money isn't everything. Money is not all it's cracked up to be." Betty takes a drink of buttermilk and then sets her glass back on the table. I start to ask her how she'd know, but then I don't. I used to fight with Betty all the time, but I'm past that now. "You can have all the money you want, but money can't buy love. Isn't that right?"

And Larry says, "That's right."

"Of course, you've got to have some money," puts in Flora. "Isn't that right, Mama?"

Mama looks up, but Mama is hard of hearing and she just shrugs.

"You have to have some money," Flora says louder, but before Mama can give her opinion, Betty says, "Of course, you do. Just look at Shawnelle Parks and Fenton March."

Just then I tip my drinking glass over and buttermilk goes everywhere. Flora rolls her eyes over to me sideways, little blue slits of eyes, and she smirks. She covers up the smirk with her napkin, "Ahem."

As soon as I've finished mopping up the buttermilk and sit back down, Betty goes on, "Shawnelle has made her bed and now she's lying in it," she says. But that's too explicit for Evaline and she says, "Betty!"

Betty shrugs, "A figure of speech."

Flora says, in a loud voice, to Mama, "Mama, you heard how Shawnelle run off with that no-good Fenton March." And Mama nods.

"Everybody's heard about it, see," says Flora. "Whether they can hear or not."

And then Betty says, "Virgil down at the post office he says Shawnelle's husband doesn't have to give her a red cent now that she's gone and done this and he says she don't deserve a red cent neither and he says that's what everybody thinks."

"How would Virgil know what everybody thinks?" I say.

Betty shrugs, "Everybody who comes in the post office, that's what they think."

"Shame on Fenton March is what I say," puts in Bob. "Shame on him running off with that girl and him without any prospects."

"Taking her reputation away," throws in Larry.

"All a girl has is her reputation," says Mama.

"What was she thinking?" asks Flora, and she sticks a chicken leg into her mouth.

"If you think thinking has anything to do with it, then you're naiver than I thought," says Betty.

"He isn't even cute," says Flora.

"How can you say that?" I say, a little too loud. "He's gorgeous!" But then they all turn to look at me.

"Gorgeous? Are we talking about the same man?" Betty lifts her eyebrows.

"We're talking about Fenton March. Is that who you're talking about?" says Flora.

"Who else?" I ask.

Flora glances at me from across the table but she's my little sister and she won't look at me straight on. She looks away, but she says, "Shawnelle has ruined her life, that's all I can say."

"Excuse me," I say, and I get up from the table and

walk out of the room and I go to the bathroom and shut the door. I lock it behind me and sit down on the commode. I put my hands over my ears and shake my head back and forth. I rock my body from side to side, like Irvin Decker's horse that he never let out of the stall. I bob my head back and forth and open my mouth and make my face go like I'm screaming my head off. I can feel the little blood vessels around my eyes breaking open again, but I don't stop. I lean forward with my mouth open as wide as it will go and my breath held and my face like it's screaming its head off.

I know I look like a lunatic, but nobody can see me. There's nobody there and, to prove it, I swing my arms around. What I said before about cameras on me and everybody watching, from all over the world, is just something I made up. I start to feel like I could scream out loud and nobody would hear me. I could walk through the house, screaming, with my face the way it is, swinging my arms, and everybody would keep eating and saying, "Please pass the gravy."

Then I get a hold of myself. "Dear Lord, please send Billy. Please send Billy Lee, in the name of Jesus, Savior of the World." I know I'm praying for a sin, but this is important. "I'll do anything you want. Please let me have this. I'll never be selfish again just let me have this. This is the last thing. I really mean it. Let me have this. I won't ask again. Let me have this."

It really works too, because after dinner we're all sitting out on the porch and Billy comes walking down the street. Mama sees him coming and says, "Here's Billy, to pick up his paycheck." But I know it's really to answer my prayer. I'm sitting on the steps next to Bob, with Flora on one side of me and Larry and Betty behind me, in chairs, and Mama and Evaline on the porch swing. And here comes Billy. I know it's him from way far off. It's a different rhythm tonight, instead of row-row-row-your-boat, but I can still tell it's him.

Billy turns in at the house and when he sees me there, he gives a little jump, but then he recovers and acts like usual. "I see you're feeling better," he says to me.

"Thank you, I am."

My husband, Bob, says, "She was sicker than a dog, I'll tell you."

"I'm sorry to hear it."

"I'm fine now, thank you. I'm just fine."

"You look just fine."

I giggle and look away, "Thank you." I can feel Flora beside me, watching, but I don't care.

"She was very sick," throws in Bob again, in case that isn't clear yet. "She was not a happy camper," he says. I never know what he means by that but it's something Bob will say, not a happy camper.

"Anyway," I say, giving the signal that we're ready to move on to the next subject.

"She couldn't keep nothing down."

"Bob," I say, to give him a little warning.

"It was coming out both ends," Bob tells him. Just so Billy can picture it clearly.

I look at Bob and I think, *How could I have married you?*

"She looks just fine now," says Billy and I say, "I am fine. I'm just fine."

At least Billy can see that I'm fine.

We sit there all evening and everybody talks, except me. They talk about fertilizer, of course, because anytime you have Bob Bybee around that's one thing you have got to talk about. They talk about Eliza March's new baby boy. And then, at Mama's instigation, they talk about Evaline's cooking when half the time it's just fried chicken and anybody can cook that.

I stretch my legs out in front of me and I don't say a word.

When they've run Evaline's cooking into the ground, Mama starts in on Flora's wedding.

It's like they're putting on a performance to prove, once and for all, that I'm not one of them. You just assume you belong to the folks you're born into, but now I can see that isn't always the case.

I don't say a word. Billy can see for himself I'm not like them. He don't belong here and neither do I. But I was born here. I grew up here. I haven't hardly been away from this. The only place I ever went was St. Louis, on my honeymoon, and that is just in Missouri. And it occurs to me that the reason I was born here in Palmyra, Illinois, is so I could be here when Billy Lee come to town. Like if I had a train to meet and this is where I had to wait.

And then this thought comes to my mind. I think Billy might stand up there in front of everybody and say how we're in love and nothing else matters. I can just see him doing it. Like how you watch a movie you've already seen and you're just waiting for the next part. I can see it the same as that, like it's already happened and I'm just waiting for everybody else to see it too.

They'll be stunned, I think, stunned. Here I've been living beside them every day of my life and they never had any idea how different, how lonely, and out of place I've been and won't they feel sorry then. I never knew what love is, I'll say. I never knew what love is, I like that phrase so much, it's so much the right phrase, that I'll say it two or three times. So when the story gets told again, all over town and all over the county and all through time, they won't leave that part out.

Then I'll go straight inside and get my pocketbook. I won't even pack a little bag.

It'd be better if Billy had brought his truck. If he had his truck then we'd drive away and leave everybody sitting on the porch, speechless. I'd look straight ahead at the road in front of me. We'd be out of town before they could get a word out of their mouths.

Maybe Bob Bybee will run after us, I think, grabbing hold of the window where I sit with my pocketbook in my lap. But then I decide that he won't. He'll just keep sitting on the porch, saying nothing, right along with everybody else. For one thing, he'll be too stunned. Like when Howie Doogan's little sister got hit by a car on Walnut Street and everybody froze and didn't know what to do.

Anyway, they'll realize how it's fate, me leaving with Billy Lee, it's Kim Novak and William Holden, and nobody can stop it. Or like when you find out there's no Santa Claus and you don't argue about it because suddenly it all falls into place. Suddenly all the little things you knew, but never let yourself think about, they add up.

By the time I get to the edge of Palmyra, I'll have forgot all about them.

"You should have been here for Lucy's wedding, " says Flora. "You were only two weeks too late."

"Isn't that something," says Billy, and he winks at me.

"Her bridesmaids wore peach-colored semi-formal gowns," says my Mama. "Peach colored to match her complexion."

"Peaches and cream," I say, so Billy will know she don't mean orange.

All night I wait for a chance to say something private to Billy but all night someone is there, stopping me from it. Finally at the end of the evening, the Bodells stand up to leave and Evaline runs inside to get something they forgot. Mama goes in too, to get Billy's pay. Everybody else is walking around talking and saying good-bye, not realizing they're supposed to be thwarting the inevitable, and me and Billy we're side by side for an instant.

I say, "I have to see you alone," and he looks at me, surprised. Here I am, beauty queen, married to one of the richest men in the county, got everything going for me, and what I want is him. He must figure he doesn't have a chance, is what I think. He must think I really was taking a walk on the Fourth of July, like how I told him. Drunk, is what he must tell himself. She didn't really mean it, is what he must think. He must figure a girl like me who can have anybody she wants, Miss Subfreshman, first runner up to Miss Freshman, Miss Sophomore and Miss Senior and Miss Corn Festival, a girl like that, the best looking girl in the whole county — what chance did he have. And I was married, too, don't forget. That's what I say to myself. Married too, don't forget.

He doesn't know what to say.

"When can I see you?" I ask. He's forgetting we don't have all the time in the world. "Alone!" I say, so he gets the picture.

"But Bob." He tips his head toward Bob who's standing by Larry Bodell, out at the car, and I look at him too, wondering what kind of thing that is to set against my feeling. Like if you have a scale and on one side you put Bob Bybee and on the other you put this feeling I have. Any fool can see which side goes down.

"So what?" I say. "Bob? So what?" It's the best I can

come up with.

"He thinks the sun rises and sets on you," Billy says, and that rings a bell but I can't think why.

Evaline has come out of the house and she's standing at Larry's car, talking to Betty. Any minute she'll look up and recall her duty, which is to keep me from ruining my life, and she'll charge over here.

"Bob leaves for work at seven."

Bob thinks the sun rises and sets with me. Where did I hear that before?

Evaline looks up now and her eyes settle on the two of us, off to the side alone, and she doesn't say good-bye to Betty or nothing but just hurries right over.

The sun rising and setting — they're the exact words Evaline said to me, that day in my room with the chicken soup, and now I can see how she used them with Billy too, how she got to him with stories of my poor husband, Bob. And I look at Evaline, hurrying towards us, and I think, *Traitor!*

"What are you doing?" she asks, looking at me.

"I was just asking Billy here to come over to my house," I say, and I smile at him but he doesn't smile back. I let the moment stretch out. I look at his face but it's calm. Evaline though, she looks from his face to mine and she's pale and worried.

"You know I've been trying to find somebody to look at my sink," I say, and I laugh. "I figured Billy here, being a handyman and all, might know what to do." I press my hand into his arm. "Bob sure don't."

## Chapter 9

"Tomorrow I've got a doctor appointment in Springfield." I tell that to Billy while he's working at the cafe and I'm sitting at the counter. He doesn't say anything, but looks at me with his black eyes. "I've got to go to the doctor," I repeat. "On your day off."

"I hope you're not sick."

"No, I'm not." Billy has made me a free chocolate shake and I'm drinking it through a straw. "Do I look sick to you?"

"No, you don't."

"Well, I'm not sick," I say. "I'm over-excited." And when I say that last word, over-excited, I lean forward and look at him, eye to eye.

"Bob thinks I need calming down." I put my lips around the straw and I drink my chocolate shake. It's two o'clock and most of the customers have left. It's the hot time of the day and I'm sitting in front of a fan but it isn't cooling me down.

"Bob thinks I need medicine to make me relax."

I look up at his eyes and then I look at his mouth and

he looks at my eyes too and then at my mouth. I'm waiting for him to make the next move. He's had time now to
think it over, but he doesn't say anything. He makes more
coffee and then he makes more tea and then he gets out
the toothpicks and fills the toothpick tray and the whole
time I'm watching, ready to say yes if he'll ask the question.

Usually guys ask the question before you have time to
ask it to yourself first, but Billy doesn't do that. He goes
in the back where Babe does the cooking, and he's gone
for a long time. When he comes out again and I'm still
there, he looks surprised, like maybe I just come in for a
chocolate shake and what reason is there to stick around,
now that it's gone.

Maybe I could be patient if I had all the time in the
world, but I don't have all the time in the world. I'm not
getting any younger, for one thing. And anyway, I think,
sitting at Babe's Cafe, Billy isn't like the guys around
here. If you've been all over, the way Billy has been, you
don't stay in a place like Palmyra, Illinois. Only reason
someone stays in Palmyra is they don't know what's out
there. Here today, gone tomorrow, that'll be Billy. Not
like the boys around here. The boys around here, they
don't go nowhere. They might talk about going someplace — they might say how they're going to Springfield
or to Chicago or they might even talk about going out
west, out to California, but then they don't. Something
always comes up. They have to get their car fixed first or
work out the planting season or they have a wedding to
go to or hogs to butcher or something, something, something. Boys around here they'll talk about it for months
and years but Billy one day he'll just up and go.

I sit here thinking, *What can I do? What can I do?* and

just then my husband walks in the door. The door jingles because Babe has put bells on it, and I turn around in my seat. So does Virgil, down the counter. Billy looks up and he moves a little bit away from me, saying, "Hi there, Bob, what can I do for you?"

It's two o'clock, the middle of the day, and I don't know why Bob isn't out in the field like he is every day at this time, but I don't ask.

Bob says he'd like a double cheeseburger and fries. And him ordering that way, it's like a knife in my heart. It's like going to a funeral and hearing the nails being put in the coffin. Double cheeseburger and fries. I think to myself if Bob would order something different one time, if one day he'd ask for the fish sandwich or the BLT, if he'd have a chef salad with turkey on top, then I could almost stand the idea of him being my husband.

Two months ago, I was getting ready to marry Bob Bybee and he was my crowning glory, my Mama said, and that's what I thought, too.

I sit on my stool, twisting it back and forth. One minute you can feel one way and the next, it's something else. I've been sleeping most of my life, I think, but now Billy Lee has woke me up and I'm only afraid I'll fall asleep again.

"How's my lovely bride?" says Bob.

Before Billy come along, my life was like the dateline Miss Petefish drew on the blackboard in history class. One thing and then another. In a line.

"You worried about the doctor?" says Bob, in a low voice, like it's a secret.

"What I'm worried about is the drive all the way to Springfield on my own and getting lost. You know how I am with my directions. And in the state I'm in —"

"Do you want a cheeseburger, Lucy?" I'm noticing how Bob Bybee can't go more than about five minutes before he has to mention eating and I say, "No, I don't."

"You already had a chocolate shake?"

I push my empty glass away and turn to look at Billy, who's now clear to the other end of the counter next to Virgil. "Billy —" I call out.

Everybody is watching me. I look around at all their faces, Billy, Bob Bybee and Virgil and I think, for a second, that they see what I see. It's like I'm Kim Novak and William Holden shows up but I already married somebody else.

But then Bob says, "What is it, Lucy?" and he nudges me.

"I'd like some of your soup, Billy," I say.

"The soup du jour?" Billy says.

"What is the soup du jour?" says Bob.

"Creme of tomato, like always."

"Creme of tomato soup right after you had a chocolate shake, honey?" I don't say anything back. At least I can eat what I want to eat. At least I can do that. "You always like the cheeseburger," Bob points out.

"I guess I don't have to be the same every day."

"No, you don't."

"I can change my mind if I want to. Just because I used to like something doesn't mean I'm stuck with it forever, does it?"

"No, honey, you go ahead and get what you want."

I look over at the window to the kitchen and an order is sitting there, must belong to Virgil. It's a BLT. I think how BLT sounds good and I say to Billy, "Give me a BLT too, please. And a chef salad with turkey on top."

Bob is watching me with alarm on his face, but I don't bat an eye. "A fish sandwich sounds good too, don't it."

Billy opens his mouth, like he's going to say something, but then he just looks at me and he looks at Bob, and he decides he isn't touching this, not with a ten-foot pole.

"Ain't that a lot of food, Billy?" says Bob, wanting to recruit him to his side, but Billy pretends not to hear. He's writing it all down. "Billy, ain't that a hell of a lot of food?"

But Billy don't join in. He shrugs his shoulders. "That girl must have a big appetite," he says.

"I do. Oh, I sure do."

Bob sits there eating his cheeseburger and I eat my soup and neither of us says a word for a long time. "I'm glad you're going to see the doctor tomorrow, Lucy," he says, at last, and I wonder if this is his way of getting in the last word about my dinner selection, or if it's a new topic.

"I wish you could drive me there, Bob. I don't like driving in all that mess. You get so many cars going everywhere and it's hard to concentrate, Bob. And you start feeling like you're sliding on ice, like the tires could slip right out from under you."

"Those are new tires."

"Like the road where it turns don't turn at all, but just ends."

"That doesn't sound right, Lucy."

"Like any minute the car will shoot into the next lane."

There's a little window, back behind where Billy works, and it leads into the kitchen. It has a shelf and when Babe is done cooking your food, she throws it there. You don't see her, as a rule. You might see her hand, if you're looking. But today I notice that before she puts up my food, my chef salad with turkey on top, my BLT, my fish sandwich, first she sticks her head out, to look. Aunt Babe has brown hair pulled back from her face in a pony-tail, so it doesn't get in your food and make you sick. She's a big woman with a big face and eyes that don't dart around but settle where they want and stay, if they want to, and now they settle on me. I look right back. She looks and I look.

"You know the car won't go anywhere you don't point it, Lucy."

I make my lips into a little smile before I look away.

"You heard about that woman and her two little girls getting killed over by Mt. Sterling the other day, didn't you read that?"

"I'd drive you there myself, but I got the man from Cenex coming."

"Cenex. I never heard of such a place."

Billy puts the food in front of me and it's a pile, I'll tell you. It about fills up the counter.

"It's not a place, it's a company, honey. You know. It's the herbicide man." Now he looks up at Billy, who's still arranging my food. "We got the herbicide man coming."

"Daddy Lyle will be there."

"Honey, we've been talking about this all week. I've got to be there too, with Daddy Lyle."

"Can't he just show Daddy Lyle and Daddy Lyle can show you?"

Bob has finished his food by now and he pushes the plate away. "Honey, we've been talking about it all week."

"Oh," I say. "All week. You've been talking about it all week. I guess I forgot. If I ever knew, I don't know now. I guess I'm getting absentminded, Bob. Here you've been talking about something all week and I never even heard a thing."

"Calm down now, honey. We'll just ask Evaline to drive you over."

"Evaline, huh."

"Your sister."

"She isn't much better than me, Bob."

"She is too, Lucy."

"Not for getting lost, she isn't."

"She drives all the time!"

"Oh, Evaline she might be fine out in the country but when she's in the city, with all those streets and no landmarks, why she's just as lost as anybody. She doesn't get much practice going out. You know her, home all the time. And she's the nervous type, Bob. She's the one who needs a doctor appointment for nerves. Oh, going with Evaline is as bad as going by myself, only I got two of us to worry over instead of just one. This is not going to work out, Bob. We'd better forget the whole thing. I'm not sick anyway. Do I look sick to you?"

Bob leans his face into his hands. He's thinking, I can tell. Finally he says, "Let's do it another day. I'll call and change your appointment to a day when I can come too."

I start eating then. I eat like somebody who's thinking things over and he watches me. I eat my BLT first of all. Bob will eat part of one thing and then he'll skip over to something else and then he'll go to the next pile of food and shovel some of that in, like he can't make up his mind. I'm not like Bob. If I decide to eat my BLT, then that's what I'll do. That's what I do now, with Bob looking on. After it's all gone, I pick up my napkin and wipe my fingers off. "I think it's tomorrow or never, Bob. I think that's the meaning of why it isn't working out. It isn't supposed to work out, is what I think."

"It is working out. We're working it out."

"I can't go with you and I can't go by myself and I can't go with Evaline neither," I hold up one finger at a time, until I end up with three.

"You mean you can't go with Evaline?"

I tilt my head to one side and give Bob a look, what did I just say?

"What about your sister Flora?"

"No."

"No," Bob repeats but he says it to himself, not to me, and he whispers it. "No."

I pick up the fish sandwich and eat it, without saying a word. Then I wipe my mouth.

"Of course, Evaline never does get out. She never goes anywhere. She just mopes around the house, is what she does. It'd do her good to get out —" I start picking at my chef's salad now. "Bob, I don't see why we can't find somebody else to drive us over."

"I still don't know what's wrong with Flora," he says.

"It would just make Evaline's day if Billy was to drive her over —" I say.

"Drive the two of you over?" says Bob.

Billy has got all the counters cleaned out and arranged by now. He looks up from below us, where he's squatting down.

"That would be asking way too much," I say. On his day off and everything. I lean over the counter to look at Billy. "Mama has got you working like a dog over there, I know it."

"Your Mama always does right by me."

"Oh, my Mama's got a heart of gold, I tell you. And she'll give you the shirt off her back. But Mama hates to ask a favor. That's just the way she is. Hates it. And Mama, she's been worried sick about me. She's such a worrier, isn't she Bob?"

But Bob, instead of jumping in, stops to think, is Mama what you'd call a worrier or not?

"Of course, nothing's wrong with me," I lean forward, talking in a loud whisper in case anybody else is listening. "Not a thing. I'm as strong as a — as strong as I can be. Healthy, that's what I am. I mean, you can just look and see for yourself." I pause to let Billy look and he does. He looks at me, standing up now, wiping his hands on his apron. Elizabeth Taylor, he's thinking. Kim Novak. "Mama will feel so much better to hear it from a doctor though."

"Could you take Evaline along and do something special with her while Lucy is seeing the doctor?" says Bob. "She don't get out much." Billy and me are still looking at each other and Bob's voice is far away like he's in a tunnel.

"Evaline ain't much to look at, but she's got a nice personality," I say, and before they can start arguing with me, out of politeness, about how Evaline looks, I add, "She's cooked all those meals, special for you."

"We wouldn't ask at all, if it weren't an emergency." Bob leans forward and grips the sides of the counter with his hands.

"You already do so much for us," I say to Billy, and he looks at me. I take a bite of my chef salad and smile.

## Chapter 10

Come to find out Evaline has plans for the next day. She's going over to Whitehall to help our Aunt Janelle and there's just no way she can back out now, it's so late. Aunt Janelle is the widow woman of Mama's dead brother, Uncle Roy.

"You can put it off a day," I say.

"She'd done had the hogs butchered today."

"They can wait."

"They'll be ready tomorrow and that's when I told her I'd come, tomorrow morning, and I'll be there all day long and you know it."

"The Dunavans they've waited up to a week after they butchered."

"The Dunavans are the Dunavans and Aunt Janelle is Aunt Janelle," she says, and I'm not going to argue about that. "Aunt Janelle has a way of doing things and that's the way she does them."

"I don't know why you got to be there."

I think now Evaline will point out that she's the best hog processor in the county, which is a big source of pride for Evaline who don't have much else going for her, but she doesn't. "You knew I was going over there," she says, sighing. "Mama and me have been talking about it all week long with you sitting right there, listening."

"That's right," puts in Mama, taking her side like she always does.

"I guess I just haven't been paying attention."

"Lucy's a little absentminded right now," Bob points out.

And Evaline says, "Is that so?"

"We're hoping the doctor will straighten her out."

"What kind of doctor?" Mama wants to know.

"He's a nerve doctor. For her nerves."

"There's nothing wrong with her nerves," says Mama. She's thinking of her Aunt Sue. "All my girls got strong nerves."

"I don't think Billy should drive you all the way to Springfield," Evaline says and she gives me a look to tell me she knows what I'm up to, but the look I give her back, it's just as innocent as can be.

The next day I get up early and fix Bob a big breakfast like Mother Bybee always does, three eggs, over easy, and pancakes and four pieces of toast, sausage. I don't make him biscuits.

When he leaves, I go upstairs to get ready. We have a big bathtub, porcelain with claws for feet, and I bathe. My body is just the way I want it. Everybody says how I'm unhappy all the time and always think about what I don't have and always want what isn't mine, but they're wrong. I look at my body and it's perfect. Even my arms are perfect. People don't realize how important your arms are. Now if you have fat arms, like say Mavel, Mavel Runels, she has these fat arms and she can't wear anything without sleeves. She's got to cover them up so people can't tell. If you've got fat arms like that and you go to raise your hand up, then the fat moves all around and everybody sees it. Or maybe you've got arms like Sadie down at the five and dime, covered with black hair so it makes people think of monkey arms and then you've got to shave them.

After the bath, I comb my hair. My hair is chestnut color. It has red and black and brown and blond in it. It has every color. I comb it out and towel it dry. I pluck my eyebrows, which are dark and don't have to be painted on, and I curl my eyelashes and paint my fingernails and toenails and put on mascara and lipstick.

We've got a full-length mirror on the back of our bathroom door. I stand in front of it, looking at my face, and I say to myself, "You look good!" I say, "Wait til Billy Lee gets a load of you!" I say, "You're going to make it out to Hollywood someday and you're going to walk down the street and somebody is going to snatch you up. Put you right in the movies. Won't that show everybody. Uh huh."

I step back and look at my whole body in the mirror. I look at my skin and it's soft and white and it doesn't have one thing that isn't just like how it should be. And I tell myself it's like I've got a ticket and it's stamped *Anywhere you want to go*.

I wait outside for Billy, sitting on the porch swing. The Dunavan's horses are down at our end of the pasture. They're quarter horses and Appaloosas. The Appaloosas have brown or black spots on their rumps, except one of them, the mare. She's black, but her spots are white. She's the prettiest one, I think, and I like to watch her. Sometimes she looks back to tell me she knows I'm watching but it doesn't make any difference to her. The other ones will show off, but she acts the same as usual.

They're Nez Percé horses, Billy tells me when he comes. Purse, he says it, like the pocketbook. He drives his old truck and I sit all the way on the other side of the seat and act like what we're doing is driving to the doctor and he's just somebody who's taking me there. My Mama's hired handyman. I stretch my legs out and I see Billy look down at them and then he looks away, watching the road. I roll down the window and let the air blow over me and I lean my head back and think how we got all day long, me and Billy.

"I guess your sister couldn't come," he says, looking at the road in front of us.

At first I can't think what he means, but then I remember Evaline and I say, "No, I guess not." I lean my head out the window a little bit and the wind blows so hard I can't keep my eyes open and my hair blows everywhere. I pull my head back in and I say, "She's busy."

We drive north past the cemetery and then head east until we get to the county road. All the county roads are laid out on a grid, one mile apart, which is something to do with how flat it is, like the top of a table. Thirty-six miles to the township, my daddy used to say. No hills or nothing to get in the way.

We drive that flat straight county road until we get to 125, outside of Rushville, to get to Springfield. We pass over the river near Beardstown and Billy says, "Will you look at that." I look down and there's nothing there. Two horses, one white and the other bay. In the horse games us kids used to play, looking out the window on trips and counting horses, a white horse was twenty-five points but today it doesn't count for anything. "The Illinois River," Billy says.

We cross the river and we pass through Walton Springs and we go on down the highway until we pass through the town of Philadelphia and that name makes Billy laugh but other than that, we don't say anything.

After a while, Billy begins to hum a little song. It's the Buffalo Gals song which is the same song my sister has sang to me all her life. Buffalo gals, won't you come out tonight —

"That's a song my sister sings."

Most people they will throw something in. They'll say, uh huh, oh, is that a fact. But Billy doesn't say nothing.

"When we were little girls, me and Betty and Flora, we'd lay in bed at night, with the windows open and all the nighttime sounds coming in and scaring us, and Evaline would sing us songs and tell us stories. She's the oldest one, you know. She about raised us."

"What kind of stories? Like fairy tales, you mean?"

"Fairy tales and then stories she'd make up, too. Like she'd tell us — I was afraid of thunder when I was little — and Evaline she'd say how it wasn't nothing but an old turtle pulling a wagon down the dirt road. The one that runs by the Filson place. He had that wagon filled up with rocks that kept rolling out and the thunder wasn't nothing but that. It was just because the turtle filled his wagon too high."

Billy laughs.

"And she'd sing to us, too," I add, to get him away from thinking of me as someone convinced by that old turtle story. "She'd lay in her bed next to ours and sing the buffalo song and we'd lie there thinking about how we were buffalo gals. We didn't know what it meant but we liked it, the other girls and me."

We're almost to Springfield when Billy asks what part of town the doctor's office is in.

I just look at him. I look and look but I know by now if I'm going to have a patience contest with Billy, then he'll win every time, so I say, finally, "I don't want to go to the doctor."

"You don't?"

"No, I don't." I say that kind of mad because I'm tired of being the one taking the lead all the time. I'm waiting for him to take over, but he just isn't doing it. "There's nothing wrong with my nerves. For one thing."

I have to remind myself about the fact that I was Miss Freshman and all the rest. Miss Corn Festival and everything else. And I'm married too, to the richest family in Pike County outside of the Winklejohns, and who would want to marry one of them. There's the name, for one thing. Winkle-john. First thing I'd do if I married one of them, is change the danged name. That's what I told my sister Flora.

We're in Springfield now and I point down the road. "There's a Holiday Inn, up ahead."

I can hear Betty's voice. *She made her bed,* it's saying. *She ruined her life is all I know.* I'm not going to let Betty tell me what to do, I think to myself. "Pull in."

We stop at the Holiday Inn and then we sit there, like he thinks I'm going to be the one to do everything. I've got us this far and now it's his turn.

"Well?" he says.

And I say, "Well, what?"

"Did you want to stop here for lunch, Lucy, or something else?"

We're sitting in the parking lot and I can see the big yellow Holiday Inn sign with its happy letters and I can see the smaller sign that tells us they also have food. "What do you think?"

Springfield is a big city. It's the capital of Illinois. It's the Land of Lincoln, is what everybody says. And it's big, like I said. They don't know who you are over here in Springfield, not like Palmyra where you walk down the street and everybody you meet knows more about you than you do yourself. If they see me going into a motel over in Springfield, and they see a man going in too, they're going to think we're Mr. and Mrs. John Smith, if that's what we say. They're going to think we're visiting from out of town. They're not going to bat an eye.

Billy pulls the keys out of the ignition and he sits there, jingling them and looking out the window, like he hasn't had time enough yet to work this out and now he has to stop and do it. I look at my watch, showing him I don't have all day.

"I'm not ready for lunch," he says, finally.

"I just had breakfast, myself."

And instead of following through on this, Billy just sits. He doesn't know what to do next. He puts his hands on the steering wheel and taps his fingers, like he's thinking — but this is not the time for thinking. Any thinking he had to do could have been done before. I don't have time to sit here and let him catch up on it.

"Guess we're not hungry then," I say, and I slip my shoe off and snake my foot over so it reaches his leg. It only touches the thick material of his pants, but Billy jumps. He won't look at me at all. He's looking straight ahead at the motel, the long row of doors, the big Holiday Inn sign with its friendly yellow letters, his hands tapping out a rhythm on the steering wheel. I reach up and take one of those hands in mine and I look at it. I turn it over and look at the lines, like my sister Flora will do, to read your future, but I can't tell anything. I take his hand then and I put it on my knee, where my skirt ends and there's just skin, my nylon stocking and, under it, skin. He doesn't move his head but Billy's eyes creep down to see what his hand is doing. And I move his hand up a little ways so it's higher and the other hand stops moving on the steering wheel now, like it's watching, too. And I move it just a little bit more. Neither of us is breathing. Nothing is moving, just our hands, going a little further and a little further.

"I'll get a room," he says, suddenly, and I don't even act surprised, like I had meant to, it has drug out so long. I just think to myself, it's about time.

He throws the door open and leaps out. He goes to the office while I wait in the car. I look at the doors of all the motel rooms, all in a line, and I think how me and Billy will walk inside one of them. And that thought seems bigger to me than my wedding day. It seems giant.

When Billy comes back finally, he has a key in his hand and then we go inside.

The room is dark, with venetian blinds that are closed and thick curtains, pulled shut. I take off my shoes, sit down on the bed and lean against the wall. I put my feet up and cross them at the ankles. I've got nylon stockings on and I like the way they feel on my skin, slippery. I like the way they sound when I rub them together.

"Do you believe in astrology, Billy?"

Billy is walking around the room. He gets a drink of water from the bathroom. He walks over to the TV set. He walks back and forth between the closet and the bed, running his hands over his hair. He doesn't look at me once. Finally he gets out a cigarette and lights it. He sits in the orange plastic chair across from me.

Billy lays his cigarettes on the nightstand and now I take one and hold it in my hand. "I don't believe in astrology," I say. "But I believe in fate." I roll it in my fingers and put it in my mouth, unlit, pretending to smoke, inhaling and exhaling. "What do you believe in?" But he doesn't answer right away. "You believe in anything?"

"I never slept with a married woman before," he says.

"I only been married a few weeks is all, " I say.

Billy looks at me. He's been afraid to look but now he does. He settles his eyes on me.

"A few weeks isn't nothing when you think how long I've been alive," I add. "I mean I've been unmarried way longer than I been married so I'd say I'm more unmarried than married, really, when you think of it."

I rub my legs together and the nylons make a soft slippery sound.

"Besides, I don't love my husband. How can I be married to him if I don't love him? You tell me that. It's a marriage on paper, is all, when you don't love someone. You going to let a marriage on paper stop you from getting what you want?"

I sit up and unbutton my blouse. "Somebody ought to get what they want," I say.

He puts his cigarette out but he isn't watching his cigarette. He stands up and comes to the bed. He lays down next to me and when I start to say something, Billy puts his finger over my lips and then he puts his mouth there. We're on top of the covers, up close to each other. They don't wash those top covers is what I hear and I think of that now, laying next to Billy. I put my leg up over his leg and feel the nylon stocking slip against his pants.

## Chapter 11

After that I can't get Billy out of my mind. Everything I look at and everything I touch gets turned into one more way to think about him. I think about his hands and his breath and his legs against my legs and his skin and my skin and all of it from the beginning to the end, over and over.

I stay home during the day and wander around my house. I sit out on the porch. I sit in front, on the porch swing and I watch the Dunavans' mare. Or I sit out back. We got a screened-in porch back there, and a big old couch where the Bybee cousins used to sleep on summer nights. At dinnertime, I cook supper for me and Bob.

I ain't going to chase him. Let Billy think that one time is all I needed and now I'm finished with him. Let him think about me and Bob, just married, over here in this big house, alone all the time. Maybe that's why I don't come around anymore, I'm so busy being a newly-wed that I don't have time for nothing else.

On the morning of the third day, I say to Bob he better call Billy and tell him to come see about the leak in our kitchen. It's early morning, 5:30, and Bob is on his way to his Mama's house, Mother Bybee, because everybody knows I don't feed him enough and his mother she has got ham and eggs and sausage, bacon, potatoes, biscuits and gravy all piled up on a plate, waiting for him.

Bob claims he'll take a look at the pipes this evening, but I say, "If you haven't done it yet, why should I think you will now?" I say, "You get somebody in here to fix that leak this minute!"

He looks at me, surprised. He never knew I took such a personal interest in plumbing.

"Lucy, that leak ain't going nowhere."

I can see the kind of man he is, the kind to put things off all the time, the kind to hope problems will just take care of themselves, which they don't do, ever.

I go out on the porch and sit down in the porch swing, with my arms crossed on my chest, and he follows me there. I say to Bob how I'm not going one more day without somebody in here looking at the pipes. I say, "I'm not going to have it!"

"Give me the car key, honey."

"I'm not stepping foot in that house until somebody is here to fix the leak."

"I can't call somebody at 5:30 in the morning," he says, which just goes to show you he isn't thinking very hard.

"Billy he gets up every morning by now. He drives his Aunt Babe out to her cafe every morning about this time and then he has a cup of coffee with her and I'll just bet that's where he is right now."

"Well then, he's getting ready to work, ain't he?"

"He doesn't work breakfast for Aunt Babe on Wednesdays and you know this is Wednesday, don't you?

He doesn't start working until lunch time. Maybe about eight he might go by my Mama's and do something for her, but right now he isn't doing nothing. The way I see it, this is the best chance we got to take care of our problem and you know, Bob, the best time to take care of a problem is now, before it gets too big. Your folks give us this house and the least we can do is take care of the problems it gets, before they get too big. Your granddaddy built this house, Bob, with his own two hands, you remember."

Bob is stuck now. He's moving back and forth on the porch, thinking of his granddaddy building this house with his hands and he's thinking of the big plate of food setting over there at Mr. Lyle Bybee's house with his name on it, getting colder and colder every moment. He's thinking of the car key, which is in my pocket.

"How do you know Billy can do plumbing? You ever hear of him doing it before?"

"He's a handyman, Bob," I say and I'm astonished that Bob hasn't thought of this before but has to be led through it. I'm thinking maybe my husband is slow witted too, on top of everything else. "Don't you know why they call it handyman? It's because he's handy, Bob, handy with his hands and any man who's handy like that, he'll know how to fix a leak, Bob, in the kitchen. It's like how a cook can make hashbrowns and they can make eggs too. It's just part of what they do."

The phone rings then and Bob goes inside. I can hear that it's his mother, calling about the plate of food which is getting cold. I can hear him tell her about the leak and I hear him say he'll be there shortly.

When he comes back outside, I hand him the car key. "You just tell him I said it's an emergency."

A little while later, both men pull into the driveway, Billy in his truck and Bob in his car. They come into the house. Billy sets his toolbox down and gets on the floor. He sticks his head under the sink while Bob and I stand watching. He starts poking around, laying on his back with his legs sprawled out, just like I've seen him before, his hips pressed down. I stand there looking at him, wondering how it is men, who think about sex all the time from what I hear, how they can lay right on your kitchen floor with their hips pressed down and their legs sprawled out apart from each other, and how they can do that right in front of your eyes and you look at their face and you can see they're thinking about plumbing and nothing else.

Bob starts pacing up and down and finally he says to us he's going to work and he says, "Thank you again," to Billy and he kisses me on the cheek, just like every day, and says he'll be home for lunch, which is twelve o'clock.

Bob hesitates. "Lucy," he smoothes his hair back, "I could give you a ride to your Mama's."

"I got so much work to do here, Bob."

Billy pulls himself out from under the sink. "You leaving?" I can see that Billy's surprised at this, that he's expecting Bob to stand right here and chaperone us, but he doesn't say a word then, just slides himself under the sink again and goes back to what he's doing.

I wait for a while, watching him, and then I go to the living room. I walk back and forth. I look out the window at the Dunavan's horses. I walk to the mantel and straighten out the little pictures we've got sitting there, and the knickknacks. I can hear Billy in the kitchen, banging on the pipe. I look at myself in the mirror over the mantel. I push my hair back from my face and I run my finger over my lips. Then I go back to stand in the doorway and watch him, in my kitchen, in the same place where I stood so many times, thinking of him. He's got a special kind of wrench and he's closing up the pipe with it.

I go over to where he is and I squat down. I've got a summer dress on, blue to match my eyes, and I pull it back up on my thighs. It's July and even though it's not seven o'clock already we're sweating. He's got the pipes closed and now he sits up, looking at my legs.

"You ever had anything in your system before," I say, "that you had to get out?"

But Billy doesn't say whether he has or not. He stands up and I stand up and the whole time we're watching each other. Then he shakes his head like something is loose inside and he's jiggling it around. Billy turns to look out the kitchen window, at the driveway outside.

"He won't come back until noon," I say. "He never does."

"He will today," says Billy.

I'm not going to argue and I'm not going to try to get him to do anything, neither. Let him take a turn at trying for a while. Me doing all the trying has got him thinking he doesn't have to do any.

I move away from him. "You haven't ever seen my house before, have you?" I go over to the cupboards. "See these here?" I open and shut a cupboard door, showing him, "These are made of cherry wood. From cherry trees."

"This floor here," we look down at the floor we're standing on, "it's not linoleum, like how most people put linoleum in their kitchen. This is tile. These are tile floors. Everything in the house is the best money can buy. Even the sink here. You must have noticed, being a handyman, it's not just a regular old sink. And look at this here," I say, pulling him through the swinging doors and into the dining room, to our table.

It's a big table and the wood is dark and shiny and it's always cool to the touch.

"This here's made of mahogany." I rub my hands over the smooth table top and Billy puts his hands there too, but he isn't looking at the table, he's watching me instead. "Mahogany doesn't grow around here," I tell him.

And it's true. They bring it from far away, from jungles.

"The wood is soft," I say and our hands lie on it, side by side, "but it couldn't have started out like this. Somebody must've rubbed to make it so smooth and soft."

I lift my hands up now and move over, closer to him. "They cut it out of the jungle and they hauled it all the way here just so folks like Bob and his wife can have a pretty table to set their dinner on. Isn't that something? When you think of it."

Suddenly I pull him by the hand. "Come out here," I say, taking him through the kitchen and then out back, onto our screened-in porch. "I got something I want you to help me with." I motion him to the big couch that sits there but he's looking at me, doubtful. "Sit down, please." I motion him with my hands again. "I need your expert, professional opinion. I want you to —" I duck back into the house. I stick my head back outside. "Do you want something to drink? I got lemonade."

"No," he says, and I can see he ain't sat down but he's not leaving neither.

I go back into the kitchen and rifle through my drawer.

"I got some beer," I call out, but he says he doesn't want that neither.

I hurry back to the porch with the house drawing in my hands. See there, I got a real reason, and I sit down and now he sits beside me, and takes the pictures from my hand. "For an addition," I say.

He studies it a while and gives me a questioning look.

"For our house," I say. "And what I'm wondering is if twelve by twelve is big enough or do we need twelve by fifteen?" I move over to look closer at the drawing and his eyes slide from it to my legs and they stay there. I open my knees a little so the side of my thigh is touching the side of his thigh.

We could lay down on this couch, if we wanted, it's that big. Nobody would see us neither unless they walked along the back, and nobody ever comes that way.

"You ever hear the expression the grass looks greener from the other side?" says Billy, handing the blueprint to me and standing up.

"My daddy his favorite saying was you made your bed, now lay in it. That's what my daddy would tell me, if he was alive still," I say, not getting up, crossing my legs.

But Billy doesn't want to say anything about laying in bed and he doesn't answer me. He feels around in his pockets, looking for a cigarette. "You ought to try to make things right with your husband, before you go and chuck everything for something you don't even know what it is."

"I know what it is."

"You don't know what you're wishing for."

"I do too."

Billy moves into the kitchen and I get up and follow him. He starts putting his tools away. He has a metal toolbox and he puts away his wrench and some little pieces of pipe he brought along.

"Lucy, you're a beautiful girl," he says. I try to look

modest and a little surprised, like maybe I haven't noticed it. Maybe I haven't heard about it all my life. Maybe I look in the mirror and I don't even see what I'm looking at. "You think that's the best thing about you, but it isn't." Which sounds like him saying I'm stuck-up, but his face doesn't look like that.

And he moves over towards the kitchen door and opens it but I get my pocketbook and follow him out. We walk down the back steps.

"I'd be fooling myself if I thought you'd be happy with me," he says, walking to his truck. He sets the toolbox in back and then he stops to face me. "You go on in now," and he nods to the house, but I don't move away from him. This is too good to be true, he's thinking, and I got to show him how it's not. It ain't too good to be true if we got the nerve to make it so.

"We might get away with one time," he says, "but this is a small town and everybody finds out everything and your husband, Bob —"

"I don't want to hear another word about my husband, Bob. He ain't my husband anyway."

But Billy isn't going to argue about that.

"You have to stay here."

"I don't have to do nothing. That's what you don't understand about me." And then I march right over to his truck and climb inside, shut the door and sit looking out the window in front of me, like the only question is when will he get in, too.

He comes to my window and stands looking at me, but I roll up the window and lock the door. I pull a piece of gum out of my purse and put it in my mouth, while he just stands there.

At last, he comes around and gets in the driver's side

but, instead of starting the engine, he sits looking straight ahead, trying to work things out. "You can't be in my truck like this."

I twist the rearview mirror around, so I can look in it, and I start putting on my lipstick. "I never knew you was such a worrier, Billy! Jeez! Maybe you're giving me a lift. There isn't anything wrong with the handyman giving me a lift when I need a ride and it's such a hot day." I draw out that last part, hot day, and lift my hair up off my neck, when I say it, to show him how hot it is. It's early morning but it's already a scorcher. "And, anyway, why do you care? They can't do nothing to you."

He's got his two hands on the steering wheel, but Billy hasn't started the engine yet.

I've got my arm up on the side of the seat and I've got my lipstick on. Now I look at the rearview mirror again and run my finger over my lips, making sure the lipstick has got everywhere. Then I turn back to him, showing him my face again.

Billy sticks his elbow out his window now and looks away from me, looks ahead of us where the Dunavan field curves around and the horses graze sometimes, but they aren't there today. It's just a plain, empty field with nothing in it.

I hear the sound of gravel and turn to see Bob, pulling into the driveway. We don't say a word then, me and Billy. We sit, looking ahead of us until Bob parks his car and comes up to the window. He comes to Billy's window and he doesn't even mention the plumbing but stands, looking in at us.

"Lucy needs a ride to town," Billy says and Bob bends down to look at me, over on the other side of Billy. And to me he says, softly, "You come on now."

*Chapter 12*

That same evening Bob and me are sitting at the table in our own house. I've made dinner, but it hasn't turned out exactly right. I've made creamed chicken and I've made the recipe my own, same as what Evaline does. I didn't have all the ingredients so I've adjusted it, like how Evaline says a good cook will do.

We got mashed potatoes on our plates too, along with boiled cauliflower. Everything on our plates is beige, except the bread, and that's white with a little slab of yellow butter.

I notice Bob is picking at his food, separating it with his fork and putting some of it in a pile on one side of his plate and putting some of it on the other. One side he's eating and the other side, he's not.

"I guess the cream was more important than I thought."

"No, it's just fine," says Bob, like I can't see how he's made those two piles on his plate. "What is it anyway?" he says and he dabs at his mouth.

"What is it?" I throw my napkin on my plate, even

though I haven't hardly touched my food yet. Creamed chicken is about Bob's favorite meal. Evaline fixes it for him at least once a week. It's like if his own sister come through the door and she don't even look familiar.

"Oh, I know it's chicken," he says, like that's something to be proud of, how he can tell chicken from beef. He takes a leg then and sticks it in his mouth, making grunting noises the whole time, like now I should be happy.

"It's the same thing Evaline fixes for you," I say, giving him a hint. "It's only your second favorite thing in the world."

"The first being you."

"Humph."

Bob is gnawing on the bone of that chicken leg with his eyebrows down low and I can see he's thinking hard. Really concentrating. "Is it Chicken Almondine?"

"Do you see any almonds? There have got to be almonds in Chicken Almondine, just like there's got to be chicken in it. That's why they call it chicken-almond-ine."

"Isn't that what I said?"

"Creamed chicken!" I shout. "It's creamed chicken."

"Oh," he says, "my favorite."

"It's the same thing Evaline makes for you."

"I can see that now, I sure can."

I keep waiting for him to ask about the cream because I've noticed by now that Bob will pick out the most irritating things he can find to say to me, but he doesn't. Instead he says, "You ought to get Evaline's recipe for this. Cream of chicken."

When he says that, I bust out crying. I'm not crying over the cream of chicken. I'm crying because I only want to sit across the table from Billy and hear him say please pass the pepper. I only want to look up and see his face, that's all. I only want a small thing, Billy Lee, I only want to see his face. I want to hear his voice. I want to feel his face brush against my face and I want to hear his voice saying things to me in the dark. I only want what nobody in their right mind would want, a man with no money and no home and no prospects. I'm crying because now that I finally know what I want, I already got something else.

Bob says, "Oh, Baby, I'm sorry. I'm sorry. I'm sorry. I'm sorry." He comes over to where I'm sitting and puts his hands around my shoulders. " I'm sorry."

For one second, I think he knows what he's done. I think we've forgot about him being my husband and me being his wife and this is our house and how we're sitting down for dinner. I think we've let the outside of everything go. What he should say to me and what I should say back and the feelings we should have and what should come next and everything. We've let it all go and it's just the deepest part of him and the deepest part of me and nothing else. For one second, I think he understands what he's done to me and to what I might have been and the life that was waiting for me, if only he hadn't come along first. I think he knows all those things, for one second in our kitchen while he stands behind my chair, with his hands on my shoulders. "I'm so sorry." But then I realize he's only talking about the creamed chicken and I push his hands away and say how he doesn't understand nothing. Then I put my head down on the edge of the table and bawl my eyes out.

Bob moves my plate away and pulls my hair out of the mashed potatoes. He says, "You're a wonderful wife." He says, "I'm so lucky to have you." He says, "I think I'll call my mother and have her come out and sit with you."

"I'm all right. I'm all right now. I've just been over-wrought, you know. I don't know what's got into me."

Bob sits back down at the table and he starts to shov-el all that beige food in his mouth and smash it together and I think, now, on top of everything, I get to watch him eat. But I'm not going to let myself get carried away again, no. I pick up my fork.

"The mashed potatoes are real good, honey."

People would say that I'm having an affair and they'd think they knew all about it. Doesn't everybody know what that means. They'd talk about it up and down the aisles of the five and dime. They'd stand in line at the PO, talking about it. Stop each other in the street. They'd whisper it in Babe's Cafe. Discuss it at the laun-derette and beauty shop. Call everybody they knew on the telephone. But not one of them would get it right.

And then, because I've got to hear his name out loud, I say, "I'm so happy with the work Billy done here this morning."

I wait for Bob to agree, but instead he takes a mouth-ful of food. Before he's finished swallowing, he's put another bite in.

"I don't know if you appreciate what a good worker he is, Bob. And coming over here first thing in the morning like he did, why, Bob, we're lucky to have a man like that."

Bob doesn't say anything to that. I start to clear the dishes but Bob says, "I guess Evaline couldn't go with you on your doctor trip."

I'm half standing up but now I sink down in my chair and look at him. "To Springfield? Why no, Bob, she sure couldn't."

Bob has a piece of bread and he's using it to mop up

every last thing on the to-eat side of his plate. I sit watching him do it. I'm breathing hard.

"She had to help Aunt Janelle with the hog processing, it turns out. My Aunt Janelle —"

"I don't think he should be coming around all the time."

My heart skips a beat now. I've been aware of its rhythm ever since the name of Billy has come up. Ka-blunk, ka-blunk, ka-blunk. And now it misses one of those beats, but outside I keep my face calm and still. "What do you mean by that?"

I put my hands on the table and stretch my fingers out. "It isn't easy to find a hard-working man, Bob. A man that'll show up on time and do what he has to do and not make a fuss about it."

"You oughtn't been in his truck alone."

"Why, Bob, he was giving me a ride, like I asked him to. I remembered, soon as you left, how I promised to —"

But Bob interrupts me. "He ain't like us, Lucy."

Which is what I already have found out.

"He's so good to Mama. He's very polite. I don't know if you ever noticed how polite he is, Bob."

"We don't know nothing about this fellow, Lucy."

"Why, Bob, he's Aunt Babe's nephew and we've known her all our life!" I start to get up from the table to show him the subject is closed but he leans forward now and whispers.

"He ain't even white!"

I sit back down in the chair. "Ain't white?" I look at my own hands, lying against the brown table, white and soft.

"He's Injun, Lucy."

I hesitate. That isn't the same as colored anyway.

Colored will really get you in trouble, around here. I don't even think it's as bad as Mexican, but I'm not sure.

"You can tell by looking," says Bob. He gives a nervous laugh, "Injun."

"Indian," I say, because the other word makes it seem like Bob Bybee is calling Billy a nigger and I'm not going to have that.

"You wait til your brother Jimbo gets wind of this," he says.

"Jimbo? This isn't nothing to do with Jimbo."

But Bob puts back his head and snorts. "Jimbo don't want a — Indian, who isn't even white, over to his Mama's house every day, eating with his sisters at the kitchen table and sitting out on the porch and such."

"Jimbo doesn't have no say around here anymore," I tell him, but I'm thinking of Billy and I'm thinking of Indians. I never saw a Indian before, except in the movies.

"I don't know how you can tell he's Indian," I say. "Lots of white people have black hair, Bob, and dark skin. Olive, they call it. Having a olive complexion.

"Anyhow, his folks come from Pearl and there aren't no Indians around there. Only white people in the whole county, same as here."

Bob lets out a big sigh. He says, "Daddy Lyle was over to the auction in Pearl this morning and he found out all about it."

"Oh, Daddy Lyle found out," I say, sarcastic, and I get up from the table and begin clearing the dishes. I go into the kitchen and the swinging door shuts behind me.

"Everybody else will find out, too!" he calls after me.

A big window was built over the sink so when I wash dishes I can look out over the fields. On this night we've had a little summer rain, and while I stand at the sink, I can see a rainbow. It looks like you could go down to the Dunavans' house and there it would be, like you could walk right under it.

I can hear Bob getting up from his place at the table. It's a sound like someone moving large pieces of furniture around, a piano maybe. He comes in the kitchen. "Daddy Lyle said his Mama run off with a Cherokee boy to Oklahoma and never come back — and that's what our friend, Billy Lee, come from." Bob comes into the kitchen after me.

"Run off? Was she already married?"

But Bob says he doesn't know. "They run off!" he shouts, throwing his arms in the air. Maybe one day it'll be me and Billy he's talking about and he'll sound just the same. I think how he'll hate me then. I think if he'll hate me then, it's almost as good as him hating me now.

"We don't want any trouble, is all," says Bob. "You know how prejudice people are, around here."

"How can you be prejudice against something you already killed, a long time ago?" I ask, but I'm talking to myself now. I start washing the dishes again. I'm looking out the window at the farmland, at the rows of soybeans to one side and the Dunavans' fence on the other, and I'm thinking of when the Indians lived here and what it must have looked like then.

"You ought to be the one to tell Evaline."

"Evaline? What's she got to do with it?"

"It's clear why he's over there so much, Lucy, and it ain't to help your Mama with her carpenter ants neither."

"Lord! You think he's after my old maid sister, a guy like Billy Lee? A guy like Billy, he don't go for somebody like Evaline, Bob. A guy like him, he wants something exciting —"

"I'll tell you, he better not be going for nothing around here, exciting or not!"

"Why don't you go sit down?" I say, impatient now. I don't think I can stand another second with him next to me. The whole time he's here, it's like somebody is poking me with a stick. "Go on, sit down."

But he doesn't go. Instead he opens the refrigerator. You might think that the sound of the refrigerator, when it's opened, is always going to be the same, but it isn't. It's different, the way different people do it. And the way Bob does it, the way he pulls the door open and the sound he makes doing it, it's disgusting.

He starts making a sandwich behind me while I keep washing the dishes, looking outside at the rainbow which is still there. I can hear the twist of the mayonnaise jar and the rattle of the lettuce and the sound of Bob cutting into the ham. I can hear him piling tomatoes on that sandwich, and cheese and pickles. I can hear his feet shuffling on the floor and I can smell his scalp and the smell of diesel on his hands and I can hear the rumble of his stomach and the sound of his spit filling up his mouth and the sound of his teeth tearing into the sandwich and then the sandwich in his mouth, getting smashed up. I can hear him swallow. I can hear the sound of his eyelids coming down over his eyes, like if the white part has got too much liquid in it. But I don't say a word.

Bob leans against the stove. He wipes his mouth off with the side of his arm. "You don't give Evaline enough credit," he says. "You know she's one heck of a cook," but that makes him think of the creamed chicken and he hurries to add, "and she has a real pleasing personality."

"She's almost thirty years old, Bob, and she ain't exactly what you call a looker anyhow."

That's Bob's word for it, looker. "She's built like a horse, for one thing."

"Like a horse? Built like a horse?" Bob repeats back what I just said, and I sigh, loud.

"She's shapely, is what she is. Yes, your sister is real nicely shaped. Shapely, is what I call it."

And I cannot believe that here I am again arguing about the form of my sister's body which I've seen every day of my life. "If I say she's a horse, then she is!" And Bob doesn't argue, but he doesn't agree, neither. "You ever seen her thighs?" I say, but he doesn't say whether he has or not, so I let it drop.

But Bob doesn't know when to quit. "If Sheila Garber can find herself a husband, then Evaline sure can," he says, but I'm washing dishes, ignoring him.

"Roberta Mosser!" he shouts. "Roberta Mosser with that big long nose she got herself a husband. She married that Hughes fellow has himself eight hundred acres. An only son, too. Sometimes it pays to wait and see, Lucy." Bob wipes his mouth with his sleeve. "He's got half his crop in soybeans this year but I don't think that's a good idea," says Bob.

"Billy Lee doesn't like my sister, is all I'm trying to say!"

Bob is a little slow following conversations and he has to mull this over. "But he does too, Lucy, everybody says so." Bob says that after about an hour.

"Everybody says so. Well, it must be true if that's what everybody says. If everybody says so, then that must be the way it is. Bob Bybee, if everybody said it was time to go jump in the lake would you go jump in the lake because everybody is right when everybody is saying so? Is that what you'd do?"

I look at Bob's blue eyes. They look like rabbit eyes. They look like eyes that are blind, like the blind little eyes of a newborn creature and not a tiger, either, a mole, maybe or something that lives in a hole and is timid. They're timid eyes and he doesn't have hardly any eye-lashes on them and his hands are all red from the sun, and burnt. I think how delicate he is and how I hate him.

## Chapter 13

All I ever had to do before was take my clothes to the launderette and somebody wanted to marry me. All I had to do was walk down the street and somebody was leaning out his window. I didn't have to do a thing. I didn't have to do nothing, is what I'm saying. All I had to do was lift my foot off the brake.

I can see what I'm doing wrong with Billy. I've got to let him come to me. I've got to let him figure out what he wants and the only way he can do that is if I stop showing him what I want. If I keep wanting it so much then he'll just go on letting me do all the wanting, without him having to do any. If I want him to do his share, I got to do less.

I'm not going to see Billy for a while, I decide, not until he comes to me. I'm going to ignore Billy. I'm giving him the silent treatment. I've got other things to do. I am who I am, Lucy Fooshee, Lucy Bybee now, Mrs. Bybee with responsibilities and such.

Now Bob, he wants to be with me every minute. The less I care for Bob, the more he cares for me, like what's happening with Billy only the other way around. The meaner I am, the nicer he is. And on and on. Like there has to be a certain amount of each thing and if you don't supply your half then the other person will throw in double.

After three days of the silent treatment, Bob suggests we go for Sunday breakfast to Aunt Babe's. I could have gone on for another day or two just like I was but this is Bob's idea and me not going to Aunt Babe's just so I can avoid seeing you know who only meant I was thinking of him, in the first place, which, as far as he was concerned, I wasn't. And anyway, how can Billy know I'm ignoring him if I ain't around?

We're getting dressed to go. Bob stands on one leg to pull his pants on and it's all he can do to keep from falling over. He says, "I think your Mama ought to get Littleberry Howe to do her chimney work."

"Littleberry Howe?" I'm turned away from Bob, getting my clothes on, but now I turn around to look at him. "Why, you know Billy is Mama's handyman, Bob. You know Billy is —"

"You can't just get anybody to do a chimney, Lucy. Ask anyone. They'll all tell you —"

"Just anybody!" I shout. "Littleberry Howe is useless, Bob. I don't want my Mama having that man do a thing. I don't want him at her house. Bob, where would she get such a notion as Littleberry Howe?" I pull my blouse on and start buttoning it.

"I told her myself he may not be good for much, but Littleberry Howe is about the best there is for chimneys."

I think I mentioned how loud Bob is, no matter what he's doing. When most people get their clothes on, they don't make much noise, but Bob does. You can hear everything he's doing. You can hear his pants when he pulls them on. You can hear him button his shirt. Even when he combs his hair it's like he's scraping metal around. Bob has got red hair but he's not Irish. I don't know what kind of other people have red hair. Whatever kind they are, that's what Bob is.

"Billy isn't going to be around forever," says Bob. "He ain't from around here, remember."

Like I might forget for a second how Billy Lee is different than the rest of them.

I sit down at the dresser mirror. I got a big dresser with a mirror on it and a chair to sit at so I can brush my hair and put on my face and squirt perfume on my neck and see myself do it the whole time. I can see Bob in back of me, fumbling around.

"He's got a lot of work to do yet, Bob. And I don't know how it is in your family but in my family we finish what we start, Bob." I don't say whether the we I'm talking about is the Bybees or Fooshees. "We see a thing through." I start brushing my hair, but I'm watching Bob in the mirror behind me.

"I'm not having him do the easy part and then, when it gets hard or it gets to something he don't like, he goes on to do something else. That isn't the way we operate around here, Bob. We finish what we start. We make a promise and we keep it, don't we Bob? We do the whole job and not just pick some things we like and leave the rest for someone else to worry about, isn't that right?"

But Bob isn't listening. I can tell by his face that the last thing on his mind is what I'm saying. He's thinking about his clothes because Bob is someone who has to think things most people wouldn't bother with. Most people would just get their clothes on without interrupting their thoughts about it, but Bob has got to tell himself each of the things he's doing. He has to think about the fact that he's pulling his pants on and they're blue and he has to think about putting his shirt on and look how white it is and he has to think about his socks and on and on, you can imagine for yourself. Thoughts that are too boring to think, that's what Bob has in his mind. I know these things because sometimes I hear him saying them out loud. He forgets himself and he'll start muttering under his breath the things he thinks all the time. I won't go into it.

All the church-going people are half done with their breakfasts when we get to Aunt Babe's. There are two seats at the counter and we take them. Most people, once they get married, sit at one of the tables but Bob and me, we still go to the counter. Billy comes right over.

He says good morning and he pulls out his little note-pad to write our order down and he says, "I haven't seen you for a while."

But I just look puzzled, like I ain't sure what he's talking about. Didn't I just see you the other day? I might be thinking.

Bob orders three eggs over hard, a double order of toast, hashbrowns, ham and bacon. I order a chocolate shake and Bob says, "A chocolate shake for breakfast, Lucy? That doesn't seem right."

But I ignore him.

When the food comes Bob eats his eggs and I sit watching Billy. I haven't ever seen a man who looks the way he does and who can do everything just perfect, the way Billy does.

I tell myself how we're lovers and it's a big secret. It's between me and Billy and nobody else. I think like right now, at this minute, we're pretending to be two people who haven't never done the things we done. But then I think it's like if you won the Miss America contest but couldn't say it to anybody. What good would it be then. When you have a secret and you can't tell nobody about it, after a while it's like it isn't even true in the first place. It's like you're making it up. I look at Billy and think how he's making me feel like I'm making it up and I want him to stop.

I say, "Billy, are you eating at my Mama's house for dinner this evening?" But he says, "No, ma'am, I'm not. I've promised to take my Aunt Babe out for dinner."

"Why don't you bring her on over to Mama's house?"

Bob looks at me like that's a funny thing to say. All this time I been thinking how not to say any funny things, but right now I don't care.

Billy says, "That's real nice of you, but I think I'll have to decline your offer."

I say, "My sister is cooking barbecued ribs."

Billy says, "We've got other plans, thank you."

"Evaline is making sponge cake too." I say the sponge cake part loud so Babe in the back can hear, because Babe is big on dessert.

Billy moves down the counter to take money from Harriet Walsh.

I lean around Bob to call out, "If you don't come, we're going to have too many barbecued ribs and then what will we do?"

Bob has stopped eating and he's frowning. He's shaking his head at me like you do when you don't want to say something out loud, but I'm not looking at him. I'm looking at Billy Lee's profile. I'm looking at his hands.

"We'll just feed spare ribs to the dogs, is that what

you're saying?"

But Bob says, "No, Lucy, we'll save them for tomorrow. We can eat ribs for lunch, isn't that right now." And he thinks he has settled it.

"At least come for sponge cake." I see his Aunt Babe peeking out of the little window that separates the eating area from the kitchen. I can see her head poking out and she's peering around trying to see, like she don't recognize my voice and she's got to get a look at who's talking.

I never noticed how stubborn Billy is but now he says how he'll have to take a rain check.

"Rain check," I say to Bob. "That means no, now don't it?"

Bob says, "It means later, Lucy, like how if it rains you put something off."

I roll around on my stool and look out the window. It's the middle of summer and not a cloud in the sky.

"Why don't you order some food, honey?" says Bob, thinking if my mouth is full of food maybe I'll shut up for a minute. "I'll have me a apple pie a la mode with black coffee, Billy." He calls out and then nudges me, "You go ahead and order too."

I look over at the window to the kitchen and Babe's head is gone. An order is sitting there, a plate of short stacks and a BLT. I think BLT sounds good and I say to Billy, "Can I have a BLT please, with sweet pickles?"

"Sweet pickles on a BLT?" Bob says. Like now I proved something they had been worried about all along. They had only feared it but now everybody could see it was true.

"I guess I can have sweet pickles if I want. I guess it ain't like asking for the moon."

Billy is cutting a piece of apple pie and a piece of walnut pie for Lloyd and Frank Garber. I can see that he's pretty good at pretending I'm just another girl come in for a BLT.

He gives me my sandwich and I start eating. I think to myself I better calm down. I think I'm all excited and I better just calm down.

Now that everything is normal again and Bob is eating his pie a la mode and all he's thinking of is the food in his mouth and Babe's head is back in the kitchen and Billy is filling the napkin holders, now that everything is like that, I guess I can talk again.

I say, "Billy, we still got that leak in the kitchen."

Right away Bob starts to choke on his pie a la mode and I got to hit him on the back to get him to stop.

I say, "You know, Bob, we still got that leak." I turn to Billy, "That leak is still leaking."

"He tried to fix it once, Lucy."

"He didn't try very hard."

Billy looks up from the napkins. "I'm not much of a plumber, Mrs. Bybee," he says.

I think he said the Missus part a little louder than the rest. I listen again, like how you can hear words echo after they've already been said, and I think sure enough, he said that part louder than the rest.

Anyway, if I was just trying to see him I could go to my Mama's house. Everybody knows that. He's at her house about every day. I'm just being friendly, the way we are around here.

I don't have to say nothing, if that's how everybody is. I don't have to say a word. I eat my sandwich. I drink my shake. I cross my legs.

I say, "Bob, I sure am glad you like your new tractor," just to get him going and Bob starts to tell me about it.

He can talk about his tractor all day long. He doesn't care if you talk back or not.

I drink the shake down. I think how I love Billy Lee so much I could eat him up. Which is what you hear mamas say to their babies sometimes but I really mean it. I could just eat him up! I let the milkshake dribble out of my lips, and just then Bob says, "Lucy!" and I swallow and pat my mouth with a white napkin.

I look down at the print my lips have made on it. I slide it across the counter and leave it there so it's just the print of my lips in brown, looks like it could be blood, looking up at Billy.

## Chapter 14

My sister, Evaline, is an old maid and old maids are not like other women. Old maids think about sex all the time — from lack of sex, they think about nothing else, and thinking of nothing else they notice it even if it ain't there and if it is there, why they smell it out, like dogs, with their noses in the air, sniff sniff.

And Evaline, from lack of sex, from being an old maid, from being alone and knowing she always will be alone, it's her destiny to be alone, from those things, she has turned secretly mean. Nobody can see it but me. In Palmyra you get stuck with what you were. What you were is all you are and all you'll ever be. So Evaline, she's stuck with being nice and nobody but me will ever see different.

Evaline has her eyes on Billy and she'll do what she can to try and get him.

She don't understand how guys like Billy, they don't go for horsy, sweet girls even if those girls can cook a fine chicken dinner. You can go down to the store and buy yourself a chicken dinner, if a chicken dinner is what you want. They got other kinds of appetites.

Evaline won't leave me be. If I'm at Mama's house, she's right beside me. If I'm inside, she's there, too. If I go out, she's next to me. One day I set out from Mama's to go to Aunt Babe's and Evaline won't take no for a answer but she has to go too. She brings along her little dog Foxie.

"We all like Billy Lee," Evaline says, walking along.

"We sure do."

"Billy Lee is a good worker," she says.

And I agree, "Yes, he is."

"He's a nice-looking man, too," Evaline adds.

"No mistake about that."

"Course, looks aren't everything."

"No, they're not," I agree.

"Pretty is as pretty does."

"You're right there, sister. It's what's on the inside that counts."

Evaline isn't looking at me while we walk. She's watching Foxie, who's running ahead of us and going down alleyways and coming back and running up people's porches and hiding behind their shrubs. She can't take her eyes off that dog.

"Most men don't know that," I say. "Most of them are looking for a pretty face. No matter what their own face looks like!" I don't mean to discourage her, so I add, "But remember, all you need is one."

Evaline walks along. She throws another stick for Foxie and Foxie chases it. She stops to look at Mrs. Runels's cherry tree.

"Look at Roberta Mosser, how she got married and her with that big nose."

"I'm not worried."

"Sheila Garber didn't get married until she was thirty-two."

"If I never do get married, it won't be the end of the world."

"That's right."

"Don't matter much, one way or the other," says Evaline.

"Cheryl Dick, she was thirty-one."

"Don't matter if you pass thirty by or not, is how it looks to me."

"Roberta, she married a Hughes too, from over to Buckhorn," I remind her.

"That's right, Roy Hughes."

"The Hughes family, they go way back, almost as far as us Fooshees, you remember."

"I wouldn't marry Roy Hughes if he was the last man in the county."

"Oh, you wouldn't," I say.

"No, I sure wouldn't."

"Looks aren't everything."

"I don't care about his looks."

"You ever seen a neck as long and skinny as the one he's got?" I wait, but Evaline can't seem to think of an answer. "And the hair on that man's body! Why, I seen him one time without his shirt on, out in the field, and I'll tell you Roy Hughes has got hair, you know the Hugheses they got that thick black hair, he has got it growing everywhere. On his shoulders and on his arms and on his back from one side to the next, he's got hair, like a monkey, he is." I hesitate. "But that's nothing to hold against him. He can't help the hair that got put on his body."

Evaline shrugs. "I don't mind all that."

"You seen it?"

"No, but I can picture it quite clearly now."

"Picturing is one thing and seeing is another."

"It's his meanness I can't abide. Why if I ever met a meaner man, I can't think of it now."

"Ain't nobody meaner than Rusty Hogg," I tell her.

But Evaline doesn't want to argue about who's meaner, Rusty Hogg or Roy Hughes.

We're at the edge of town now and there's the highway and across it is Babe's Cafe. I can see the sign and Billy's truck parked out front, with all the windows rolled down. The parking lot is full. I open the front door and Evaline says to Foxie, "You sit, girl!" and we go inside.

It's lunch time and all the tables are taken, but we don't sit at the tables anyhow. We walk on by the tables saying, "Hey there!" because this is Palmyra and everybody knows everybody else in Palmyra. It's hot inside, even hotter than outside, and everybody is talking loud and smoking cigarettes. The windows are open and you can hear traffic going past on the highway.

I sit at the counter and Evaline sits next to me. We've got summer skirts on and no stockings, sandals, and blouses without sleeves. I can feel the heat from my thighs, where they lay close to each other. I can feel the heat from my arms, where they touch against the sides of my body. And the heat on the back of my neck, and the wetness there, where my hair hangs down.

I lean my naked arms on the counter and look across the room at Billy. Billy is standing, kind of slouched, with the yellow, tobacco-stained wall behind him, and Lester Egree across from him with a plate of eggs, leaning forward, trying to get what Billy's saying. His face looks like it must be a joke, he's ready to laugh. I can hear the sound of Margery Johnson's voice on top of all the other ones. I can smell cigarettes and fried bacon and hamburgers.

"A piece of apple pie," I call out. "And Evaline wants a chocolate shake."

Billy goes through the swinging doors and into the kitchen. When he comes back, he's carrying the biggest piece of pie you ever saw and he sets it on the counter in front of me, alongside Evaline's shake. Everybody in Aunt Babe's is calling out they want something.

I pick up the fork to take a bite and, while I open my mouth, Billy's standing there, watching. My lips close over the pie and I can taste the apple on my tongue and all the time Billy's looking at my mouth.

Margery Johnson's voice is yelling, "Can't nobody get a refill around here?" but Billy doesn't move.

I run my tongue over my lips.

I can hear Margery. "Goddamn it, Babe, you better get some help around here!" she's yelling so Babe can hear, clear back in the kitchen.

"Billy!" whispers my sister and Billy looks up.

"Right," he says, looking around, and then he walks away and starts pouring coffee and taking orders, refilling waters, handing out plates of food, while I sit, eating my pie.

"He's a good-looking man," says a voice behind me, and I twist around on my stool to see Mavel Runels and Eliza March standing behind us.

"He sure is," says Evaline.

We all turn to him now. He isn't like nobody any of us have ever seen.

Mavel and Eliza are standing behind us, with dollar bills in their hands. Billy sees the money and he starts writing in his little notebook, adding up their food.

Mavel leans in between me and Evaline. She says, "You are one hardworking man," and she bats her little eyes. "I see your pickup down at the Fooshee's house day and night, seems like."

Before Billy can answer, Evaline jumps in, "I never seen a man who could do the work Billy can. Oh, and Mama — she's got him working like a dog."

Billy tears the bill out of his little pad and hands it over to Mavel. He's smiling like he has a secret they don't know and, even if he told them, they still wouldn't get it.

Mavel's got her eyes fixed on Billy and her smile is stretched from one side of her face to the other. "Must be hard to work in the dark," she says. She's got her red lipstick on.

Mavel feels me looking at her. I'm looking at her lips, how she's used a liner to make them bigger than what they are. She can feel my nasty thought and now she twists her face around to mine.

"You sure aren't spending much time at your own house, Lucille," she says.

"She's such a help to Mama," says Evaline, but they ignore her.

"Must be hard to keep up a house as big as the Bybee house." Mavel smiles at me with her big yellow teeth. "All that dusting!"

"And you never there to do it," throws in Eliza.

"There's the garden —" says Evaline, but Mavel interrupts.

"I heard," says Mavel, bending forward even more so now we're looking at the tops of her white breasts, "that Mrs. Lyle Bybee is throwing a hissy fit!"

"You're not keeping that house up, is what everybody is saying," says Eliza, quickly. "They say you're always at your Mama's house. You and Billy Lee, both!"

"You know how people talk," says Mavel.

Nobody says nothing. Evaline and me are turned in our seats. Billy is stopped in front of us. The girls, Mavel and Eliza, standing behind us, Mavel tilting forward, showing off her little breasts. It's like a game of freeze and someone has called it out, "Freeze!" and that's how we each wound up. I've got a fork full of pie in front of my face and my mouth just starting to open. I could get myself a low-cut shirt and push my breasts up, if I wanted, if I needed to show off like that, I could, I'm thinking, but I don't. Only reason I don't is I don't want to.

But Evaline isn't thinking of Mavel's breasts and she laughs a phony laugh and tosses her hair back like she's being casual and she says, "They can't stay away from my cooking!"

I can hear people in the diner shouting, calling out articles of food or names of condiments but we ignore them.

"You know it's the way to a man's stomach," says Evaline, and she reaches across the counter and sets her hand on Billy's arm. And Billy, he doesn't shake it off. He doesn't look surprised but he stands there, calm, like he isn't surprised by that hand, creeping like a old snake on him. Maybe it's been there before, is what his face says.

Mavel and Eliza are just shocked by the notion of my sister, Evaline, setting her hand on the arm of someone like Billy Lee. You don't go doing that out of the blue, they're thinking. They stand there, pale and outraged. Evaline Fooshee! Of all the people! Well, they're thinking, this goes against all reason.

And when it's too much for me — when I can't bear it and I start to open my mouth to set them straight, Evaline's other hand travels over to my leg, secretly, and gives it a pinch.

"Billy, would you bring me and my sister a BLT, split in two?" Evaline says smiling, and fluttering her eyes, and he turns back to work.

"Too bad he don't have any prospects," says Mavel, once he's out of earshot.

She's dying of jealousy because of that little hand of Evaline's touching his arm. She's dying, but it's for the wrong thing.

"Or good family, neither," adds Eliza.

If they could only see what me and Billy done together they'd lay down on the floor of Babe's diner and they'd just stop breathing. If they could look at my mouth and tell where it's been. Oh, they'd curl up and die.

Mavel and Eliza finally leave and it's just me and my sister, together, saying nothing.

I eat my pie. I smash it up with the fork so it's all mushed together, flat and brown, and I eat it. Evaline, beside me, doesn't say a word. We don't look at Billy when he walks by us. We look straight ahead.

Finally I say, "If you got out more, Evaline, maybe you really could find yourself a boyfriend."

"From the look of other people's marriages, I might be doing myself a favor staying single," she says.

"You just keep telling yourself that," I say, licking my fork.

Evaline picks up the menu then and sets it on the counter in front of her and she starts reading it, like she don't know every word in it already. I ignore her. I eat my pie slow now and I look around. I look at all the people in Aunt Babe's and it's like they're strangers and not people I walked among all my life.

"You don't really think he likes you," I say, low. "You don't really think so."

I wait but she doesn't say what she thinks. She leans forward like she just found something real interesting in Aunt Babe's menu and she can't miss a word of it.

I poke my fork in my pie. It's flat and all smashed together. "It may be true for some men that the way to their heart is through their stomachs but —"

"Would you shut up!" she hisses. And Evaline never says a thing like that so I do shut up, I shut right up.

Evaline has got to the end of her milkshake now and she makes little slurping noises, getting the last of it, and I start to say to her how she ought to go easy on the milk shakes — think of Mama, I start to say — but I stop myself. If she wants to wind up looking like Mama, then let her go ahead.

Billy brings the BLT to us, on two plates, but he doesn't look at me when he does it. He walks off and he starts doing the next thing. He has got a white T-shirt on and his hair wet with sweat brushed back from his face and he has got a apron on and in his back pocket a rag for wiping down counters. His back is to us and I'm watching his neck and I'm thinking how it's like a salt lick somebody has left in the woods and I'm a little deer, just come up on it.

Pretty soon some people come up, Lowell Hopgood and his cousin, they come up and start talking to us and for one second Evaline forgets about me. I sit smiling at them, next to Evaline who's smiling too, and I see, from the corner of my eye, Billy going back into the kitchen, the doors swinging shut behind him.

"Excuse me, I have to use the rest room," I say, and I follow after him.

Billy's in the kitchen, talking to Aunt Babe. She's standing at the grill. She's got about two dozen eggs on that grill, all cooking at once, and when she looks up to see me, she jumps in surprise.

"I came to use the rest room," I say. The rest room is through the kitchen. I can see the door from where I stand, but I don't move towards it.

Aunt Babe looks from Billy to me and then back to Billy again. She doesn't know what to do.

"Billy," she says, looking at him, searching his face.

Billy looks back at her and then she wipes her hands on her apron, takes the little notepad Billy is still holding in his hand, and goes out through the swinging doors.

I know what he's going to tell me. He's going to say I can't behave like this. I'm going to ruin everything. I can't make a scene in public. What will everybody say. But I'm sick to death of thinking of everybody else and what they'll say.

Billy looks over at the grill at all them eggs cooking away. He moves over to them now, and picks up the spatula, and I move with him so we're both standing at the grill. The heat's coming off it and the smell of eggs and grease.

"Billy," I say, just to feel the feel of it in my mouth and he looks at me, at my mouth and then at my eyes and then back down at all the eggs, their yellow yolks sticking up, staring right back at him. He starts flipping the eggs over, one and the other, the next one, the next, all in a line, and he doesn't break a one.

I'm watching his chest how it moves up and down with his breathing and how now it's moving like he's been running, like he's been lifting heavy things, like he's really working hard, instead of just holding a little metal spatula and flipping eggs over easy.

He looks at me and he's going to say for me to go on out now. I lean forward to hear him, over the sound of the refrigerator and the stove and all the little motors in there, and the sound of the eggs, cooking. I lean forward. He's going to say everybody out there is waiting. Everybody out there will know. They're watching the clock. Everybody in town will hear. And then he shuts his mouth again.

He sets the spatula down and looks at me. He looks at one thing at a time, at my eyes, at my forehead, at my mouth and then he takes his hand and brushes the hair back from my face where it's fallen, and looks at me like he hasn't seen me before and he puts his finger on my lips and traces their outline, first one and then the other, and he slips his fingers into the side of my mouth, and I taste the salt from his finger and he kisses me but he doesn't take his finger away but kisses me over it and when he pulls his mouth away the finger is still there only now he moves it from the side of my mouth down to the bottom and he traces my line of teeth and then the line of my jaw and then his hand moves to my hips and pulls me towards him and I fall forward into him and we stand like that, with our hands on each other and I can't tell where I'm touching him and where I'm touching myself and I begin to sob and I'm saying, "Oh, oh," and the door flies open and it's Aunt Babe but I can hardly understand that, that now Aunt Babe is here. She's shoveling the eggs from the grill as fast as she can. They're burnt. I can smell it.

"Damn it, Billy. Damn it," she's saying but whether it's about the eggs or me, I can't tell.

*Chapter 15*

The next day I hear how Mama is sick with the stomach flu and I go by her house, to help out. The heat hasn't let up a bit. It's as hot as it's ever been, as hot as anybody can recall. I go over to Mama's house and here Evaline has got Billy chopping firewood. On this day, when nobody can't imagine ever being cold enough again to want a fire, Evaline has got him chopping wood because she wants to sit on the front porch and watch him.

Evaline is on the porch with her red cotton skirt on, pulled up to show her white legs. She's got her shirt rolled up. Her eyes are glued on Billy and he's cutting up hedge posts for firewood. He has his white T-shirt soaked through with sweat and he keeps on working. Whack, whack, whack.

While Evaline, all this time, is watching him from the porch, red in the face and breathing hard, slapping her legs back and forth together.

"Well, look who's here," says Evaline when she sees me. "Come to help, I suppose."

"Where's Flora?" I say.

"She got a ride over to Whitehall, to see Aunt Janelle."

"Aunt Janelle still sick with the milk leg?"

"That's right," she says, pulling the skirt down over her knees.

"Why don't you go too, Evaline? You know how Aunt Janelle just loves you. You know Flora could use a hand when she's at Aunt Janelle's." I sit down next to her on the porch. Foxie comes to jump on me but I swat her away. "Does you good to get out. That's what everybody says."

Evaline smoothes her hair back. "I have a lot of work to get done."

"Oh, a lot of work," I say.

"Anyway, I am going. I'm going over there to pick up Flora and I'm taking Aunt Janelle some dinner. You know how she hates to cook. I'm taking her dinner and I'm staying to visit. I don't know why you don't come along. Looks like you got nothing better to do."

"I've got my own house to look after now." Everybody knows Aunt Janelle doesn't have any use for me and I never did like her, neither.

"Oh," she says, "and when are you going to start doing it?"

"I've got my laundry in the car, I beg your pardon."

"And what about your new washing machine?"

I could get in a fight right now but I stop myself. I go back to my own thoughts.

"Why have you got him out here in the heat of the day?" I say, at last. He's taken off his shirt and his skin is shiny with sweat. "He ought to wait until the sun gets lower to do that kind of work."

"He *is* under a shade tree."

Billy lifts his arms and then he swings them down and he swings his hips too, at the same time. He bends forward into the wood and then back and forward again into the wood.

"Why don't you wait until this evening to do that, Billy?" I call out.

"Billy is just fine," says Evaline.

Billy stops and wipes his face with his hand. "I'm just fine," he calls.

"What'd I tell you?" says Evaline.

"No use him killing himself."

"Does he look like he's dying?"

We both look at him now, at his big arms that swing up into the air, at his hands, at his legs that pull forward and then back, his hips that lean and pull back and then thrust forward. Instead of waiting for my answer she stands up and goes on inside and lets the screen door slam behind her.

By the time Evaline leaves for Whitehall, Billy's out back, putting in a window for the porch. I go back there too, with my laundry to hang up. A little breeze is just coming off the prairie.

First, I hang up the sheets, mine and Bob's, our white cotton sheets, all bleached and perfect. I can't dry those sheets at Bob's what with the dust from the fields blowing everywhere. Perfect and white. I put clothespins in my mouth while I set the sheets on the line, even, and each time I take a pin out of my mouth I slip my eyes over to Billy and he's looking. I've got red lipstick on, even though it's only a weekday and I'm not going anywhere. The next thing I see in the laundry basket are Bob's big old underpants and I poke them down to the bottom. I pull out a slip that belongs to me, a cream-colored silk half-slip, that kind that starts at your waist. I don't look up now. I look at what I'm doing. Maybe I've forgot all about Billy Lee. Anyway, he's supposed to be working. Mama wants a new window for the back porch. Then I hang up my whole slip, which comes all the way up to cover my breasts and is lace on the top. Then I pull out my first pair of underpants, which are cream colored with a lace border around the waist and around the legs. I hang up three pair, just alike, and then I pull out the last pair, which is white silk.

When I've got them all on a line, I look up at Billy who isn't even pretending to work now, but just watching me. I hesitate, watching him back, and then I reach for my brassieres.

Billy goes over to the pump then and starts working it, up and down. I'm not looking at him but I can hear the sound of the metal pieces, rubbing against each other. I hear the water pouring out and Billy is sticking his hands under the stream of water, splashing it on himself. When he's finished with that he comes to where I'm standing. I'm behind a sheet now. It's moving a little in the breeze and he comes back behind the sheet and stands next to me. Anybody looking can see our feet down below.

"Can I see you again?" he says.

I start to point out how he's seeing me right now, isn't he, but I don't. I hesitate. I'm risking a lot, in case he hasn't thought of it. I'm risking everything. What does he have to lose? He doesn't have nothing.

"Oh sure, let's go in the house," I say, sarcastic, but his face doesn't change. He lets it go by. He's standing there, waiting. Anybody looking at our feet, down below, would wonder what it is the handyman has to say to me that's lasting so long. I think that to myself, but it's an automatic thought that comes out of habit and nothing else. "Where?" I whisper.

This is the day Billy and I begin meeting in the cemetery. The cemetery is his idea. It's right outside of town. You walk along like you're going to Bob's house, like maybe it's a nice day and you've decided to walk, and then you swerve south at the last minute and wind up at the cemetery. Or from Bob's, you can go to the barn out back and not far past the barn you can get to a little river. That river goes right through the cemetery. There's a little woods alongside the river and on both sides of it are cottonwood trees. They have a good smell right now. You can smell them clear to Bob's house if the wind is out of the southeast.

First Billy leaves and then I wait twenty-five minutes. I hang up my clothes and pace in the yard. I look at my garden and I sit under the oak tree, looking at the space where he stood a little while ago. I'm being a fool, I say to myself. This is not pretending. This isn't something I'm making up. It's not a story I'm telling to myself. But it's like I'm in a dream and I know I'm in a dream and I keep saying to myself wake up but I don't. And the funny thing is, I don't mind. I don't want to wake up. I don't want to stop myself. I don't want to change the way I feel. I only want the time to go away so I can see him again.

After twenty-five minutes, I go inside. I tell Mama I'm taking a little walk. I tell her, "I'm leaving you a pan right here to throw up in," and she just looks at me. I pick up an old paperback book and take an apple from the kitchen.

I walk along like I'm walking home and then, at the last minute, I swerve. Nobody is around. I walk through the black iron gate. When you drive by you can see through the gate of the cemetery to the first few rows of tombstones, but you can't see the rest. Back behind the regular graves is the old pioneer cemetery where you can't hardly read any of the names, and some of the stones have fallen over or been knocked over. Back behind the pioneer cemetery is a little woods with thick brush and cottonwood trees and, in one corner, gingko trees. And way back, behind the woods, is the little creek that runs through the Bybee property.

I'm just through the entrance when I hear a car, so I sit down by the Doogan family monuments, which aren't far from the road. I open my book and pretend to read. I take my apple and bite into it. Mr. Maurice Quigg, he drives by on the road and looks over. I cross my ankles and lean forward, like this is a real good part of the story and I can't think of nothing else.

I hear his car go on past and I close my book. I walk back behind the Doogan monuments, the big ones for the old people and the little one, where Howie's sister is, and I go on and on, down to the old settler monuments that you can't hardly read, and then back where the monuments fade out and there are only cottonwood trees and gingko trees and Billy Lee.

Billy has a blanket spread out on the ground, back in the brush, almost hid. I don't know what I was expecting. I mean you aren't going to find the Holiday Inn back here. This is just the old pioneer cemetery, I know that, and I have no reason to be surprised but I'm surprised anyway. I'm surprised by the blanket laying on the ground, back in the bushes. I'm surprised by the way the air feels back there, nasty. Like big eyes watching us. Even in the shadow of the trees, it's bright and nasty feeling. This isn't how I picture my love affair with Billy Lee. The old pioneer cemetery, with dead people under us and an old blanket down on the ground and the blazing sun, like if we're a couple cows out in the field and can't even tell where we are.

I stand there thinking how this is a Hogg thing to do, to meet somebody in the bushes of the old pioneer cemetery in broad daylight.

"Somebody'll see us," I say, still standing back from him.

"Nobody comes here," he says.

"Boys might come here. They might come here poking around, the way they do. Smashing up old cemetery plots and writing bad words on them, and they might fall right over us. Or they might get down on their stomachs and watch the whole thing, just so they can go to school and tell everybody about it."

But Billy motions to the brush and to the ground. "Nobody's been here for a long time." After he says that Billy sits there quiet as can be. He gets tired of watching me after a while and looks the other way, like we've got all the time in the world.

"I don't like it here."

He turns to look at me again.

"I'm not a cow, you know. I'm not a dog." I start to say I'm not a wild Indian, but then I don't say that. I been meaning to bring up the Indian thing but I think maybe this isn't the way to do it. I'm waiting for him to say how I agreed to it. Go home, if you don't like it. But Billy doesn't feel like he has to say a word.

What I should do is turn on my heels and go stomping away out the cemetery, with him following and calling for me to come back! But the things that have worked for me before, they don't work with Billy. So instead I move over to the blanket and sit down on it. I've got a skirt on and I spread the skirt out in a circle around me and cross my legs at the ankles, like if we come here to have a picnic.

"See those trees?" Billy points up to the big gingko trees above us. "How did they get here?"

Which is a funny direction to take off in, if you ask me. "They're not from here," he says.

"No, they're not. They're from someplace else. I have no idea." After all I been through, to bring me here to the Palmyra Cemetery and strike up a conversation about the danged gingko trees. "An old lady name of Farrell, like how you say a cat has gone feral but spelled different, she planted them but she's dead now for a long time. Probably buried right under us with all the other dead bodies," I say, in case he isn't thinking of what we're sitting on top of. "She come here from whatever place that is that's got gingko trees and she planted them around the graveyard, way back a long time ago for her dead husband so he can look out and think of home, I guess."

"I thought they came from Japan," he said, but I'm not going to argue.

The gingko trees are tall now and wide. They have a funny name — gin-ko — which is more like a sound than a name. The trees have small leaves that are shaped like fans, like if somebody took sheets of paper and made them into millions of tiny fans no bigger than a man's finger. In fall, they turn yellow.

"Are you afraid of this place?" he asks.

"I don't believe in ghosts, if that's what you're thinking."

"Listen to how quiet it is."

I roll my eyes at him. A graveyard, what do you expect.

And then he pulls me over to him and lays me down

on my back, so I'm looking up at the branches of the trees, over us. He pushes the hair away from my face and smoothes my skirt down around my legs. And while he's doing that, he takes the palm of his hand and he runs it over my skin, over my legs and my thighs and my hips and he puts his hand up under my skirt and he puts it on my belly and it lays there like a little animal fallen asleep, like a little cat maybe. And after a while it wakes up and it goes up to my breast. It isn't like the hand of Bob or the hand of Hammer, nervous and fussy, but it's like the hand of someone setting out on a trip. It's the hand of an explorer wandering around, looking to see what there is.

I found out that time doesn't just run in a straight flat line going out but it also runs in thicknesses. When I look back over the time Billy and me spent like we did, under the gingko trees back near the dead pioneers, Mr. Farrell and the rest, when I count up the days, there aren't many of them. There are just a few, really, when you count. But each day was thick. Each day was bigger than any other day. Each day was worth about a year, at least. And when I think about the things we did there, in the little woods back off the highway under the trees, when I name the things we did, they're like the things anybody else might do. When I say the things we talked about, I guess other people have talked about the same things. We've got the same bodies as anybody else, don't we. We've got the same mouths to speak with. If you just looked at the outside, you'd think it was something anybody else might do or say. Oh, it would be big news in Palmyra. Everybody would talk about it, but they wouldn't know what it was. It was different than anything else.

I start taking walks. Sometimes I walk from Bob's house. I go to the barn and I walk along past the shed where he parks his truck and on down to the creek. I follow the cottonwood trees to the cemetery, where Billy is waiting. You live in a town like Palmyra and you notice any funny thing the minute it happens and you talk to everybody about it because people have to talk about something, don't they. So I'm careful. Sometimes I walk from Bob's, like I said, but sometimes I walk from Mama's. You can walk from Mama's like you're going to Babe's or you can walk like you're going to my house. Sometimes I walk like I'm doing one thing and sometimes like I'm doing the other. Sometimes someone will stop and they'll want to give me a ride and they just won't take no for an answer.

I go in the afternoon sometimes. Or I go after Billy gets off the breakfast shift at Aunt Babe's. I go every day, if I can. I go to the woods and see Billy there, under the trees, and it's just him and me and nobody else and nothing else, like if the rest of the world ended there, like there is a line and on one side is Palmyra and everything else and on the other, just me and Billy.

My sisters, they don't leave me alone but they want to be with me all the time. If I say I want to walk to the store, then they want to go to the store too. If I say I want to walk alone, they kick up a fuss.

"I just like to walk," I tell them.

"You never liked to walk before," says Evaline.

"You always drove," says Flora. "You always drove before."

"Before what?" I say, but they don't answer. I see the look Flora shoots Evaline and Evaline's eyebrows going down to tell her that's enough.

"Then let me go along," says Evaline, one day. "I like to walk, too."

"I need to walk alone," I say. Flora rolls her eyes at Evaline but Evaline pretends she doesn't notice that. "Can't somebody be alone if they want to?" I say.

"Oh, alone," Flora repeats after me, but Evaline says to her, "Just be quiet now!"

We meet almost every day. Some of the days we hardly speak and other days we don't hardly shut up. I tell Billy everything there is to tell. About my life, growing up in Palmyra. We grew up with my brother Jimbo and us four girls. Evaline was oldest, of course.

"Evaline never is going to get married, that's what everybody says. She isn't much to look at," I add, in case he's wondering why not.

"Looks aren't everything," he says.

"Pretty is as pretty does is what our Mama always told her." Billy is laying next to me, naked, and now I put my face against his skin. Billy has skin that smells so good. I breathe it in. I put my tongue on it and taste the salt taste of sweat. "She's a big girl, that Evaline. Guys don't want a girl as big as they are." I look up at him to see what he's thinking, but I can't tell. "She's built like a horse." I'm waiting for him to defend her and he doesn't but he's smiling like I've made a joke. "What?" I demand. "What's so funny?"

I tell Billy about growing up. I tell him how we used to sit on the porch in the summertime, same as now, and the little kids chased lightning bugs in the yard. If there was a moon you could look out over the prairie and it was so pretty. "Now the little kids," I say, "they'd catch lightning bugs and bring them to me and I'd pull the wings off and put the shiny part on my finger, like they were wedding rings." I hold my finger out and we both look down at it. It's the finger with Bob's ring on it now, and we look for a moment before I pull my hand away and put it behind me. "The crickets would be out in the field," I continue, "rubbing their legs together and the frogs, too."

I tell him everything on my mind without thinking first should I or not. I just open my mouth and talk. I tell about my daddy who was mean and my brother Jimbo who's even meaner. We were taught you never say a bad word about each other outside the family. You can say what you want inside it but outside you got to present a united front. I tell him about my Mama's family, the Hoggs, and I tell him about Hammer Johnson who killed himself one day and everyone said it was my fault. I never talked this way to anybody before.

Billy isn't a big talker, but sometimes he tells me about himself. He tells me how his mother, Aunt Babe's sister, run off with a half-Indian man, name of Joe Eaglekiller, and that was Billy's father. He tells me that name one of the days in the cemetery. I'm laying on my back, looking up at the gingko trees. I can see a little bit of sky behind them and it's as blue as anything I ever seen.

"Eaglekiller," I say. We've rolled off the blanket and are laying in the tall grass. There are ducks flying overhead and Billy's watching them. He doesn't say nothing. "Isn't it funny how a white person's name, like any of them names over in the cemetery, you don't get any ideas from listening to them. Gillespie, Johnson, Fooshee. John-son, that means son of John, now doesn't it? But that doesn't paint no pictures in your mind. You hear a name like Eaglekiller and you get a picture. You know here's somebody with a history." I say, "Fooshee, now what does that mean? Foo-shay, like two little names stuck together." I touch his face. "So why do you have your mother's name?"

But he doesn't say.

He says, "If you look hard enough at any of them names then you'll see they all mean something or other."

"Lee, that ain't much of a name neither. Billy Lee. Bill Lee. Like you got a stutter."

"It means something though."

I wait to see if he'll tell me what it means and then I say, "General E. Lee, we had a cat named that once."

"There's a river in Ireland named Lee," he says. Billy's big on geography. "Maybe the name comes from that." We lay there, and then he says, "Anyway, the point is every name comes from some place and every name gives you a clue."

I say, "There's a bar over in Beardstown, Pooch Filson's place, and the whole wall on one side and the whole wall in back is covered with arrowheads. Pooch is a collector. Everybody is all the time digging up arrowheads in their fields, when they plow, you know, and they give them to Pooch. But there aren't any Indians." I say that last part soft and put my mouth on his skin when I say it.

"Where are you going when you leave here?" I ask him.

"I got work any time I want out in Oregon, on the barges," he says and then he adds, "but I like California, too."

"Take me out west with you," I say, but he doesn't say anything back. I've got my head in his lap. I can hear a chickadee in the trees above us. They make a little sound like chhchh ch. I can hear the gingko leaves rubbing against each other.

"Don't leave me here alone," I say. I sit up and look at him and say it again. I'm not fooling around. "Don't leave me here alone."

"I won't."

"You mean it?"

People think they know what love means, but they don't. Until you know, you just have no idea. You think you know, but you don't. And when you do know, then nothing else matters. Nobody in Palmyra knows. I've lived with these people all my life and now that I know, I can tell none of them do. It's like one of those dog whistles you blow and nobody can hear a thing, but all the dogs bark and whine and go crazy. And whenever Billy is around me that dog whistle is blowing and nobody else bats an eye.

Billy says it's an irony how I got married just two weeks before he showed up. Irony, he says, is what you call something that should have gone one way but then it went the other.

With most people it doesn't matter too much who they marry. One is about the same as the other. Any of my sisters could have married half a dozen boys from Palmyra and nothing much would be different for them. Oh, they'd live in a different house. They'd live in Arenzville, instead of Buckhorn. They'd drive a Ford and not a Chevy. Their children would have brown hair, instead of blond. But everything else would be the same. They'd sit at the table eating the same food, saying the same things, they'd go the same places, have the same opinions, put the same things in their cupboards, have sex the same way and make the same noises while they had it, and it would all be the same, the same, the same, the same. Betty could have married Buster Filson or Lance Decker and it would be the same. Same with Flora, only there aren't many as rich as the Winklejohns. Everything with Flora will be the same anyway, only a nicer version of it.

But with me and Billy Lee, it's like we get to have different lives from what we had before we met each other. Maybe they look the same, but they're different. The feeling of everything is different. What can I say except that? Different. You sit in the bath and it's different. You lay in bed, you walk, you eat, you look out at things, and it's all different. Even alone, even with Bob, it's different. Just knowing I live in the same world as Billy makes that world a wonderful place.

To everybody else, me and Billy are just two people. He works for my Mama, that's all they know. And if they drive by and I'm standing on the sidewalk talking to Billy, I'm probably talking to him about insulation or firewood or plumbing. I'm standing a ways off from him and my face looks like the face of someone talking about such things and his face looks like that, too.

I see Billy at the store and I say, "Why hello there, Billy Lee," and he says hello back and we go on our way. I drive past his house, where he lives with Aunt Babe, and it's like I'm driving by any old house in Palmyra, and no different. If he's outside I wave my hand and he waves his hand and nobody looking would have any idea what those hands mean to each other and what those hands know about each other. I come to Mama's and find him working out back and eventually I go out back too, because that's what I've always done. And sometimes Billy is so busy with his work that he doesn't say a word to me, but sometimes he says how nice my garden is looking or what a beautiful garden I've got and how he loves the smell of my garden. And sometimes Evaline or someone else is with us, Mama or Flora, and they don't bat an eye.

## Chapter 16

One day I go to Mama's house and it's empty. I go through all the rooms. I can hear Billy out back, sawing. I stand in Mama's room and look out her window and he's there, at the sawhorse, cutting a six by four, back and forth.

I kneel down at the window and watch him. Everybody would say I wronged Bob when I took Billy to the Holiday Inn motel and laid in the bed with him there, but that wasn't nothing compared to this. My real adultery is here at the window when I watch him work and I don't want anything else and nobody else and I know that I'll never go back to Bob and who I was when I was with Bob. I'll never sleep with Bob again, I tell myself. I'm not his wife anymore, if I ever was.

And suddenly Billy feels me watching and he stops and looks up. He sees me in the window and he just looks.

Then I stand up, slowly, with him watching, until I'm framed by the window and he sets his saw down but he doesn't take his eyes off me, and he smoothes his hair back with one hand, still watching, and I'm looking back, smiling, and I take hold of the hem of my blouse and I lift it, slow. I lift it up over my breasts and I thrust them out towards him and then I laugh and he laughs, too.

He laughs and I laugh and he stands up then and walks to the pump, taking his shirt off on the way and throwing it on the ground. I stand watching at the window while he pumps the handle. You have to pump it up and down and then the water pours out and, while it pours out, he ducks his head under it and then splashes it on his face and his arms.

"Where's Mama?" I call out to him.

"In Jacksonville with your sisters for the whole day," he says. "Gone shopping."

I look up at our neighbor's house, Mrs. Hobbes, but that's a habit only. I don't care if Mrs. Hobbes is watching us. I don't care if she's taking pictures. You have to know what's important and I'll tell you right now, Mrs. Hobbes and everybody else, they don't measure, they don't count, they're nothing — when you set it next to this, all of it is nothing.

"Mr. Lee, I think you better come in here and look at my plumbing!" I say. I lean out the window, laughing, but my shirt is down now.

And Billy comes inside, laughing.

We go to my room, where I used to sleep with Flora. My little bed is still here, across from Flora's bed, against the wall, and the dresser, where I kept my clothes. And the room, with him in it, seems suddenly small, a child's toy room, with low ceilings and walls too close to each other. For a moment we stand, looking around us. Looking at the bed, where I slept all my life and the floor, where I played with my dolls, and it seems to me that he can tell anything he wants, just by looking around him, and I want to rush in and hide things. But then I look carefully. There's nothing I don't want him to lay his eyes on, nothing to stick in a drawer, nothing to distract him from.

There are two windows and I go to each of them, closing the blinds and pulling the curtain shut. I take off my shoes and the floor is warm against my feet. He comes into the room and he doesn't say anything but he goes to my old dresser and touches the top of it. There's a picture, sitting in a frame on the dresser. It's a picture of me and my sisters and Jimbo, when we were little kids. We're standing, lined up, on the front porch. Jimbo is younger than both Evaline and Betty but he's bigger than any of us. Billy picks that picture up and looks at it. It's like he's forgot I'm standing next to him. He studies the picture and then he takes the tip of his finger, softly, and touches the one that's me.

We take off our clothes and let them drop onto the floor. He sits on the edge of the bed and I stand in front of him.

"I have a game I like to play," I tell him. "I made it up. I pretend I'm a famous movie star. I'm so famous everybody is just dying to find out about me. And I pretend someone is making a movie out of my life and everywhere I go, there's a camera pointing at me."

He lays back on the bed and I sit next to him.

"I pretend that everything I do, just sitting here, pushing my hair back from my face," and I push my hair back, to show him, "licking my lips, sighing, looking at you, is being watched." I put my leg over his hips and I climb up on him, "and a director is saying, Get in close now!" I lean forward and rest my belly on his belly and my chest on his. "Slow it down," I say. "Be sure to get the mouth, " and I kiss him. "And all over the world, people are watching me on their TVs and they're all pointing at the screens and saying to look!"

"Are you playing that game now?" says Billy, smiling, and I sit up on him and I make my hands into a frame and giggle.

"Down at the hardware store, Chuckie has the TV on and everybody is looking at it."

He pulls me over then and rolls on top of me. "Shhh," he says.

"And over at Rhonda's House of Beauty the TV is on and all the ladies are pushing the hair dryers back from their heads," I say quickly. "Isn't that Lucy Fooshee?! they're saying. What is she doing? Who is she with? For God's sake!"

And then it seems like all my life has been a game I was making up, like I've been sitting on the floor down there telling myself stories, and only now something real is happening. I can feel Billy's hands and his skin and his breath. I can feel his heartbeat, where it lies against my chest. And I think this must be how Gloria Quigg felt the day she stood up in church and yelled, "Hallelujah!" And then I think I am yelling. I think I'm yelling and shaking, my eyes are back in my head and spit coming out my mouth.

When we're quiet again, laying side by side, I touch my mouth but it's dry. I listen for the echoes of my yelling, but it's quiet. And I wonder about myself, how I can't even tell what my own body is doing anymore, I can't tell what's coming out of my own mouth, or what I'll do next and I think I should mind these things, but I don't.

Billy slides his head down to lay it on my belly. I have a heart beat there, he says.

When I'd fool around with Bob or with Hammer, it always seemed like my mind would start to wander. I'd find myself thinking of what somebody said or what I needed to buy at the store or sometimes I'd start making lists, grocery lists, shopping lists, lists of what I had to do. I just couldn't keep an interest up. And the things they did — those things seemed far off, like they were happening to somebody else, and not to me.

With Bob, even before we got married it got to where I'd tell myself, this is the part where he does such and such and this is the part where this happens and next is the blah, blah. You get so you know all the parts. You get so it's a story someone is telling that you heard too many times before. You aren't going to be surprised. You could fall asleep and then wake up and you'd know where you were, which part you were on and which part would come next.

After a while, Billy sits up and looks around my little room. There's a picture over my bed of an angel, with two little children, and he looks at that. He's sitting with his back against the wall and he pulls me up to sit next to him.

I lean my head on his shoulder. Outside the window I can hear a car driving past. It goes on by and doesn't stop. "Take me out west with you," I say. "I want to go with you, out to California or someplace. I never seen the ocean before. I want to go someplace with an ocean."

"You're somebody who wants whatever they don't have," he says.

"What do you mean don't have? What is it I don't have?" I wait, but he doesn't say. "I'd want what I have if I had the right thing." I wait again, but he doesn't talk. "You got to have the right thing to start out with, and then you can want what you have." He puts his palm on my leg and we both look down, at it. "I never had a chance," I say. "You give me a chance and I'll show you how happy I can be with what I've got." He slides his hand around my thigh. "But first you've got to give me what I want."

"Come here," he says, and he pulls me around to face him, to straddle him, and we start all over again.

I've heard this can happen but I never seen it before, how some guys can go two times. Girls say Glenn Pinshaw can, but I never seen the point of it before now.

He's got his hands on my hips. It's hot and we're sweating. I can hear our breath and I can smell our bodies, salty and sweet, and for a moment I look down to watch, but it's too much. I shut my eyes and there's just his hands on my hips and the movement and the feel of him and then I begin to sob and he hesitates but I put my hands on his hands to show him keep going and we do keep going. We're at an edge and instead of running over it we stay there at the edge, we run along it, we stay with it, we push against it, we stay there until finally we can't hold back anymore and we let it go. And I fall over on the bed, panting and hot and dying of thirst.

After a little while, Billy rolls out of bed and stands up but he doesn't dress. He goes to my dresser and picks up my hairbrush and turns it over in his hand.

"What if your husband Bob finds out?" he says. "Your husband Bob," he calls him, like there might be more than one husband and he wants to make sure I know it's the one named Bob he's talking about.

Billy walks to the window and opens the curtain a crack, to look out. You can see the side yard from there. You can see the woodpile and rose bed. You can see the Burr Oak tree.

"A town this small," Billy says, "he's bound to find out."

"Shawnelle Innick, she run off with Fenton March when this happened to her." I sit up and put my feet on the floor. "She was married to someone she didn't love and then she fell in love with Fenton and they run off." I straighten out one leg and look at it. "They're very happy, is what I hear, the both of them."

Billy lets the curtain fall shut.

"Bob's not my husband anymore," I say.

"You married him."

"I don't fool around with him."

Billy crosses his arms in front of his chest. "Fool around? What do you mean, fool around?"

"Sex," I say.

"Oh, Lucy," he says. Then he goes over and gets his underwear and pulls it on, like this is something he can't hear naked but has to get dressed first. "You don't have sex with your husband?" he says.

"He's not my husband anymore."

"Don't do this because of me," Billy says, and now he pulls on his trousers, zips them up, buckles his belt. He starts walking back and forth in the little room. "Jesus!"

I stand up now and begin to dress. I put on my underclothes and then my skirt. I pull my blouse on and button it, while he paces.

"You only been married a little while," he says.

"If it was you married to someone else, the wrong person, you wouldn't do it neither," I say, but he looks at me, confused, and I'm not sure if that's true.

"The wrong person?" he says, stopping now in the middle of the floor to watch my face.

And I don't see how he can ask me such a question.

"Yes!" I say. "The wrong person. Wrong, wrong, wrong! I don't feel nothing for him. How can he be my husband if I don't feel nothing for him?"

"Why did you marry him? Why did you do it? What were you thinking of?"

"I waited til I was twenty-two!" I shout. "I waited forever!"

Billy pulls his shirt on. He begins to button it but I go to him and move his hands aside, and I button it myself. I start at the bottom and work up.

"He's a good husband, isn't he? You couldn't hardly ask for a better husband." His head is turned away from me.

"Oh, he's a good husband, all right," I say. I've got his shirt buttoned but I don't let go of it. "And he loves me so much." I pull him forward so he's face to face with me. "He's counting on me settling down, don't you see? Everybody is. There's no one around here who hasn't. We all settle down."

"There's nothing wrong with settling down," says Billy.

But I don't argue with him. I let go of his shirt. "You might think everybody is so nice and all, you might come into town and think that. But side by side with that niceness is something mean and hateful. They're nice, so long as you do what they want."

I cross the room to the window and pull the curtain open. There's no breeze from the window. It's still and hot and I'm thirsty. The sun is shining through the window onto my face.

"Don't leave me here with them," I say.

I hear him move towards me. I feel his hands around my waist and his breath on my neck. He touches my hair.

He puts his face against the back of my head and I lean back towards him and open my eyes.

"Goddamn!" I say. "Goddamn it!" I say, and I whirl around. "It's Betty! It's Betty's car, out there!"

And we hear the screen door slam. We hear footsteps through the house and they don't hesitate but walk straight down the hall. We're froze, listening. We can't move. We watch the door knob turn and the door is thrown open and it's Betty, standing, red faced, furious, with her big pocketbook slung over one arm and her hands clenched.

We're standing too close together and now we move apart.

"I knew it!" she says.

I shake myself a little bit and recover. "I guess we don't have to replace the window then, Billy?" but he looks at me, blank. "And this here crack," I point to the ceiling and he looks up and Betty, still in the doorway, she looks up, too. "you say it's normal for a plaster ceiling to crack like that?"

He blinks at me and I give him a look. "Yeah," he says, "structurally it doesn't mean a thing."

"Well, that's a relief!" I exclaim. I look at Betty and wink, "I was afraid the roof was about to fall in but I guess it's not."

Before I can congratulate myself too much though, Betty turns to the bed and our eyes follow hers. The bedspread is half torn from the mattress, blankets crumpled, pillows thrown to the floor, the bed pushed away, crooked, from the wall.

*Chapter 17*

Betty is mean and she'll tell. She's gone home to Buckhorn but she'll be back and there's nothing I can do about it so I push the thought of Betty out of my mind. Enjoy each day, I tell myself, and when you get to a bridge then cross it.

I like being by myself now. I like to sit at Bob's house on the porch alone and watch the Dunavans' horses. I like to have the whole house to myself after Bob's gone to work in the fields I like the feeling of all the space and emptiness and the quiet and the loneliness around me. I like to feel how full that is, the empty space, like the space where Billy doesn't say anything, but it's full of something so sweet you can almost taste it in your mouth. And sometimes, when I'm at the house and Bob's gone, I run through the house showing myself how big it is and how nobody's there, not anywhere, and I think of all the distance around me and how far it is to someone else. The further away everybody else is, the bigger I feel, like I can expand into that space, all the space between me and everyone else, I can fill it up. When I explain that to

Billy, he doesn't say anything, but I don't mind.

The more I want to be alone, the more Bob wants to hang around me. Suddenly Bob wants to be wherever I am. If I'm outside, he's there, too. If I'm in the kitchen, he comes in. If I want to go to the store, he thinks he'll go along. If I'm in the bathtub, he's knocking at the door. If I pull up in the car and sit there for half a minute, listening to a song on the radio, Bob is out on the porch, calling to me. If Bob didn't work twelve hours a day, I don't know what I'd do.

One day I'm at Mama's, in the garden. Billy is working on the porch, ripping the old siding off it. On days like this, it's almost like we're married. Like he's the husband and I'm the wife, out in our yard on a hot summer day.

I like to tell myself stories about where we are and what our lives are like. We're in California and later we'll go to the beach and lay on the hot, white sand. And in the night we'll sleep together on our own bed and we'll leave the window open and the curtains.

It's August and I've got fat red tomatoes in the garden, dying to be picked. It was only last month that was the Fourth of July with Billy and me out by the road and Flora coming by. But I can't hardly believe that. It's more like half my life.

You think time is always the same, but it's not. You think it's tick tock tick tock one two one two forever, but you're wrong.

A shadow falls over me but I don't turn around. I hear the voice soon enough.

"Why, look who's here!" says Betty.

I'm weeding the squash and I don't look up.

"It's so kind of you to trouble yourself about Mama

now you're married and have your own house." Betty puts her hands on her hips and looks down at me. "And such a nice house too. I'd think you'd want to spend more time there, nice as it is. You must have so much work too, what with all them big rooms to take care of and all those knickknacks to dust and I know how particular Mrs. Lyle Bybee is about her things."

"I don't worry about Mother Bybee."

"That's good," she says. "You got enough to worry about."

Betty has a big straw hat on her head and she pushes it back, away from her face. She's looking at Billy. He's got a flatbar and he's tearing strips of rotten wood off the side of the porch. "You don't want to get people talking, is all I'm trying to say."

"Why should anybody be talking?"

"You here all the time, instead of out at your own house."

I've got so much squash, we'll never eat it all. "I got the garden here to take care of."

"Gardening, uh huh," she says, and she sits down beside me, tucking her pink skirt all around her legs so nobody can see up it, like they would want to.

Betty never will pitch in. I'm pulling weeds and throwing them in a pile behind me. She sits on the grass. Betty's hands like to sit in her lap and do nothing.

"What kind of gardening were you doing the other day?"

I wear little brown lady's gloves in the garden to keep my hands nice, but now I take them off. "I don't know what you're talking about."

Betty sighs. "You live in a little town like Palmyra and anything you do, somebody will notice it."

"That's a fact," I say. "Somebody will notice and go sticking their nose right in it."

I weed all my romaine. I don't care if Betty doesn't help. When she has helped, she's pulled half the topsoil up anyway.

"I remember the day before Shawnelle and Fenton run off," she says. Shawnelle she was married to Buck Innick, before she run off with Fenton. "And I was driving through town, the day before it happened, and I see Shawnelle out front of Babe's Cafe, standing in the parking lot. She's talking to Fenton. They're standing by her car and they aren't standing any closer together than I would stand if it was me talking to him but, even so, I know something is unusual. Maybe they're talking a little too long, I don't know. Maybe it's the way their faces are. Something. Anyway, I realize, just minding my own business, I realize something unusual is happening and it wasn't twenty-four hours later that they run off with each other. Run off." Betty pauses. "You just can't keep a secret in Palmyra."

I lean back from my work. "They're very happy, is what I hear."

"Oh, they are."

I push the sweat from my forehead and look her in the eye, level, and she looks back at me. "You know them big moles Shawnelle had on her face?" I say. "Well, I seen her sister at the Post Office and she told me that they fell off now. That's what Shawnelle's sister told me one day at the Post Office, that after Shawnelle fell in love with Fenton and run off from this place, then her moles just fell off."

"Those big moles of hers?" says Betty, surprised. Shawnelle she always had big moles on her face, all her life.

And Betty sits there for a while, pondering this, but then she recovers herself. "We're not like the Innicks! We come from good family." She starts in on how the governor of Virginia was our great great great grandfather's brother, or some such. Larkin Fooshee was a minuteman in the Revolutionary Army. But I hold up my hand, to stop her. "Anyhow," she says, "we've got our family name. The Fooshee name," she adds, in case I'm wondering which one.

"I know it isn't the Hogg name you're talking about."

Our Mama is a Hogg and don't nobody brag about that name. Not just how it makes you think of a pig but how, if you live around our parts, it calls to mind a set of people not much better than the name they got.

"Do you know that Billy Lee there," she nods suddenly at Billy, like now she's starting a new subject, "why, he ain't even white."

I don't say anything.

She hesitates, "I used to think he was Italian, but he's not Italian. Nor Greek. I always thought Italian myself. You know, like Frank DiPirro who came down from Chicago that time to marry Fannie Lou Gertler. Wop, is what Daddy used to call it," says Betty.

My palms are wet and I wipe them on the side of my pants.

"Not that I'm saying there's anything wrong with being Italian," she adds. "Nor Greek neither, for that matter."

"I don't know that I ever seen a Greek," I say.

"Not many Greeks around these parts." Betty's hat has a bow that ties under the chin and now she unties it and ties it back again. "Mostly white people around here."

"Greeks are white."

"That's right," she says, "and so are Italians. But anyhow, Billy Lee — his father isn't any of those things, is what I hear. He's Indian."

I've been squatting but now I sit on my knees. "Then he's the first Indian I ever met."

She leans forward, "You know how prejudice people are, around here."

Betty tips her hat back, away from her face. She's sitting cross-legged on the ground with her pink skirt all tucked in around her legs. She fidgets with her hat. She unties and ties the ribbon. She takes the end in her mouth and chews it. I can hear her breathing beside me. The sweat is pouring down her face and she wipes it with one hand.

"If Jimbo did his job around here, like how Daddy would've expected, then we wouldn't have this trouble in the first place. Here Mama is spending a fortune on a hired man when it's Jimbo's job to see to Mama."

"Mama thinks it's good for Evaline to have a man around here," adds Betty, nodding to Billy. "I told her Billy there is Indian, but you know Evaline is thirty years old now and I don't think Mama cares. And so I said to her, I said, Mama, would you want Evaline seeing a nigger? I said, it's the same thing only you don't know better, and she said, it's not, and I said it is too. And I said to her, just because Evaline is thirty now don't mean she has got to take the first thing that comes along. But beggars can't be choosers, that's what Mama thinks." Betty looks at me with eyes as round and hard as marbles.

And now we both turn to look at Billy, across from us. He has tore all the siding off the wall and is putting it in two piles, one to keep and one to haul off. We can see the muscles in his arms and back and the motion of his hips and it's all perfect and Betty knows that too. Watching him work is like seeing something private and I want to call out to him to tell him stop.

"You wait til your brother finds out!" Betty whispers, mean, in my ear, and low, like we're in a room full of people and someone will hear.

"Jimbo?" I say. "There ain't nothing for him to find out."

## Chapter 18

Bob won't stop bothering me about sex. I got the smell of it on me all the time, the smell of having it or the smell of wanting it, and that keeps Bob in such a state. At night he pushes against me but I don't feel nothing about his wanting, not even sorry. I don't feel nothing but irritated. How he can want me so bad when I don't want him at all and then bother me about it, day and night, pushing against me, pulling me towards him. Isn't he good to me? he wants to know. Isn't he good? He's nothing to me but I don't say that. And I don't feel any more obligation towards him than I do the man down at the Texaco.

He thinks I ought to see the doctor, like not wanting him is a form of sickness and I better go see somebody about it. Or see the preacher. We never go to church and here he wants me to tell the preacher such a thing. Or I ought to talk to my Mama. He has all kinds of ideas. Bob is not usually an idea man but he comes up with ideas now.

One day I'm on my way to Aunt Babe's Cafe. It's late August and there's no breeze anywhere. It's still morning but already the sun is beating down on my head. The concrete burns through my shoes. When you look out you see heat waves coming off everything. All the dogs are stretched out in the shade, sleeping. The cats are all holed up someplace dark. No birds in the sky and not a cloud anywhere you look.

I'm at the parking lot of Aunt Babe's and inside, when I open the door, I'll see Billy.

A car pulls in behind me but instead of parking, it slows down, following me. "Hey!" I turn around, slowly. "Hey! Where you think you're going?"

Jimbo is driving and he's got his head stuck out the window. His face is big and red and he has little flat eyes. He's got a cigarette in his fingers and while I stand froze he takes a puff and blows the smoke out.

"Going to see your nigger boyfriend?"

He veers into a parking spot, opens his door and leaps out, slamming it shut behind him and hurrying to stand in front of me. Jimbo seems even bigger now than he was before, if that's possible. He's a big, hard-looking man, takes after Mama's people, the Hoggs.

I look up at him. You can't be afraid of Jimbo. Even if you hide it, he can tell. Jimbo don't have much going for him, but he knows one or two things and he knows fear.

"Why, Jimbo, what a surprise," I say. I have always been his favorite sister and now I smile up at him. "Mama will be so happy to see you. You ain't been home for a long time, Jimbo."

Jimbo is easily confused and so you've got to hit him with different things. You've got to pretend he never said nigger boyfriend and if you pretend hard enough he might even doubt it himself. He might start thinking he only thought nigger boyfriend and never said it out loud which is why you're so calm and just smiling up at him and talking about Mama and such. Jimbo is someone who can only hold about one thought in his mind, so what you do with Jimbo is you replace the thought he has, that you don't want him to have, with something you pick out yourself.

"I seen Grace Ellen at the store the other day, Jimbo, and let me tell you, she has got fat!" Grace Ellen being his old girlfriend who dumped him for Wyman Scott and got him started on his road to pure meanness. "Lord!" I say, knowing he'll get a kick out of that.

"I'm going to kill him, you watch and see." Jimbo's hands are at his sides and he opens and shuts them.

A car pulls in the lot and parks but we don't look at it. The car door opens and shuts and someone walks past and we hear the door to Aunt Babe's and the little bell that rings when somebody opens it, but we just stand, looking at each other.

"Wyman's not worth killing, everybody knows that."

"I ain't talking about Wyman!"

"Let's go to Mama's," I say and I take his arm, but he shakes me off. "She's been dying to see you."

I take his arm again, but he jerks away from me. "You married the Bybees, don't that satisfy you?"

There's something nasty about the way he uses the word satisfy. It seems wrong coming from my own brother, Jimbo, and I'm quiet. I can hear my heart pounding in my ears and I'm hot and dizzy and if I open my mouth, I think, I'll throw up.

But this is just Jimbo, who's nothing to me, I tell myself. This is Jimbo, who's nothing. I think about me and Billy, and I think how all of them have been thinking the same thing, but what me and Billy are, they can't know it. They can only think of what they are and think they know the rest, but they don't know. I look towards the cafe and think of Billy inside working, innocent.

"If Mr. Lyle Bybee finds out." Jimbo puts his face close and I can smell beer. "If Mr. Bybee takes a notion to, well, he can make it hard on all of us." I can't think clear enough to know what Jimbo is talking about, hard on all of us. "Them Bybees own about half the goddamn county," he says.

"Don't you cuss at me."

"Them Bybees can do about anything they want to, if they want to!" Jimbo throws his cigarette down and grinds it with his foot.

"Give me a ride to Mama's. Come on and we can talk," I say. "Someplace cool," I say. "Let's go to Mama's and have a beer." I lick my lips. "I'm about to die in this heat."

But then a bad thing happens. Jimbo looks up and he recalls where we are. He looks around at the parking lot.

"Let's go," I say, trying to head him off, but he won't move.

He nods towards the cafe. "Is he in there?"

"I don't know what you're talking about," I tell him.

"He ain't even white, Lucille!" I can smell beer on him, on his breath and on his body where he sweats it out.

"Come on, Jimbo," I pull his arm towards the car. "When you get mad you always get in trouble, you know that."

But he shoves me away hard.

"If you're looking for Aunt Babe's nephew, he's at Mama's putting up siding."

Jimbo's face is shiny with sweat.

"Did you screw him, Lucille, did you screw a nigger?"

My eyes travel over his face, slow. His face is fat but hard and his nose is swoll up, red and mean looking. He has stupid little eyes set back too far in his head and they don't blink. He doesn't look like a member of the superior race. This is Jimbo Fooshee, I remind myself, my own brother, but that thought doesn't stop me from hating him. We stand like that for a long time, out in the parking lot in the blistering sun.

"Yeah, I sure did," I say.

I don't see his hand coming at me. It hits me hard in the face and I fall back. I fall onto the ground, onto the burning hot parking lot and I'm surprised but I jump right up.

Jimbo is ready to charge at me — he doesn't care if you're a girl or not — but the door of the cafe opens and Billy comes outside. He grabs at Jimbo.

"Get inside, Lucy!" he shouts at me. "Get inside!" but I don't do it.

Jimbo whirls around and swings at Billy but he misses. He's a big man and Billy comes in close to him and hits him on the jaw and Jimbo lets out a yell and he grabs hold of Billy and throws him into Pete Egree's blue Fairlane and Billy rolls on the hood but twists away, out of reach. I can hear people pouring out of the cafe and gathering around but I don't look at any of them. Jimbo goes after Billy and I charge at him, but somebody grabs me and holds me back. Loyd Garber from the bowling alley wraps his arms around my shoulders and holds me.

It's been quiet, just the sound of breathing and falling and arms flying out and hands, but now Jimbo grabs hold of Billy's shirt and begins pulling him back and forth, shaking him. "Nigger!"

"Stop it, Jimbo!" I shout, from behind the arms of Mr.

Garber, kicking my feet.

I can feel the confusion of the crowd. Nigger?

"He don't look like one," I hear somebody say.

Billy brings his hands inside, between Jimbo's and pushes them out. He takes hold of one of Jimbo's elbows and pulls him around and then down so that Jimbo trips, stumbles, falls sideways onto the ground and then rolls onto his back. Billy jumps down on top of Jimbo, on his chest, and he jabs his fist at his face. He hits him over and over and Jimbo's mouth breaks open and starts bleeding and I think to myself I hope he kills him but men's voices are saying, "Break it up!" to Billy and they start to move in, to stop him now.

Mr. Garber is pulling me away and Pete Egree is helping him. I'm kicking and trying to get back but they take me to Mr. Garber's car. They throw me inside and Mr. Garber gets in his door and Pete Egree sits on the other side of me and they take off. I reach across Pete, like I'm going to grab the door handle and jump over him and get out of that car and run back to the parking lot, but Pete holds my arm. He holds it longer than what he should. He holds it all the way to Mama's house and then he lets go.

Evaline is out on the porch, waiting, like a dog who knows when something is wrong. She takes me inside and I hear the men shouting to Mama while my sister gets ice from the freezer and makes a pack. Evaline wants me to lay down but I won't lay down. I can hear Mama on the porch outside telling Pete and Mr. Garber how she don't know what has got into Jimbo, to get him acting this way.

"I'm going to kill that Jimbo," I say. "I'm going to kill him!" I'm moving through the house, going from room to room, while Evaline follows me, taking hold of my shoulders or my arms, and I shake her away. I start to go out the back door but she won't let me. I'm crying and won't keep the ice pack on my face. I can hear the men drive off, Pete and Mr. Garber, and I think how Pete held my arm in the car, too long, just for the chance to do it, and now here are Evaline and Mama, following me through the house, grabbing at my arms, too. Clawing at me.

"I have to go back there!"

But now Evaline takes both my shoulders and shoves me against the wall. "If you don't shut up, I'm going to slap the other side of your face!" she says, and she doesn't let go, but holds me there, like it's me that done the bad thing and now I'm caught. I push against her and I kick at her legs and try to bite her hand but Evaline is strong as a horse and she doesn't budge.

Mama is behind her, holding one hand in the other. "I suppose someone will tell the Bybees?" says Mama, in a voice that's too quiet for her. "Oh, someone will tell everyone and everyone will know," she answers her own question. I can see her over Evaline's shoulder, pacing back and forth. Then she thinks of a new worry and Mama says to Evaline, "Loyd Garber says Billy was beating him up real bad before the men broke it up."

Finally Evaline lets go of my shoulders, but she doesn't move away. She pulls my hair back from my eyes. "You better put that ice back on your face," she says.

They don't know what to do with me so Mama runs a cool bath and they take me to the bathroom and Evaline waits while I undress. She takes my clothes and leaves, shutting the door behind her. I stand, looking at my face in the mirror and I start to cry again because of how I look, my eye all swoll up and red. And I think, this is from being hit one time and I'm glad Billy's face didn't get hit. Unless after I left, the men pulled him back and held him for Jimbo. I seen that happen in fights before. And Jimbo is one of their own. Still, I tell myself, nobody likes Jimbo much.

The bathroom window is open and it occurs to me to crawl out it and go back to the cafe to find him, or to Aunt Babe's, to look for him. Without making a sound, I push the window open, slowly, but then I look around for my clothes and, of course, Evaline has taken them out.

He told me once that he wouldn't leave me here.

I've let the bath water run almost to the top. Mama doesn't like that because it's wasteful but I don't care. I run it to the top and I get in. I sink under the water and feel my hair float around my head. I hold my breath as long as I can. The water stings my face, where Jimbo hit me.

Now it's out in the open and I'm relieved. Now something new will happen.

I sit up in the bathtub and lean my head against the side of the tub. I wish I had me a gin and tonic, I think, with a little piece of lime and a mint leaf. I had one of them in St. Louis, and it was the nicest thing I ever had that was alcohol. I don't know how it is Jimbo can drink beer the way he does. I don't know how he can stand it. And I think again, I hope Jimbo is killed but nobody blames Billy because it was self-defense and we all saw it. And I think of Jimbo when we were little and he was my brother. I try to think of one good thing, but I can't do it.

When Evaline hears me drain the water, she comes back with my clothes, and she waits with me while I dress. "Bob is here," she says.

"Bob? Bob is here? What has he heard? Has he heard about the fight? Does he know if Billy's all right? Is he leaving town? He has to leave town now, doesn't he, Evaline. Has anybody said —"

"Bob doesn't know any more than we do and don't you go asking him about it!" she whispers, quick and harsh, in my ear.

Bob and Mama are sitting in the dining room. Mama is at the table, with knitting in her hands. The needles clicking back and forth, fast. They stop talking and look up at me when I walk in and Bob comes right over.

"I come to take you home, Lucy," and then he sees my face.

"Oh, honey, look what he did!" He puts his hand towards my cheek but he doesn't touch it. "What kind of man would do this? What kind of man would hit a girl?" says Bob. He doesn't know what to do. "You don't go around hitting other men's wives!" he cries out. He doesn't want to fight Jimbo but there's no way around it now.

"I knew Billy Lee was trouble, the minute I seen him!" exclaims Bob. "Didn't I tell you?" he says to me, but I look away from him.

Bob ain't my husband and I don't have to talk to him.

We can hear Mama's knitting needles, click click click.

Evaline's got the bottom of her shirt in her hands, twisting it. "Jimbo was drunk, Bob! And someone told him Billy is spending too much time at this house, sitting inside at the table with us girls and such, and him not all the way white. Oh, he's got some wild notions, doesn't he, Mama?"

"Billy Lee's daddy was half white too," says Mama, "and that makes him three-fourths."

"I said all along —" starts Bob, sitting down at the table, but I interrupt.

"You're acting like Billy done something wrong, Bob," I say, flinging myself into the chair across from him. "He didn't do nothing wrong."

And Bob looks at me, blinking.

"He did what you should have done, he took on your role, Bob."

"Defending her," adds Mama, so Bob will be clear on which role it is I'm referring to.

"And all because Jimbo has gone and got himself drunk and started making a scandal," says Evaline.

Mama doesn't say anything but her needles are going faster, clickclickclick.

The dining room seems small and crowded, like it can barely hold the four of us. I go to the window and open the curtains but the sun comes streaming in and Mama says, "Close that thing up! You'll let in all the heat." And I shut it again.

"I'll have to get Daddy Lyle and go over to Jimbo's house in Pittsfield," says Bob, relieved a little now, to think of Daddy Lyle.

"It was Grace Ellen that done it," says Mama. Click, click, click. She's talking to herself. "He was a good boy until then."

"Jimbo never was any good," I say.

"And then she threw him over," mutters Mama.

"Daddy Lyle will be out in the field," Bob says, looking at his wristwatch. "He won't like being pulled away today." He crosses and uncrosses his legs. "But I guess there's no getting around it." Bob looks at Evaline like she might have a answer for him.

"If you go after Jimbo tomorrow, you know you'll find him at work at the lumber yard," she says. "He won't be drunk then and he's not half so brave when he's sober."

Evaline doesn't point out that Daddy Lyle is friends with the owner of the lumber yard. She doesn't mention how Daddy Lyle's little sister is married to the manager of the lumber yard, either, but we all know those things.

"Otherwise we could wind up hunting all over Pittsfield for him," agrees Bob, "wasting our time."

Bob's pretty happy now, thinking of going after Jimbo in the lumber yard, surrounded by his kin and their friends. "You don't go around hitting my wife," he says, for practice.

And then he says to Mama and me, "We're going to teach him a lesson," and it occurs to me that Bob must be forgetting how Jimbo is my mother's son, because when she makes a plead for mercy, when she says, "Just give him a talking to, man to man, that's all he needs," he looks at her, surprised and confused. "He's family, don't forget," she adds.

"He's not my family!" Bob shouts.

Although Mama will hold that remark against Bob forever, she doesn't comment on it now. She says, "Jimbo has got his father's temper." But that's too much like she's taking Bob's side against her own family and now she looks down at the knitting in her lap. "Just don't make him lose his job, whatever else you do."

"Folks like to talk," says Bob, " but then things will calm down and everybody will forget about it. Nothing will change." He runs his hands through his hair. "We just got to give it time. It'll quiet down, you wait and see." He waits for someone to say something hopeful, but nobody does.

## Chapter 19

Bob isn't one to go running off half cocked, he tells us, explaining again why he doesn't drop everything and go looking for Jimbo. Half cocked, I think, it's a funny thing to say.

Finally he leaves me in the hands of Evaline and goes off to the fields.

I have to be very patient or she'll never let me get away. It's early afternoon and I tell Evaline and Mama that I have a sick headache and I go lay down but they don't leave me alone. Evaline sits in the chair next to me, with her mending. I'm laying in my old bed, the same bed where me and Billy laid together just four days ago. I turn over to face the wall and I put my hand on the cover where we were and look at it there. Evaline is so quiet, you almost think you're alone. I breathe deep and slow, like someone sleeping, but my eyes are open and I'm looking at my hand.

After what seems like hours, I hear Evaline set her sewing down. She sighs and I hear her make that noise she makes when she stretches and I shut my eyes so that when she bends over to look at me, they're closed. I hear her move around my room. I hear her go to the window and pull the curtain to the side, to look out.

Evaline goes out of my room then and I hear her walk down the hall. I'm going to Aunt Babe's house first. That's where he'll be. And if I don't find him there, I'll run all the way to the cafe and I'll find him. I'll ask everyone I see. I won't care how it looks or who they tell.

I might go over to the radio station and tell Shirley to interrupt her program to announce to Billy that I'm looking for him and please go home right away.

I can just see the faces of the ladies at the beauty shop when they hear Shirley. "Mr. Billy Lee, would you please go home. Lucy Fooshee is waiting there for you and she's in a hurry."

I don't wait around but climb right out of bed and I get some pillows and plump the covers over them so if Evaline glances in the room, she'll think it's me, sleeping there.

Then I climb out my window, scraping my legs on the bushes underneath it, and I run out of the yard with Foxie running after me.

I run all the way down the block without turning around. I'm barefoot and the sidewalk is hot. Mr. Wells is out in his yard and he watches me go by. Eliza March's nephew rides past on his bicycle and he looks at me, too. Foxie is jumping after me, nipping at my ankles in her excitement.

"Stop it now!" I tell her and I kick at her, but she thinks it's part of my game. "You go home!" But Foxie pretends she can't understand plain English and she just barks.

I look behind us and there's nothing but the empty

sidewalk. Still, I begin to run again. I run down the street and I run around the corner and there's Aunt Babe's house and outside in the driveway Billy's truck. I run right up the front porch and I pound on the door. I feel like someone in a horror movie and the monster is right behind them and they only need someone to open the door, that's all, and they'll be safe. But then the door does open and it's Babe herself standing there.

She still has her apron on. "What are you doing here?" Aunt Babe says, Before I can say she begins to shut the door but I hold my hand against it.

"I have to talk to him," I say. "Is he here?" I push against the door and yell inside the house, "Billy! Are you here? Are you in here?" while she shoves at me and Foxie jumps against my legs, nipping.

"Go away! Leave us alone!" And she slams the door in my face.

I don't leave. I stand on the porch. His truck is out front and he's in here. I bend down and pet Foxie. "Shh, girl, you calm down." I stand up and put my ear against the door but it's too thick and there's no sound from the other side.

I turn around and look at the houses across the street. I look up and down the block. I whirl around now, desperate, but the door is still shut. I pound on it again with Foxie barking beside me and then I hear a truck pull against the curb behind me and I stop. I slowly turn around and there, across Aunt Babe's big front yard, I see Bob's truck, against the curb, waiting for me. He's sitting in the driver's seat and Evaline is next to him. They wait in the truck, not looking at me but facing straight ahead down the street.

Then Evaline opens her door and gets out. At first I

think she'll come to the porch to get me and I decide I'll run. I'll run through Palmyra and hide. I'll run through back yards where they can't drive and under bushes where they can't find me. But Evaline only waits by the passenger door, so I can get in and sit between them, and there's something about this that I can't run from.

Foxie runs across the yard to Evaline and I start down the porch steps but the door behind me opens and I turn back to see Billy standing there, looking out, seeing me and seeing Bob and Evaline.

I never seen Billy look confused before but he looks it now. He doesn't know what to think of first so he says, "Goddamn, look at your face!" which is the first I ever heard him cuss and I put my hand to my cheek.

I haven't kept the ice on it, like what Evaline told me to, and now I'm all swoll up and awful looking. And I'm annoyed at Evaline for being such a know it all.

I start to move up the steps towards him but he shifts his eyes over my head, to the truck. He's got fresh clothes on but no shoes, like me, and now he looks down at my feet like they're part of a puzzle he hasn't put together yet.

"You won't leave without me," I say quietly, taking hold of the banister. "You said that once."

I hear Foxie bark from the truck. I hear the engine running.

"I'll come for you tomorrow," he says, in a low voice. "If you're sure."

"I'm sure all right," I say, backing down the stairs. "I never been surer. Tomorrow," I say, to remind him, and then I turn and go to Bob's truck.

*Chapter 20*

The next morning I wake up early, even before Bob, and I lay in bed, thinking of Billy Lee, coming for me today. I turn my head to look out the window and the sky is still dark. I think tomorrow I'll wake up beside Billy and every day after that will seem like Christmas.

And I start thinking of the last time we were together, in my room, and what we did there. I think of him, sitting on the edge of my little bed and how I stood in front of him and I think of how I climbed on him.

I throw the covers back now, off my chest. The sun is barely up but it's boiling hot.

I think of myself on top of him, like when you ride a horse.

And I move my hand down, under the covers while I think of it.

I think of the second time, when he was sitting up, leaning against the wall with the picture of the angel over his head, and I sat facing him and his hands were on my hips.

I've got my eyes shut tight and my hand is moving.

I think of how we got to the edge which is like the edge of a cliff and we ran along it.

I'm running along it now too, alone, Bob snoring beside me. I'm running along it like how me and Billy did and Bob slides over close to me and I take my hand away for a second and shove him away and he rolls over and keeps snoring.

I think of Billy's hands on my hips and I think of how once I looked down and I think of what I saw and I arch my back and the feeling starts to explode in me. It starts out little but it gets bigger and bigger and suddenly out of nowhere out of the nothing there's a blast, an eruption, of noise and I hear Bob's hand whack! on the top of the alarm clock and it's quiet.

Instead of getting up though, like usual, Bob turns over to face me. I lay very still and pretend to sleep. Last night it was the silent treatment but now he touches my face where Jimbo hit me and then he pulls me towards him. I squirm away. I can feel my cheeks, pink from the heat inside me, pink as a baby's, and I turn them away from him.

I've got to pack my bag, soon as he leaves.

"I'm going to see to Jimbo this morning," he says, nudging me.

I yawn and stretch and wiggle further away. "You got your Daddy and his friends and your kin all around you. I wouldn't worry, if I was you."

Bob is a little deflated by this and he hesitates. "I'll show him whose wife you are." I know he has figured out this line for Jimbo and is trying it on me but he says it all wrong, like he isn't sure himself the answer to that question, and I laugh.

Bob doesn't understand a lot but he understands that

laugh of mine and now he pulls me to him and says, "You are my wife, Lucy."

I kick my feet, impatient. "Oh, Bob, go on."

And he starts rubbing his hands on me.

"Your Mama will be waiting," I say. Everybody knows I don't feed Bob enough and his mother, she's got ham and eggs and sausage, bacon, potatoes, biscuits and gravy all piled up on a plate, waiting for him. "You don't want your food to get cold."

I pull away from him and roll out of bed. "I'm going to make you some coffee," I say, and he pulls at my nightie but I pull it back and stand up. I put my robe on and tie it around me and I don't even turn to look at him, but just go on down the stairs, quiet. I can hear him in the bedroom behind me, getting out of bed. I can hear him open and shut his dresser drawer. I can hear him go to the window and push it open all the way. The sun is just starting to come up and it's already warm.

I go downstairs and turn the water on to boil. This is the last day I'll stand here, I think to myself and I start to hum. I start to sing a little under my breath, moving around the kitchen, wiping the counter and arranging things.

Bob has never been quiet but now he's got downstairs and right behind me without making a sound. I turn around and there he is, all of a sudden and I jump.

"What are you so nervous for?" he says. He doesn't have his clothes on. He's still in his pajamas. And then he makes his voice sweet, "Hmmm? Why are you so jumpy?"

And then he pulls my hand, "Come here," he says, leading me through the kitchen and out the back door and onto the screened-in porch.

"I was just putting the water on," I say. "I was making coffee."

But he leans me up against the screen and kisses me, putting his hands through my hair and messing it up. I go to pull away but he sticks his hands over my breasts, nervous, fussy hands.

"Did you forget you got married to me?" he says, and he rolls my nipples between his fingers. "Sometimes I think you did," he says.

He sticks his mouth on my mouth. His breath is sour. He pokes his tongue between my teeth. He fumbles around, pulling my robe off, grabbing at me, and pulling me and making noises and finally I twist away and say, "Are you about done?" and right away I'm sorry for that.

A look comes over his face and, if I didn't know it was Bob next to me, if I hadn't woke up next to him and seen it was him in the kitchen with me, I wouldn't know now by looking. He looks hard and cold, not like Bob, but like somebody I don't know, big and cruel looking, just by the way he holds his face, by the way his mouth is especially, thin and tight.

"No, I ain't done at all," he says, and he shoves me back onto the couch. We got a couch on our back porch and he shoves me onto it and then he fiddles around with his pajamas and finally pulls his penis out the little hole they got in front for men to pee with. It's pink and fat and I scramble to get up but he shoves me back and climbs on me. I can feel his legs between mine and the weight of him on me. I can smell his scalp and the smell of diesel that never comes off him and I can smell his sweat. I can feel his feet against my feet and his penis that he holds in one hand, jabbing against me until finally he pushes into me and doesn't wait to get moving, but moves fast and deep, pushing into me, and now his eyes are shut. When he pulls back enough, I can see his face and I can see his hips over me, thrusting, with their pants still on, only his penis out like he's in the bathroom, standing over the toilet. He slides his hands under my hips and I start to pull away, to turn to the side, "Cut it out," I say, but he pulls me back and he doesn't answer. He's leaning back and I'm watching his face. It's nothing like the face of Bob. He opens his eyes then and sees me looking so he leans over, puts his chest against my chest, his arms up over my arms, so I can't see him anymore but now my teeth are against his shoulder and I bite him. I don't fool around. He yelps then and jumps back. He falls out of me. He grabs me and turns me over, shoving my nightie up my back. And then he climbs onto my back and pulls my hips up from under me, like I'm like a dog. That's all I can think, how I'm like a dog. And he's moving faster and all I can think of is dogs and how they look, especially the male, how they look so desperate and sad. And I think this is not right.

He's holding my hips, pulling me back and forth against him. The couch slams against the wall. Back and forth. Back and forth like I've got no more weight than a fan you might wave in front of your face to cool off.

"Tell me you love me," he says, his voice like he's choking.

Back and forth. The couch slamming against the wall, loud.

"Tell me!" He grabs hold of my hair, pulling back. "Say it!" Pulling back with his hands and pushing forward with his hips.

"I do," I say and I'm mad but I'm sobbing.

"Do what?" and he pulls my hair back.

And I say it, that I love him, but it's the biggest lie I ever told and he knows it.

And he moves harder. "I can't hear you."

And I begin shouting it, over and over, my eyes shut, the couch banging against the wall and he's shouting it back to me, the same words I'm saying, and it goes on and on until finally he moans like a child, and falls on me.

Right away he gets up again. He doesn't know what to do first. He pokes the penis back into its hole and he smoothes his hair down, where it's sticking up. He turns to say something to me but my face stops him from it. I ain't afraid of you, I think. He sees my robe, on the floor, bends over, picks it up, shakes it out gently, and sets it on the couch beside me. Inside I can hear the telephone ringing. Mother Bybee, calling to say breakfast is on the table and getting cold, but he doesn't go to answer it. He stands at the back railing looking out to make sure nobody seen us. But it's just our backyard and then the woodshed back there and beyond it, cornfields and then way far back the woods and the little creek. He stands for a long time, like that, with his arms crossed over his chest.

My legs are shaking and I put my hands on them, to make them stop.

Bob walks around to the side of the porch to look out towards the Dunavan's pasture. You can see the horses from that side. I like to stand upstairs at the window and watch the Appaloosa mare and usually she'll feel me watching, when I'm there, and she'll look back at me, searching until she finds me in the window, and then she stops to meet my gaze.

I don't want Bob seeing her or her seeing him, right now. I don't want him looking at the things I look at. That view is mine, it's the only part of this house that belongs to me, and I say, "Get away from there!" but Bob only turns to me, calm, and says, "He's gone now."

I sit up and pull my nightie down but I don't take the robe he's handed me.

Bob turns again to the back field, scanning it.

"Who?" I say, standing up. "Who's gone?" and I move next to him looking out and I can tell who it is he means and then I lean forward, gagging. I heave and choke and then, bending towards the floor, vomit.

I seen people in movies get so disgusted they throw up. They see a dead body maybe and then they do it. In the movies, they just do it once and it's finished, but as soon as I finish one time, I begin to heave again and I run through the kitchen and dining room, slipping and falling up the stairs, throwing up on the rug at the top of the steps, holding my mouth with my hands, running, until I get to the bathroom and I lean over the toilet. I think I'll throw up the inside of me. I think the toilet will turn red and fill up with my organs but it's only clear and bad tasting stuff.

Bob has followed after me and he stands now in the doorway wiping his face with his big clumsy hands and saying my name.

*Oh, Jesus,* I think. *What next?*

I brace myself against the side of the toilet, shaking.

I've got to pack my things and I've got to organize. I made a list, didn't I. I have a list of things to do and things to take and I got to get ready. I can't stand around here all day. I shut my eyes and bend forward again and I think now I'll have a heart attack because nobody can throw up this many times in a row and live to tell about it. I'll suffocate, at least. Here, bent over the toilet, probably winding up head first in it, so all the ladies in town can gloat and all the holy people say how that's what happens to sinners and everybody can talk about it forever and ever, amen.

I got to get a message to Billy that what he seen, if he seen anything, was a mistake.

I look over at Bob standing in the doorway and I want to remind him of his breakfast, getting cold, but that seems out of place.

Finally I say, "Just leave me alone. That's all I want!" and I push the door shut.

The phone is ringing again and if he don't get to Mother Bybee's in the next few minutes then she'll show up here herself and that's all I need. I got a three-ring circus going right now and all I need is her to make it complete.

When I'm done I flush the toilet and start to cry. I wash my face off. It's full of red blotches and my left eye is black and blue and the cheek below it's all swoll up. I rinse my mouth out but I don't put on lipstick. I sit down on the top of the toilet seat and rest.

I'm hot and my legs where they touch each other are wet with sweat. I reach the sink from where I'm sitting and run water over a washrag and then I take that washrag and I rub it over me. I rub it over everywhere Bob touched.

I can smell the smell of what's happened. I can taste it in my mouth, a sharp, metal taste. I can feel it everywhere. I look at my hands, resting on my legs, and they won't hold still. My legs are trembling.

When I've been with Billy, I can feel it later on my body. When I've been with him then it's like my body is a field where deer have laid down the night before and slept. You ever seen it? The grass bent down, soft, showing the mark of their bodies where they've slept, like a nest. And when I've been with Billy then my body has felt like that, a field that deer have laid in.

Sometimes out in the woods, I've come across the place where hunters have been. They'll stop and gut a deer, right there. They'll cut its legs off and its head. And you can find a spot like that, if you're unlucky, the grass red, the legs of the deer tossed to the side, the long tube of intestine, the red insides, everything bloody and hot. A thing took apart doesn't look nothing like it does when it's whole. And the spot where deer have laid down to die is nothing like the places they've slept.

I can't hear Bob anywhere in the house. It's silent there, the silence of nobody home which is different than the silence of someone there but being quiet.

I open the bathroom door and I go out.

I phone up Aunt Babe's Cafe and I tell her, when she answers, to have him call me. I say, "Tell him it wasn't what it looked like. Can you remember? Tell him I'm waiting for him, like what we said." But she doesn't promise me nothing and I know this is like a message in a bottle thrown out to sea only with less a chance of getting anywhere. I call Evaline, but she ain't home. Flora answers and I say, "Please, find Billy Lee and tell him I'm waiting for him. Go find him!" I say. "Do this one thing for me. "And she says she will but I don't believe her, neither. I call the March house and I ask to talk to Stanley who's twelve and sees everything that goes on. I say to him, "Stanley, if you get this message to Billy Lee I'll give you twenty dollars, you hear me?" and I tell him what to say. Stanley March is my only real hope, a twelve-year-old boy, that's what it's come to.

I got to wait here for him, like what I said. If everybody just does what they say, everything will work out.

And then I start to get ready.

I pack my bag and I put on my favorite dress, which is

red. I pin my hair up, off my neck, and I go to the front
porch, to wait. I have the bag with me and I set it at my
feet. I sit on the porch swing and I wait. A blue truck drives by on the road and I stand up, sliding my dress down
with my hands and laughing a little out loud, but it's not
his and I sit down again. I'm wearing my red summer dress
and my hair is pulled back in a French twist. I'm not in a
hurry. I begin to hum a little bit and to rock myself. My
stomach is settled but I ain't ate all day and I can't think
of ever being hungry again. He'll get my message, I say to
myself. Maybe he wasn't even here in the first place, I say.
Maybe Bob was talking about something else, he's gone
now. Could be anyone. Could be a stray dog.

I sit and watch the horses. Sometimes the horses will
buck and chase each other and sometimes they roll in the
grass on their backs, with their fat bellies in the air and
their thin legs sticking out, but today they're just grazing.
Their heads bent down. The sun is shining on them and
they have their smooth summer coats so they're glossy
looking, like metal.

I sit all day. I sit while the sun moves across the sky.
I'm not going anywhere. Soon as I leave the porch then
he'll pull up. Billy has a lot to do, getting ready and all,
arrangements and everything. I never went anywhere further than St. Louis, Missouri. I don't know what all you
got to do for a big trip like the one we're taking. You got
to get the truck ready, I know that. You need plenty of oil
and you want to start with a full tank of gas. I sit on the
porch swing and I think of all the things you must have
to do first, before a trip like this one. You got to get your
money out of the bank, if you got any in there.

I sit all day. I don't eat a thing. Cars and trucks drive
by, every now and then, but I stop jumping up when they

do. My hair falls down from my barrette but I don't put it back up. In the late afternoon the sun hits the porch directly and it's in my eyes but I don't turn to face the other way or move to the shade. The sun burns my arms and legs but I don't move away. I'm going to be right here, waiting, when he comes. He said he'd come and he will. He didn't say morning and he didn't say afternoon neither. Tomorrow, is what he said, and that lasts all day. I think it lasts until five o'clock, I tell myself. I look at the sky and it ain't five yet. It ain't even four.

Finally though I get up and I walk around to the back porch, to where the couch is. The cushions are still all squashed down and one has fell off onto the floor. My robe is still laying there and now I pick it up and fold it. I stand where Bob stood when he first grabbed at me. From there he could look out over my head and see anybody approaching from the back and they could see him, too. And then a thought occurs to me and I run inside. I run up the stairs, two at time, and I go into our bedroom and walk to the window. From our window you can see the backyard and the back field and you can see the trees that line the creek, where Billy would have walked. You could see him, coming, if you looked. I stand at the window, dull and blank. And I remember Bob coming up behind me in the kitchen and his face, mean and red, and his pajama pants and how he pulled me outside to stand on the porch and I recall the pressure of my head against the arm of the couch, and the couch itself hitting against the wall, over and over, and I think of my voice calling out what Bob made me say, and him shouting it back.

I hear something coming down the road and I run down the stairs and out to the porch. But then it gets close and it's not a truck at all, but a car, and it turns in my drive and I see it's Evaline. I don't move. I got my bag in plain view but I don't hide it.

I walk to the edge of the porch and watch Evaline pull in and park. Her face is tight. The car door makes a sharp sound like a gunshot and I jump. I stand on the edge of the porch, hugging my arms to my body.

"What happened?" I shout, because Evaline is taking way too long getting to me, but she doesn't say.

Evaline waits until she's right in front of me and even then she doesn't talk. She climbs the steps. I never noticed before how slow Evaline is. She finally stands right in front of me and Evaline still hasn't said a word but she's got bad news written all over her face.

"What's happened?" I say again and this time I take her arms and shake her a little, to wake her up.

"Jimbo lost that job of his," she says, pulling back from me, and I hesitate, reminding myself, that's Jimbo, she's talking about, your brother, and his job is at the lumber yard. "Mama is just beside herself —"

"What about Billy?" I interrupt. "What about him?"

She looks at me, confused, like I asked such a obvious question she can't believe she has to answer it. "Why, he's gone, Lucy."

She's wrong, I think, he'll be coming down the road any time, any second, and I strain to listen, could be I can hear him right now and I look over at my bag, to make sure I'm ready. I put the hair back in its barrette.

"He left early this morning," she says. "First thing."

## Chapter 21

Every morning now I'm sick. I open my eyes and lean out of bed and throw up in a pan Bob has set there. They leave Saltines on my nightstand but I don't eat. They sit and watch me, Evaline or Bob or Mama. Somebody is always watching, sitting in the chair beside me, looking. Mama brings her knitting and I hear it beside my head click click click.

Evaline has moved into the house and she has put a little cot beside me so she can watch me even while she sleeps. Bob sleeps down the hall, in a extra bedroom, a bedroom for one of our children. We got three bedrooms for all our children. Even without the addition, we got plenty of room for all those Bybee children who will never be born. We got the rooms, waiting for them.

Sometimes when I'm just about to sleep or just coming out of it, I think I hear those children. I hear them running on the stairs. I hear them singing. The girls jump rope outside and the noise of their laughing and the rope hitting the ground and their jump rope songs float up into the air and into my window.

*Cinder-rel-la dressed in yell-a*
*Went up stairs to kiss a fell-a*
*Made a mistake*
*And kissed a snake*
*How many babies did she make*

They bring Doc Hyde to look at me and they all wait outside, Bob and my sisters and even Mama, wait out there to hear what he'll say. And when he leaves, Bob doesn't say a word to me, but I can look at his face and see how pleased he is. Now we'll put all that behind us, he's thinking. Now he's got me. He says everybody tells him my own Mama went a little crazy every time she was expecting. Don't I recall the way Betty acted when she was expecting, he says.

"Expecting what?" I say, but he doesn't answer. "Expecting a letter?" I say, but he walks out of the room. I can tell by looking at his back that he's smiling. Female trouble, he says to himself, and he's smiling fondly. Isn't that cute? He's thinking, the little woman.

"I'll tell you what I'm expecting," I shout, but I'm talking to an empty room. Then I quiet down, thinking of that word expecting. I'm expecting, I think. I'm expecting any minute Billy will pull up in his old truck and come running up the stairs for me.

"I'm expecting, all right!" I shout, and I kick at the covers.

"Can't you count?" I yell, but I'm alone.

Billy can count, even if Bob can't. Everybody in town knows when I'm due and Aunt Babe will tell it to Billy, sometime in a letter maybe or on the telephone, and he'll do the math and he'll come. He might come in the middle of the night, for all I know. I leave the window open and sometimes I drag myself there, while Evaline sleeps, to sit, looking out. At night nobody in Palmyra goes anywhere and it's silent and dark. I sit at the window and watch the road to Palmyra and I think how I'll walk away and never look back. My Daddy was born in Palmyra at the house my Mama lives in still, and my Mama grew up about a mile north, on a farm. And my aunts and uncles they live around here and my cousins. It's the only thing I ever knew but it's nothing to me.

Billy will figure it out, I tell myself. He'll go over that scene again and again, tormenting himself with it, and then one day he'll notice something wrong. He'll notice Bob's hand, pulling my hair back. He'll move his eyes to my face. He'll replay Bob and me moving to the couch and he'll think, wasn't that a shove? He'll hear my voice shouting to Bob and he'll know I don't mean it. He can tell everything about me and he can tell when I mean something and when I don't.

I got to give him time to put all the pieces together, shove, hand, open mouth, voice, eyes. To make out the picture, like pieces of a puzzle you pick up and hold in your hand. Maybe you get two or three pieces put together and you think, oh, that's a bird, only it won't be birds, what he'll find. He'll figure it out.

And once he gets it figured out, Billy might want to find a house for me. He wouldn't do what Fenton March done to Shawnelle, make me sleep in a car and then find some dirty room over a bowling alley with a toilet down the hall. He'd start us out right.

I lay in my bed here at Bob's house sending myself to him. Thing is, I don't know what direction to go in. South, towards St. Louis? And how far? Over to Iowa, or further? Billy used to talk about working on the barges, too, in Oregon on the Willamette River — will-am-it, three syllables — and that's how I begin to imagine him, standing on a barge with his hands on his hips looking back at me. I see him waving at me while I stand on the bank.

Billy said he'd come but I can't recall him saying exactly when. I was standing on the steps at Aunt Babe's house, with Bob and Evaline and Foxie back at the truck, waiting. And then did he say tomorrow he'd come or did he just say he'd do it?

I try to ask Evaline, but she didn't hear nothing. She don't want to talk about him anyway. She tells me to just be quiet about Billy Lee. Just shut up, is the way she puts it. And when I tell her to shut up herself and I kick my feet around, she pushes me into the pillows and says, "Listen here, now. You have got to snap out of this!" and she says it so fiercely that I just lay there, silent, and look at her.

Now that I can't defend myself I can see how Evaline really is. Now that she can do what she wants.

She sits on my bed and says, low, so nobody can hear her if they're down the hall, "If you don't watch out you're going to wind up back at Mama's house with a baby to take care of! You'll be back at the five and dime with Sadie Pinshaw! If they'll take you back, which maybe they won't. So you better just snap out of it and behave yourself, hear me?"

I lay in bed with the throw-up pan beside me and I think anyhow maybe it's a good thing he left me here right now, the way I throw up in front of everybody. Mama says all the Hogg women went through what I'm going through but I don't believe her. If it was the truth then the Hogg family would have died out a long time ago is what I think.

One morning after Bob has left the house, I lift my head up without having to bend it over the pan. Evaline is sleeping beside me, her mouth open and spit running out the side of it. Which is enough to make your husband hate you, if you did have a husband. But Evaline never will have a husband, so she don't have to worry about it. No man will ever wake up with Evaline. No man will ever watch her sleep. No man will ever touch her skin the way it wants to be touched. But then maybe all skin is not the same. Maybe if it never wakes up it can lie on your body alone without once thinking what it's missing. But once it knows, then there's no forgetting.

I climb out of bed and get dressed. I have got skinny, I can see that now. Now that I put my pants on, I see how skinny I am. Bony. I can feel my hip bones, how they jut out, and my ribs too. My stomach is still almost flat and I set my hand on it. I stand in the mirror and look at my breasts and then I pull a blouse over my head and a sweater, too.

I sneak down the stairs and find my coat and then I go outside. It's November and the colors are gold and red. It might snow anytime, but it hasn't snowed yet. The sky is bright blue against the autumn colors and I go down the front porch steps and I start to walk. I can't remember the last walk I took. I've hardly stood on my feet. I walk along. I can smell the river. I can smell the dirt. You forget how dirt has a smell. Today it's a cold, damp smell. It's a brown smell. I've forgot my mittens and I put my hands in my pockets and walk.

I walk along the Dunavans' fence line and the horses follow beside me. They've got their winter coats. The air is cold and comes out of their nostrils in swirls of smoke. I go over to the fence and talk to them and they gather around, sticking their long soft muzzles at me. They have big, red nostrils and wet brown eyes. I pull some brown grass and offer it to them. It's the same grass they can get themselves but they think it's special, sitting on my hands like a present, and they eat it like they're starving, pushing against each other.

I start to walk again and the horses follow alongside me, nickering. My feet make a hard cold sound but their hooves are soft.

I cut through the Dunavans' cornfield, walking towards the river. The smell of the water is so strong I could shut my eyes and find it. And you can hear the sound of the water a long time before you ever get there. Billy said that all rivers lead to the ocean but I'm not sure I believe that. To get to the ocean you have to cross through Missouri and Kansas and all the western states and keep going. So I don't know if people mean that when they say it or if it's something like the axis through the center of the earth — just a nice way to look at things.

I walk through brush, through bushes and weeds and trees, to get to the path that runs along the river and leads in a roundabout way to Aunt Babe's. Most of the land is flat and bare but down here it curves and I'm finally hidden. Birds fly out of the bushes when I pass and squirrels jump across my path. I lean against a tree to rest and then I squat down and put my head on my knees.

I stay like this for a long time, thinking of what I'll say to Aunt Babe when I get to her. She's the only one who can help me now. She has got everything in her hands. It's all up to Aunt Babe, who would think it? Aunt Babe who I've known all my life and never took no notice of.

I got to find the words that will put her on my side, or at least, get her off the side that's against me. I think if I can only say the right words then she'll give him my message. I ain't going to tell her how I'm being held prisoner, because that's too outlandish for her to believe. And if I said what Bob had done she would only think I deserved it anyhow, and ain't I his wife in the first place.

I stand up and I tell myself to get going.

It's less than a mile from Bob's house to Aunt Babe's cafe when you cut through the field and go down to the woods and cross the river. Still I cover that distance slow. I only stop to throw up once. I creep along the ground like something wounded. Animals, when they get hurt, why you might as well shoot them, is what Jimbo always said. You find a bird out in the woods with a broken wing, you might as well step on it. But you don't want to start thinking of yourself like a bird with a broken wing, flopping around on the ground. There will always be somebody like Jimbo there to step on you, if that's what you are.

I straighten myself up. I'm out of the woods and in sight of Aunt Babe's. I push my hair away from my face. Oh, I ain't brushed my hair all week. Now it's full of leaves and there are bits of twigs tangled in it. But I walk with my back straight and I toss my head. A few cars are going up and down the road. Never mind the hair. I'm still myself, Lucy Fooshee, I'm still her. And that name of mine, it's a lucky thing like a rabbit foot in my pocket that I can put my hands on whenever I want. I stride across the parking lot. I haven't looked up at the cars but they'll have looked at me. By now half a dozen people are on their way to report sighting me.

I go straight inside Aunt Babe's. The door jingles when I open it and all the customers swivel around to look, casual, because that's what they always do, but then they're surprised. They're shocked to see who it is, Lucy Fooshee. They can't believe their luck to be here now, when I walk in. A first-hand account. That's what they'll have.

I stand in the doorway for a moment, looking around. I open my coat. It's warm in here and I unbutton it and let it fall open. You can't see my belly yet, but I can feel it. If you look at me, I look about the same but I can feel my belly like if it's full of something. I can feel heat there and I can feel fullness and weight. It's heavy and it never lets me forget about it. I stand in the doorway with my belly and for once I feel more powerful because I've got it.

I walk across the room, slowly, while nobody says a word, nobody talks to each other and nobody speaks to me. I go right over to the counter and stand at my usual place. I hesitate but then I sit down on my stool.

I can smell the cigarettes and the coffee, the eggs frying. I can smell hamburger and French fries and blueberry pie. I can smell the grease from the kitchen and the shaving lotion on the men and I can smell the women and for a moment I feel my stomach lift up but then I make it go down again. Nothing is going to happen in here today that I don't pick out to happen.

Aunt Babe is nowhere to be seen but I can hear her in back. I can hear food frying. I can smell eggs. I pick up a menu and then I hear the door open again, and turning, I see Evaline, coming straight at me looking determined and not even minding the stories that are getting framed right now to be told up and down the streets and all over town night after night, day after day until something better comes along, which might be a very long time.

Evaline suddenly remembers herself and she pauses

halfway across the room and looks around, smiling at folks. "Hey," she says to one and then the other and she keeps that grin on her face. She points it right at me as she takes the seat at the counter beside me.

"I mean to talk to Aunt Babe," I say in a quiet, civilized voice. "You can't take me back until I do. And don't you try to stop me."

"But Lucy —" she starts.

"You know how I get."

There are other people in the restaurant, like I said. There are the Egree boys, sitting at a table by the door, and there's Leander Filson and Frank Garber. Althea Runels is sitting at a table with Mrs. Hopgood. Everybody is eating quietly and looking at me from the corner of their eyes.

I stand up then and go through the swinging doors into the kitchen. I ain't decided exactly what to say to Aunt Babe, but I think it'll come to me once I'm looking in her face. She can't say no to me, I tell myself, because I won't let her. I'm not too worried. I'm going to get his address from her. Maybe I'll go there straight away, on the Greyhound bus today. I can already see myself walking up onto his front porch, early morning, knocking on the screen door. That's what I'm thinking of when I push the swinging doors open and walk into Babe's kitchen.

The doors swing shut behind me and I stand looking at a middle-aged man in a dirty white apron, with a spatula in his hand. He's standing over the grill, cooking eggs, pancakes, and home fries. He's got a row of potatoes, boiled and peeled, lined up on the counter to the side of him, with a big knife.

"Where's Aunt Babe?" I say, confused, and twisting my head around towards the bathroom door and back to him.

He doesn't move a bit. I'm not even sure he's heard me over all the kitchen noises. Maybe I haven't even spoken out loud, I don't know.

But then he says, "Gone."

He starts flipping the eggs, one, two, three, four. There are four of them. They're still runny but the grill is hot. They make a loud noise while they cook and the smell of them makes my stomach lurch.

"Where to?" I say, and he takes the spatula and picks up a pile of home fries from next to the eggs and flips it over. He presses down on it until it sizzles. He does that three times. "I ain't got all day to stand here," I add.

He pulls five white plates down from a rack over his head and sets them on the counter. "She's just gone. Moved out."

"Moved out?" I can't think what he must mean. I look hopelessly around the room but I can't see any sign of Aunt Babe. I go over to the grill and stand next to the man.

"Yep, up and moved," he adds, like that's telling me more than what he's already said. Like now he's filling in details.

I wave my hand at him. "I'll just go to her house, then."

"She ain't there, neither."

I grab his wrist in my hand and hold it but he just looks at my hand there, just looks at it like he doesn't understand what it is, like it's something he doesn't recognize, and he's trying to figure it out. I pull it away again and put it in my pocket. I put both hands in my pockets and they set there in tight round balls.

"Where is it she's gone to? You stop fooling around

and say! She's got the cafe here, she can't just run off and leave it, can she?

"She done lost the cafe," he says. He's a dull stupid man I can see that now. I can tell from his face which is closed up like only a little bit of what comes at it can get inside. "The bank foreclosed on her and she done lost it."

We're both watching the eggs now, the way they spit up oil while they cook. And then he turns back to the row of cooked potatoes, standing on the counter, and picks up the knife.

"She's always been here," I say.

"Well she ain't any more," says the man and the knife comes down whack! onto the counter.

## Chapter 22

I don't go nowhere after that day at Aunt Babe's. I don't go to town. I don't even go to Mama's. I lay in bed and Evaline brings me soup and magazines but I don't want to eat and I don't want to look at magazines, neither. I don't want nothing. Bob peeks in at me, smiling, happy now that I am quiet. "Getting better," he says to Evaline, but Evaline knows different.

It ain't fair how, things being what they are, hard already, they got to be made even harder by the jokes life plays on us.

In my fourth month, Evaline tells me it's time to snap out of it. It's almost Christmas, she says, and they've put the Christmas tree up downstairs and I ain't even been down to see it. I ought to come and sit by the Christmas tree, at least, she says. Now that I ain't throwing up anymore, it's time to join the living, according to Evaline. And to help me do it, she has invited the Bybees for dinner, she tells me, and she'll do all the cooking herself. All I got to do is sit at the table and eat.

I tell her I'd rather throw up all day than be obliged

to sit at the dinner table with Mrs. Lyle Bybee, but she just laughs like I'm being funny.

Mother Bybee and Daddy Lyle Bybee are bad enough but Evaline went and invited Bob's sisters too, Babs with the bad eye and Bitsy, red-haired, pasty skinned, mean faced girls who never would've found husbands if it wasn't for all their Daddy's money.

Evaline is in the kitchen cooking up a storm, but I'm staying upstairs long as I can. I've set the ironing board in the upstairs hallway, by the window, and I'm ironing the big tablecloth.

Outside the sky is overcast and the window itself is covered with frost. Snow has fallen during the night but it isn't pretty the way you expect snow to be. The sky is as pale as the ground. It's like a lid has been put over Palmyra and the land around it, a big pale lid. Maybe on the other side of it there is a sky. Maybe you can see the sun. But here it's just Palmyra. Palmyra on this side and everything else on the other and nobody can leave and nobody can get in. They can't get in even if they want to, which nobody does. I know that now. He doesn't want to get in. He's left Palmyra and he's left me.

I can hear all the ladies' voices, she made a mistake. Made a mistake and kissed a snake.

I'm folding the tablecloth when Evaline comes up the stairs. She's got her apron on and she has her hair pulled back and her face is pink from being by the hot oven all morning.

"Mrs. Bybee says you might iron some of Bob's shirts while you're up here, ironing anyway," she says. Mother Bybee has made her do this, I can tell. "Now you've got the ironing board out and all," she adds, to show me what a good idea this is.

Evaline slides a laundry basket towards me, full of Bob's white cotton shirts, and then she stands nervously in the hallway, facing me. I look down at the pile of shirts. They're Bob's town shirts. He sweats all the time, even just riding in his car to town he's sweating. His shirts get stained around the collar where his neck sweats. They have to be bleached, and they have to be ironed too, and starched.

I don't say nothing about the shirts. I say, "Evaline, I don't have to have this baby, if I don't want to."

But Evaline already loves this baby and she throws her hand up to her chest, her palm against her heart, gasping, and then she freezes like that.

"Gloria Quigg found somebody up in Chicago to go to," I say, but already I know the argument against that. Gloria Quigg didn't let the whole town know first, which isn't my fault, the way us Fooshees have to throw up so much. Gloria Quigg didn't wait four months.

"It didn't take long neither," I add. "I could do that, if I decided to. I could drive to Chicago myself, if I had to."

Evaline looks at me with a pitiful expression. I'm so danged pitiful, she can't even be mad at me. All our lives Evaline has been the one for us to feel sorry for but now she gets to feel sorry for me.

I turn away from her, looking out the window. I can hear the Bybee women downstairs, taking over the house. I can smell all that food, cooking. Outside it's grim and gray. It's cold and the cold and the gray go on as far as I can see.

"You'll love that baby, you wait and see," she murmurs and then I hear her on the stairs, going down.

I go to the banister and lean over, shouting after her, "Nobody can make me do anything if I don't want to do it. You hear me?"

Billy said I was hiding my beauty under a basket. He told me I could be a movie star.

And he slid his fingers over to touch my fingers, the tips just meeting, and that was the start of it.

I walk back to the window and look out, at the sad pale day.

I hear Bob's footsteps on the stairs, but I don't turn around until he calls my name. He has a shirt in his hand and he holds it out to me but I only look at him, blankly, thinking to myself, this is Bob, your husband. He gives the shirt a shake to draw my attention to it and when I look down, he shows me how it's got blue ink all over the pocket where he's let his pen leak out on it.

"Fix this, would you, honey."

Why he needs all these white shirts anyhow, I don't know. He doesn't go anywhere but maybe the hardware store. Maybe the cafe for lunch. Maybe he might go to his mother's house so she can cook for him. But he doesn't need any white shirt for those things. If he needs a white shirt then why doesn't his Mama iron one for him, or his sisters.

"Honey!" he says. "I want to wear it today."

Everybody feels sorry for Bob being married to me. Everybody thinks I'm so mean. He loves me so much and look how I am.

He's holding the shirt up at me.

I put my fingers around the shirt, looking down at it. "You want me to fix it? Oh, I can fix it." I take the shirt from his hands, grabbing hold of either end and pulling. "I'll fix it all right!" I pull and I pull and you'd think a shirt would rip apart, but it doesn't.

Bob grabs hold of me. He wraps his arms around my shoulders and I pull and twist and try to kick him, but he holds firm and he keeps holding until, finally, I get quiet. I stand still. I stand facing the wall with him behind, holding me, and we both stay that way, while below we can hear the voices of the women and the sound of cooking and table setting. I look down at his hand on my arms, dirty from being in the field. I can feel his breath on my neck. I can feel his heart against my back. And then, very slowly, he puts his face against the back of my head.

"Let me go," I say.

His hands open up and he pulls back so that I slip away and then I hear Evaline, on the stairway below us, calling up that it's dinner time.

They're getting ready to eat, Daddy Lyle and Mrs. Bybee, Babs whose eye got poked with a stick, and Bitsy. It's Sunday and they're wearing their Sunday clothes. Mother Bybee has on high heels, like she always wears, and when she walks across the room she slams her feet onto the floor. You can tell where she is, all the time. I can sit upstairs and follow her through the house down here. Marching, like a soldier. They've took over the house, like I said. Whatever part of this house was a little bit mine, isn't anymore. They've pitched their tents and set up barracks.

The table is laid out with platters of food and Evaline is walking back and forth, doing little useful things, and Bob says, "Come on, Evaline! Sit down!" but she acts like what she's got to do is too important to let her sit down. Evaline is the only one who can get the salt when someone needs it, or fetch the right serving spoon, all those small things. Only Evaline can do them the right way.

Mrs. Bybee takes my seat across from Bob and Bob looks at her, opening his mouth, but then he shuts it again. He makes a face to tell me it's not important, see,

it doesn't matter. But Bob is not an expert on what matters and what doesn't. And I think how they all feel sorry
for me but I'm the one who knows things they don't
know.

I sit down across from where Evaline would sit, if she
sat down.

Daddy Lyle says grace and everybody bends their
heads down. He says it quick and low, so you can't make
out any of the words, and when he's done with that,
Daddy Lyle puts his napkin on his lap.

He looks up at Bob, "In a couple months now, those
sheep'll be ready to sell."

Bob says, "I adjusted the carburetor on my Allis
Chalmers and it's running real smooth."

Daddy Lyle leans forward, "Howard Pinshaw has got
himself a John Deere but I think Allis Chalmers has that
beat."

Bob says, "Feed corn prices are up but soybean prices
don't look so good."

And he adds, "You do make a nice dinner, Evaline."
Evaline is more like his wife now than I am, but he don't
notice that.

Evaline says, "Lucy, eat your food." She says, "Come
on now."

Bob says, "Come sit down, Evaline! Stop fussing
around!"

I look across the table at Bob. He's stuffing himself
full of ham and lima beans and there's mashed potato in
the corners of his mouth.

Evaline says, "Lucy, you didn't look at the Christmas
tree! Soon as you finish eating, you go in there and look."
She nods to the living room.

Everybody looks at me and when I don't say nothing,

Babs says, "I hope all the weight comes off for you."

And now Bitsy livens up. "Remember how slender your sister Betty used to be before she had her little dead baby."

"That baby wasn't dead when she was born," says Bob, quickly.

"I remember your Mama, when she was a girl," says Mother Bybee, taking another helping of ham. "We didn't have nothing to do with each other, but course I knew who she was and you'd never know it but that woman was slender."

And both the Bybee girls are thrown back in their seats by this bit of news. "No!"

Mother Bybee shrugs. "Until she had that first baby."

Babs pats her mouth with a napkin. "Did she lose any babies, the way Betty done?"

But Mother Bybee has got a mouthful of food and before she can answer, Bob interrupts to say to his Daddy, "Doesn't Lucy look fine!"

And they all look over at me. The Bybee women they press their hard little lips together, but Daddy Lyle says, innocently, "She always looks fine. She's one fine looking girl." He glances around at his wife and his daughters, shrugging, "Everybody knows that." When nobody argues with him, Daddy Lyle goes on, "The Bybee line could use a little infusion of good looks," he says, expecting everybody to be pleased with this cheerful thought.

"We've got the most darling bassinet," says Evaline to the women, quickly, but they aren't thinking of the bassinet.

"All our babies have red hair," says Mrs. Bybee, looking at me.

"They have red hair soon as they're born," adds Babs.

"It's one of the distinguishing features of our family," says Mrs. Bybee.

"You can always tell a Bybee baby from his hair," says Babs, batting her eyes at me. "You go to the nursery and you don't have to ask the nurse — do you Mama? — you know by looking which one is ours."

"We're hoping for a boy," says Daddy Lyle, winking at me. "We got enough girls to last us," he adds, laughing, but his girls don't laugh back. You can't hardly blame him for not wanting more of them, I think to myself.

"Nothing like a son," I say, smiling at him.

"Now Bob, he was named after Uncle Bob from Chilicothe, made his money with hogs and soybeans," says Daddy Lyle. "A big tall man, smoked a pipe but had himself a pegleg."

"From the war," says Mama, and then she adds, "Daddy Lyle and me, we named all our children 'b' names. Barbara, Bitsy and Bob. Barbara she was named after my aunt Barbara."

"A fine woman," says Daddy, "but she married Catholic."

"She went and did that after we named Barbara," Mama nods to Babs to make sure we know who she's talking about.

"And who's Bitsy named for?" asks Evaline, when already the conversation has gone on way too long.

"Oh, she's named for herself," answers Daddy, "cause she was such a little, bitsy thing," and we all look at her now, a big red-headed girl with bulging eyes and yellow teeth.

"The girls, they've kept the tradition up," says Mama, in case I ain't drawn any conclusions from the fact that Bitsy and Babs have named their girls Brenda and Betsy.

"There are lots of good names starting with a b. That's what we noticed when we were looking."

"Ben," says Babs, to prove it. "Brian."

"Bruce," says Bitsy, and then she has a brilliant idea. "Bill — after your great granduncle, Mama, William Willard, and it's a 'b' name, too!"

But soon as the words leave her mouth, Bitsy gasps and everybody is quiet, eyebrows shooting down, heads froze, looking forward, but the eyes sliding around at each other.

Finally Mother Bybee collects herself, coughs, sticks her nose in the air and says, "Somebody already took him."

Inside my belly, I feel a flutter, like butterflies are in there, trying to get out, and I start to touch it but then I hold my hand still.

Babs says, "I hear a Mexican is fixing to open a restaurant here in town."

"Mexican?" says Mother Bybee, opening her eyes wide. "Where'd they find a Mexican?"

"Lucy, you heard how Aunt Babe has closed down, didn't you?" says Bitsy who's mean, but I don't look up. I'm looking at my plate.

"I didn't like Daddy renting to her anyway," adds Bitsy in a low voice, like she's telling us a secret.

"You know Daddy owns the building she used," she says to Evaline, and Evaline nods.

"She could hardly pay her rent on what she made in that place," says Mrs. Bybee, patting her mouth. "And there were rats," she leans forward and whispers. "We never had rats before."

"They were mice, Mama. Not rats," says Bob. "Weren't they?" he asks his Daddy and his Daddy nods.

"It was not a nice place," says Babs.

"I don't know who ate there," adds Mrs. Bybee.

"Most everybody in town," says Bob, taking another helping of ham.

"Well, there's a taco place going to open up downtown is what I hear," says Babs. "Mexican, from Mexico."

"I heard that," Bob says, "and I said, I don't know if Palmyra is ready for Mexican, that's what I said."

"No more than they were ready for Indian," smirks Babs, but everyone is shocked and they look away from each other, embarrassed, eating, eyes down at their plates.

We're each thinking of Billy Lee now, only they aren't thinking of him with a raw ache like me. They're not thinking of him with a longing that's so bad you'll bust open. You'll jump out the nearest window. You'll lay down on the floor and have a fit like Wally Hicks done in church one Sunday after the sermon. You'll jump around and try to swallow your tongue. You'll fling your arms and legs out and hunch your shoulders and your eyes will roll back in your head because it's just too much and something has to give.

I don't remember when I last felt like myself. It's like something foreign has got a hold of me, like when you're sick and that's all you are. You can't think of nothing else, just the sickness inside you. And when you're well again, you can recall it but it's just a idea and it's far away. You can't think what the fuss was about. Like when you're in pain. When you aren't in pain you don't think a thing about it. You hear about burning in Hell and you sit there calmly, with your hands on your lap, and the next minute you're thinking what will I make for supper. But when you're in it, that's all there is.

And I think suddenly of how Norman Pinshaw cut his

arm off in the combine one summer and how he'd say he could still feel that arm, years later. He wanted to warm it up in the winter and in the summer it got hot and some-times it got burned in the sun, when he was out too long in the fields. He wanted to scratch it sometimes and sometimes, when he saw you passing by, he'd lift it up and wave, only what you saw was just the stump part, sticking up in the air. Daddy called it a phantom arm. I think of that just now, Norman Pinshaw's phantom arm. Billy is like that, a phantom too, and I can feel him just the way Norman would feel his arm. And there's an itch too, that can't be scratched.

*Chapter 23*

My belly is big but it's not ugly. It's smooth and firm and round. I can feel the baby's back, the long spine that presses against me, curving. I can feel its feet, when it stretches its legs out under my ribs.

I stay home, at Bob's house, every day. I don't go to town. I sit upstairs, at my window, or sometimes I go outside and sit on the porch swing. But the porch swing always makes me think of the time I sat all day, waiting and watching the road and jumping up every time somebody drove down it. And the back porch only reminds me of that other thing. Sometime I expect those thoughts will go away, but they haven't yet. So mostly when I'm outside, I walk. I circle the house or I walk out to where the cornfield starts on one side, or to the fence where the Dunavans' horses are, on the other.

I watch the snow come and then go. I watch the birds fly away and then come back again.

In April, Mr. Dunavan's youngest boy, Will, drives the tractor back and forth, planting. He works from dawn until dusk, back and forth, back and forth, slow, in a straight line, patient, back and forth. All day I hear the hum of the motor.

I watch him from my window and think how right Will is for the life he got born into, but some people they get sent to the wrong place. They get sent to the wrong people, to the wrong time, maybe, to a life anyhow that's wrong for them. And I wonder if animals ever feel this way, a beaver thinking how it ought to have been a possum. Those are the kind of useless thoughts I have now.

I can smell the same way a dog does now. Outside, I smell the plant smells and the dirt smells, the horses, the river. When I'm inside, I can tell where someone is and where they've been and I can tell their feelings, too. I can smell fear the way a animal smells it and I can smell waiting. In my house those are the two smells, the smell of fear and the smell of waiting. Maybe if I went someplace else, I'd see that I can smell other things too, but I'm just here everyday.

Come May, Evaline moves a baby bed next to my bed. Sometimes I lean up and look into it and I try to think of a baby, laying there on the little white sheets, but I can't do it.

I don't think of it as a baby, anyway. The baby — what they call the baby — well, I don't think of it like they do, like something with a face and little hands who'll sleep in a bassinet and have a name and a voice and a life of its own.

Even though I can put my hand on its spine, even though I can feel it hiccup, can feel it roll over and stretch, can tell when it sleeps and when it wakes up, even though all these things are there to tell me what it is, I still can't believe it.

Sometimes I think I've about forgot Billy Lee. I go for

a whole hour, sometimes, and don't think of him once. I go for a day or two at a time and only think of him with a little bit of feeling.

But today, soon as I open my eyes, the thought of Billy is so strong, it's like he's in the next room and all I got to do is call out his name. All I got to do is turn my head.

I tell myself I don't want to think of him anymore but I start in anyway. What he meant when he said such and such. What I said back. What he said that proves he loved me. I've thought of every last detail and I can't think of nothing new and I've put each part together with every other part, in every combination you can find. I've set each one up beside every other one. I've took apart all his words. Listened to them over again a million times. Played them backwards and forwards in my mind. I have thought of him enough and there's nothing new to think.

Evaline has picked roses from my garden and put them in a vase beside my bed. They're yellow roses, Eclipse they're called. I used to think they didn't have a smell, but now I find that they do. They used to be my prize-winning roses, them and the Charlotte Armstrong took number one at the fair three years in a row, beating out Althea Runels every time. But old Althea, she can take the blue ribbons now. I don't care.

I ain't going back to the fair. I'm not going anywhere I used to. I don't know where I'm going, but I know where I ain't. I don't know where I belong but I know it isn't here, Palmyra.

I've been sticking money in my drawer, a little bit at a time, and I got enough now to go somewhere. I can buy a ticket for a Greyhound bus. They got those buses all over the place. You see them drive past with people inside, looking out with their calm, happy faces.

I used to think I'd go looking for him, but I don't think that anymore.

I used to think of walking up on his front porch and knocking. It was always early in the morning and I always had a small suitcase that I set on the floor beside me while I waited and I always wore a dress, but not my unlucky red dress. I don't wear hats much, but when I thought of standing on his porch, why I always had one on. Sometimes I had the baby in my arms, and sometimes my arms were at my sides. I was never fat when I thought of waiting on the porch. Some girls they wind up fat but I don't plan to. And each time I thought of it, he'd look the same way — sleepy, just pulling his clothes on, his hair sticking up, confused like you are when you're half asleep and then unbelieving. Was he dreaming? Could it be true? And then the door would fly open.

But lately when I think of it, someone else is there. I can hear her sleepy voice, "Billy, who is it?" from the bedroom.

Let him have her, I think. Let him have whoever he wants, whoever he can get. Nobody will be like me. Nobody will love him the way I do or do the things I did the way I did them. And it's like he won a million dollars and then didn't bother to go down and collect it. Let him realize that someday and be sorry.

I hear Evaline coming up the steps but she doesn't come in my room. She has the vacuum cleaner out and she's down the hallway with it.

Sometimes I can't get that other woman out of my mind. I try to think of what she might look like and every time she winds up blond haired and sweaty with a big red, jeering mouth like the mouth of Mavel Runels.

I think of her and him, doing the things we done, and

I think of them having a house together and then children. And it's like I had a life ahead of me but now somebody else gets to live it. Somebody else gets to live my life, but I don't know what I get. Somebody else gets to wake up in the morning, beside him. Gets to sit across the table from him, every day. Gets to sit beside, stand beside, sleep beside him and will she know what's she's got or not? Will she notice at first and then forget? I'd give anything for him but maybe she won't think no more about Billy Lee than what Betty done Larry Bodell, after they was married. Maybe they'll ride in the car and she'll stare straight ahead, like you see married people do, and if she thinks of him at all it'll only be to notice how irritating he is. But maybe not. Maybe she'll be wild about him, not the same as me, but in her own watered down way, crazy about him. Maybe she'll be like a wildcat when they are in bed, like how I once heard Jimbo talk about Grace Ellen. Maybe she'll scratch his back up with her long red fingernails.

Evaline is in the hallway. She's turned the vacuum off but she's hitting her hand against something. Smack, smack, smack.

And that makes me think of the day when I first seen Billy at Mama's house — the noise of the axe and our own noise we made ourselves, later, him and me. And thinking of him making that noise with that other woman seems worse than anything.

I stick my head out the door and see Evaline standing in the hallway. "Will you stop it!" I shout and she looks at me, confused, and then motions to the window.

"It's stuck," she says.

I shut my bedroom door again and now there's a spasm in my belly. I look down and see it lift up and pull together under my nightgown, tight, taking my breath away, and I stand very still, watching it, surprised. Then, when it stops, when it relaxes again and I can breathe, I put the lock on my door and lean against it.

I can hear Evaline walking down the hallway, coming towards my room. I hear her outside my door. I hear the rattle of the doorknob when she touches it and I don't move. I feel her on the other side, hesitating, and I then hear her footsteps, going away this time. I hear her down the hallway, adjusting the window to where she wants it, and I hear her on the stairs, going down.

I don't feel like someone getting ready to have a baby. I feel just fine.

Everybody said I'd be late, this being the first baby, but I ain't late yet. I'm right on time. It's the middle of May, the same time Billy came to town, just one year ago, and changed everything, and I think of the first time I seen him that day at Aunt Babe's and I think suddenly for no reason of my crown, the one I got for Miss Homecoming — a gold crown with diamonds and rubies, all fake but pretty anyhow. I used to wear that crown, just out and about, I'd wear it around like how some girls wear barrettes. And I recall how I had sat at Aunt Babe's that day wishing Billy would know I was Miss Homecoming Queen of Palmyra, and that makes me giggle, thinking how silly such an idea is.

I go over to the window and look out. It's early morning and the clouds are pink and soft. They look like something you want to lie down on, like something you want to rub your skin against. And I think of the child and wonder if looking into its eyes will be a little like looking into his and if that's true, I think, I don't mind how much it hurts. Oh, the girls always talk about how it hurts. How so and so about came apart. How somebody else like to died! But I never been scared of it.

And then, to teach me a lesson, my belly pulls together again and this time it's so sudden and hard it takes my breath away. Eliza March had a cousin over in Pekin who was in labor for 72 hours. I lean against the door with my eyes shut, thinking, let's see, how many days is that?

I put my hand on my belly and rest it there. It's hard and round, with no give, like a stone, and pressing forward, away from me, like the child expects to march right out the front of my body.

And then, quickly, the skin under my hand is soft again. It'll come back though, I think, and I wonder if there's something I ought to do to get ready, but I don't know what it could be.

I walk to my dresser. I have a dresser with a big mirror and a chair and I start to sit down but then I don't. The dresser has all my cosmetics on it and my hairbrush, my combs and barrettes and hairpins. It has perfumes and powders. At night Bob used to like to watch me sit here and brush my hair out. He liked to watch me look at myself in the big mirror. And I worry suddenly that this is his baby, from that time on the porch. Wouldn't it be just my luck. All this and I wind up with something reminding me of that, every time I looked at it. All this and it's just one more way Bob has got me. And then I feel like when you read a mystery and you find out who did it and you think, *Why of course*, I ought to have known it all along! and I think this is Bob's baby from that day he made me do it, of course it is, because that's how things work. I should know that by now. No, I remind myself, I went through this already. The timing is wrong for Bob.

I have another contraction and I lean on the dresser

this time, with my eyes shut, shoving aside my bottles of perfume and my face powder, knocking them over, to rest my hands there. I can see all the Bybees around me, with their mean little eyes and their turned down little mouths and their long white arms reaching at me. I can see the baby, round and red-haired and stupid.

When it's over, I go to the bed and lay down on my side. I oughtn't have such mean thoughts. I'm being punished for them, I think. I ought to have soft, pink thoughts and I look towards the window but I can't concentrate on what I want to find there.

I ain't going to feel it so much next time, I tell myself. I ain't going to think of the Bybees. I ain't going to think of what Bob did, but soon as I think that, it's the only thing I can think. I get confused then. I'm suddenly hot, burning up, sweat rolling into my eyes, pouring down my legs, my nightgown soaked with it, hair stuck to my face and neck, and I pull at my clothes and kick the blankets at my feet and moan, but I don't want nobody to come. I'm panting and confused and I think Bob is here with me and it's Bob pressing on me, Bob laying against my belly like a big rock, Bob tearing at me, and I want to push him off and I want to shout but it takes too much energy. Just to let it happen takes everything.

It's stronger than what I am, I can see that now. If I was being tortured I'd have given up by now. I would have said anything but there's nothing I can say to make this stop.

Then it's stopped, but it'll be back. It stops to fool you, to make you think it's gone. It stops and you start to think you're done with it. You try to tell yourself it wasn't nothing anyway. It stops and you wait, panting, looking around, listening, for it.

I think suddenly of a feral cat we had one time, living in Aunt Janelle's barn in a hole in the floor, and how us kids, Jimbo, got a stick and poked at it. And I'm like that cat with the stick poking all around me, me quiet and motionless, waiting, knowing it will stick me one of these times and all I can do is wait for it. But that's the wrong thing to think. I been thinking of all the wrong things. Bracing myself against something you can't beat. Thinking of all the things I ought not think of. And it's like a riddle I got to solve but I don't have three days like in the fairytales, I just got til the stick finds me.

And I look at my hand laying in front of me, clenched, and I open my fingers up.

I can hear Bob now, outside in the hallway, calling my name, shaking the door. "Lucy! Open this door!"

This isn't his baby. This doesn't have nothing to do with him.

I uncurl my legs. I hear myself panting, and I make myself stop. I breathe normal. I feel my face, all scrunched up, wincing, teeth clenched, and I open my mouth a little bit and make my face soft. Okay, I say, you win. I give up. I raise a white flag. I lay my cheek on the pillow. And this time, I let it take me where it wants. I go along, following. I follow it through a dark and hard place, a hot and cold place, a painful, soft, lonely, animal place, a place of the dead and the just waiting to be born.

But there's banging and suddenly the door falls open and Bob's here, and Evaline, hysterical, running at me and they yank me out of the bed, afraid, in panic, and Evaline wraps a bathrobe around me and they're dragging me downstairs to the car and when I tell them no, no they think it's the pain I'm saying no to, and they're so glad to have got there, in the nick of time.

## Chapter 24

It was first thing in the morning when Bob and Evaline drug me into the hospital, but it's almost night time when I wake up again. There's a light turned on above me, but when I roll my head to the side, I can see out the window and it's already evening. The window faces west and the sun is going down. The sky is red.

Inside, I'm in a world of white, wrapped in a white blanket, dressed in a white nightgown surrounded by white walls. There's a bed to one side of me, empty and white. The room is quiet but outside it I can hear footsteps on hard bare floors, back and forth, and I can hear wheels rolling along and it's a windowless sound, a shiny hard sound, and sometimes there's a voice.

Suddenly I think of this morning and my hand flies up to my belly, which is soft and empty. I raise myself up and look around the room. What did they do with the baby? Did it die? Did they take it away? Was something wrong?

"Hey!" I call out. "Hey!"

I listen, but nobody answers me.

Then I notice a buzzer on the wall beside me and I

push it. I push it a long time, to show them I mean business. I can hear it down the hall, buzzing, in the nurse's station. I hold it until somebody pokes her head in, a nurse, young and perky, with a nurse's hat.

"Where is the baby?" I say. "I want to see him."

"I bet you do," she says, and then she giggles.

I hear her walk away and I wait and, while I wait, I look down at my wrists and see that they're black and blue. Mavel says they tie your wrists down when you have a baby so you can't hit nobody, but Eliza March says it's so you can't touch yourself and get germs.

Pretty soon there are footsteps, and I sit up, ready, but they walk on by. And there are more footsteps and more, but every time they walk past.

I think of Lowell Hopgood's older sister and how her baby had a harelip.

Finally my door opens and that same young nurse comes in, holding a pink blanket, all wrapped up. A girl, it must be. I didn't think of a girl. I sit up and hold my breath. You can't see nothing, the way they wrap them babies up, but the nurse she pulls the blanket back so her tiny face peeks out and oh, she's beautiful.

Lips like rosebuds. Black eyebrows arching over fierce eyes. She looks at me square in the face, not blinking, staring at me like her daddy used to do, holding her eyes still, watching. "I never seen a baby look so beautiful!" I say, but I'm not bragging. And I feel tears spring into my eyes. I never seen anything so sweet and so tender, makes you want to hide her under your body and growl if anyone gets too near. Makes you want to grow claws and swipe them at the Bybees and all the rest of them.

Oh, she's too good for Palmyra. She's too good for this whole world and I feel desperate, like I have brought her here when she ought to have stayed in heaven, safe.

The blanket slides back from her head, showing me her black hair.

"She is pretty," admits the nurse, watching us.

I touch her tiny ear, like a seashell, and look at her pink fingers.

Babies usually come out looking like they just got a piece of bad news. But this baby she looks like you can't tell her nothing she doesn't already know. Most babies don't approve of what they see, but this one does. She looks around — at me, at the room, at the young nurse, and she thinks it's all just fine.

But then, the door opens again and the oldest Gertler girl, the one who went to nurse's school in Jacksonville, looks in. "Bob and Evaline are waiting to see you," she says, and she stands aside so they can come in, too. "They been here all day."

The nurses leave and Bob and Evaline come into the room now. I see them and I feel like I been caught doing something wrong, like I got a book out with pictures nobody should look at and I need to flip that book over. But they just come in.

At first it seems like Evaline is going to sit on the bed next to me, but there's a rule in the hospital about sitting on the bed. Instead, she and Bob pull up two chairs from the side of the room and put them near to me and sit down.

"Isn't she just a little angel!" says Evaline, bending forward to look at the baby. "We been at the nursery window most of the day, watching her."

"You can hold her, Evaline," I say.

But Evaline says, "Oh, Bob will want her first."

Bob stands up, pale and sweating, and he takes her

from me. He knows she isn't his. I can tell by his face that he's already reached that understanding and now he's going to make the best of it. Bob sits with the baby on his knees, his hands folded around her small head. He doesn't look unhappy. He smiles and makes little noises, soft, his head bent forward.

Evaline is perched on the edge of her chair, leaning towards them, her eyes on the baby, her eyebrows raised, smiling, saying, oooh, ahhh in a high little voice, saying, yes, indeed like the baby has said something really smart and Evaline is agreeing yessirreee and the both of them, Evaline and Bob, they've forgot all about me.

"Why look at her face," says Bob, not thinking what all is meant by that face, thinking only of how pretty it is and Evaline, says, quickly, "She looks just like Lucy." And she glances at him, "Don't she now." But she says it like she's telling something and not asking, so Bob doesn't say. I lay with my head on the pillow, watching the two of them, and I think how Evaline could take better care of her than I ever could. I never took care of anybody before, but Evaline she about raised all us girls. She knows all about taking care of people.

"I can't wait to take her home," says Bob, looking up at me. He has got his arms around her, making a shield.

"Mama and Flora were here too, but they just left," says Evaline.

Bob hands the baby to Evaline and he stands up. He puts his hands in his pockets. "My folks are anxious to visit, too," says Bob. He begins to rock a little back and forth like you see a horse do, in a stall, when it wants to get out but knows it can't. "I told them they need to wait until you're feeling a little better. I told them you like to have died," he adds. "Why you almost had that baby by yourself, can you imagine? Up in that room, alone, in too much pain to call out? Oh, it about killed you!"

And just then, the door opens and Caroline Petefish walks in, dressed up in white, a nurse now with a white a-line dress that doesn't do nothing for her figure, ugly white shoes, and a white hat you couldn't pay me to wear and she's smirking. I can see the attitude of all of Palmyra by looking at her face, by watching the way she bangs around my room, smirking, when she's just my nurse, here to serve me.

I say, "Nurse, bring me something to drink besides this water." Like she ain't important enough for me to notice. She's just a nurse, nobody, and I'm not even going to look at her long enough to see that she's Caroline Petefish who I went to school with since first grade.

But old Caroline has got more gumption now that she thinks I'm lying in bed half dead, just gave birth to a baby that ain't my husband's, and got nobody on my side that counts anymore. Now that she figures it's her and the whole town against me, she's pretty danged bold. Instead of rushing off to get my drink, Caroline sashays over to the bed and she stands too close, the way an animal does when it's pushing you around, and she says, "Sure have been a lot of folks come to see that baby you had. Why, it's a regular circus out there."

Which is a puzzle to me, at first, until I remember when Betty had her baby, the way they lay all the babies out in beds behind a big window anybody can look through. They had the babies in rows and they all looked just alike.

"What do you mean by that, Caroline? A regular circus. What do you mean by that?" says Bob.

Bob doesn't understand that you don't let someone like Caroline Petefish think she can goad you.

Caroline looks at her watch, "Feeding time," she says, and she goes to take the baby from Evaline but I say, "She ain't hungry yet," and Evaline holds the baby to her chest and won't give her up.

"She's not crying," says Bob, wanting to be on my side.

But old Caroline points up to the clock on the wall. "It ain't visiting time for the babies."

"What do you mean, ain't visiting time?" says Evaline, bossy.

"I mean it's almost 7:30 and 7:30 is feeding time, followed by changing time," Caroline says, pulling the baby from Evaline's hands. "We got rules in the hospital and there are no exceptions."

The next day all the women come. First the Fooshees, Mama, Betty, Flora, and of course Evaline. The nurses have rolled the baby in her little bed with wheels on it and she's laying beside me, sleeping, all wrapped up. My sisters and Mama hardly look at me, laying in the bed, but wander around my room, bending down to look at the baby, pulling the blanket back from her hair and then forward again, covering the hair up, pacing back and forth, chewing their lips, doing all kinds of nervous, irritating things, all the while talking to each other like I'm not even there.

"She sure don't look like them Bybees," Betty says, and Mama raises her eyebrows. "You know how they only look like themselves."

"She looks just like Lucy when Lucy was a baby," says Mama.

"That's not what they're gonna see when they look at her," says Betty.

"She's Black Irish, same as us," I hear my Mama say.

"I know that's what you been telling everybody, but don't nobody believe it!" says Flora and she's mad. She's got her arms crossed over her chest.

"The Black Irish are the Irish with black hair," says Mama, "and that's what the baby comes from, the black-haired Irish."

"The dark-skinned Irish, too, I suppose," says Evaline.

"The black-haired Irish, is what I said."

But before they can go any further with this line of thought, the door opens and Bob comes in, followed by his mother and sisters, the Bybee bitches, I call them to myself, in keeping with their traditional inclination towards the letter b.

My Mama and my sisters are pressed back against the wall of the little room and the Bybee bitches they go straight over to the bassinet.

"The nurses say she's just a little angel," says Evaline, but the Bybees don't say nothing. They're quiet, standing around the baby, looking to see for themselves how bad it is.

"She sure does have some black hair, now don't she?" says Bob's mother, Mrs. Lyle Bybee, pulling the blanket back from the baby's head, and my Mama says her bit about how we're Black Irish.

Them Bybee women they just look at Mama a long time and I can hear them thinking is this even worse than what we imagined. Finally Mrs. Lyle Bybee leans forward and whispers to Mama, "You don't mean Negro?"

"Goodness," Mama says. "Goodness, no." And she's thinking of all the other people she has said this same thing to and Mama is wondering did she start a rumor about her own family and she's thinking what next. Just when you thought it was as bad as it could be, now they start saying you're colored. "Goodness," Mama says again.

And everybody turns back to look at the baby.

"She sure don't have the Bybee hair," says Bitsy, and Mrs. Lyle says that no she sure don't.

"She looks just like Lucy," says Mama.

All the Bybees, they're bent over her with their faces scrunched up and I can't stand that anymore. I slide over in my bed and pick her up. Bob jumps up to help me, but I can do it by myself. I press her to my chest and hold my hand cupped around her head, like a helmet.

"We all had the red hair, didn't we, Mama?" says Babs.

Bitsy says, "Two days old and she ain't got a name."

"Her name is Mae," I say.

"Mae Bybee," Mama says, but Mrs. Bybee makes a strangling noise in the back of her throat.

## Chapter 25

I've been in the hospital for three days when they put another woman in the room with me. An old farm wife from Beardstown, name of Trudy Deere. Trudy Deere had a car accident and all the other beds are full so they put her next to me. She's recuperating.

I don't say a word to her. I heard her say to Evaline she has five children of her own and I know what she thinks of me, having a child that ain't even my husband's, a child that ain't even all the way white. I know what she thinks of me.

Evaline comes to visit every day and she holds the baby. She rocks her and feeds her from a baby bottle, singing.

Buffalo gals won't you come out tonight
And dance by the light of the moon
Evaline sung that song to me when I was little myself, but I don't let on that I recall that.

My sister Evaline she wants to know all about Trudy Deere, who I always thought of as Trudy Dear, but then I seen her hospital records and found out it's with the two e's, like the tractor, and I was wrong. Evaline wants to know about the accident. A spinster, she wants to hear about blood and guts. It's from lack of sex, I think. So Evaline wants to know what was it like and all that. You'd think she had more sense, but she doesn't.

Trudy Deere says they had to perform an emergency operation on her and Evaline says, "I do declare!"

Trudy lowers her voice and says that she actually died for one whole minute and Evaline gasps and says, "Well, I never!"

Trudy says she swore to God it was the truth and Evaline says, "Of course it is," but I can tell Evaline is wondering about this.

Nobody says a word for a long time. I'm laying there with my eyes shut. This is the most interesting thing I've heard the whole time I been here and now Evaline is going to let it drop. I've been listening to the price of soybeans and corn futures. I been hearing weather reports and the debate on how many bridesmaids Flora should have for her wedding, six or eight. And each one of those subjects has been milked for all it's worth. Like if the rule was to think of any possible thing you might say about each one, and to say it as slow as you can, and then repeat it at least ten times.

Finally someone says something that's worth hearing and Evaline don't jump on it. She walks to the window and looks out. Finally she says, "What was it like?"

Trudy Deere says it was like going down a long, dark tunnel. And then she stops like that's all of it. A long dark tunnel, I think. Well, maybe Mrs. Trudy Deere was on her way to you-know-where. I want to ask was it getting warm, but I haven't said a word to her and this doesn't seem like the place to start.

"It was like getting squeezed through something that's

too small," she adds. I think now she's getting dying mixed up with being born.

"And then I saw a bright light," says Trudy Deere, "And I saw angels."

"Did you see Jesus?" asks Evaline, like if Trudy Deere saw Jesus she might forget to mention it.

Trudy Deere says, "No."

"But there was angels."

"There was three angels with the prettiest faces you ever saw, like on a Christmas card."

"Is that a fact," says Evaline. She's too polite to say how Trudy Deere don't exactly seem like the kind of person angels would take a interest in.

Trudy Deere says she didn't feel like being dead yet. She says her middle daughter is getting ready to be married and there are all the preparations for the wedding. Trudy hasn't even sewed the wedding dress, for one thing. She explained all this to the angels, like they're going to care. And then Trudy Deere starts explaining to Evaline about the pattern she's picked out and it sounds just like the one Mavel Runels' mother made for her when Mavel got married. I tell you, that dress didn't turn out nothing like how it looked in the picture.

"It's a Simplicity pattern," says Trudy. Sure enough it's the exact pattern Mrs. Runels made for Mavel. I think to myself that Trudy Deere must have about the weakest argument against dying that them angels have ever had to listen to. And I'm astonished when, instead of laughing in her face, they come up with a deal.

They explain to Trudy Deere that she came down on the earth to do a certain thing but she wasn't doing it, and that was why it was time for her to die. Like if she didn't make her car payment and now the bank has sent someone to get it back.

"They said that?" says Eval0ine.

"That's right, they did."

"And what did you say?"

"I said I sure was sorry and would they give me another chance." Trudy Deere says the angels told her she could have one more chance, but she'd better do the thing she come to earth to do or they'd have to come back and get her and this time it'd be for good.

I think Evaline is never going to get around to it, but at last she says, "And what was it? What was the thing you're supposed to do down here?"

I think to myself we all know it ain't sewing that wedding dress.

We wait but Trudy Deere doesn't say a word.

I'm annoyed that the angels would talk to Trudy who is just an old farmwife from Beardstown. It doesn't seem right to me that she gets told her purpose so then she can just follow it like what you do a recipe, this and then that, without any meaning behind it. It seems like cheating. And I start to mention this to Trudy but I ain't said a word all day and why start now.

Evaline moves over to Trudy Deere's bed and looks down at her. "So what is your purpose?" she says, but the other woman is just staring out the window like she forgot all about us and her story and everything. "What did the angels say?" Evaline asks.

"Why that's just the thing." Trudy Deere looks over at my sister then and blinks her eyes and she says, "I've been racking my brain but I can't, for the life of me, recall."

*Chapter 26*

Bob can't wait to take us home, he says, but everybody knows I'll never go back there again. Now we're a
real family, Bob says. Now we've got a little girl. Next
we'll have us a son and then more children and we'll have
a big family, he says. Lucky we had us a girl first to help
out with all those other children. And everybody says
ain't he nice. What a good man. What a faithful husband,
sticking by her like this. But it's just Bob, wanting to get
what he wants, that's all, just wanting to get what he
wants no matter what.

When we leave the hospital, we go to Mama's, instead
of his house. We go there so I can recover, they all say, but
recover from what, I don't know. They give me sleeping
pills to help me sleep, but sleeping is the only thing I been
doing anyhow. At Mama's, they say, Evaline and Mama
and Flora can all help out, until I'm myself again. Myself
again, they say over and over. But I don't think I ever was
that self they're talking about.

But anyway, here we are. We're sleeping in my old
room. Flora has moved in with Evaline, down the hall,

and it's me and Mae in here, alone. Evaline has put the rocking chair in my room and she sits here all the time, rocking the baby who never cries anyway, and singing songs. And sometimes it seems like it's me in her arms, and not Mae. It seems like it's me against her shoulder.

Sometimes Evaline puts Mae in the bed next to me and leaves her here, like it doesn't occur to her I might roll over in my sleep. I might roll on the baby or I might knock her off the bed. But Evaline doesn't think of such things. She tucks her in the blanket next to me and walks out.

Bob comes after work sometimes and he sits in the room with us. "You remember how happy we used to be?" he says one day.

I think of how I used to be and I guess people would say I was happier then. Maybe I'll never be happy like that again. Once you know something, you can't unknow it and I know too much to be happy that way and anyway, even if I could I wouldn't go back to it for nothing.

"Billy Lee brung nothing but trouble," he says.

I open Mae's fingers and wrap them around my thumb. I ain't sorry for any of it. Billy Lee give me something even better than himself. He give me Mae, of course. And something else, too. I think of telling Bob how Billy Lee and what come after Billy Lee made me different and how the point of Billy Lee didn't seem like Billy Lee himself but I don't think I can say it right and, even if I could, Bob is not a big getter and he sure wouldn't get this.

"Everything was fine before he come along," he says, like I'm arguing.

"Can't do nothing about it now," I say, giving him a hint the subject is closed.

"Can't do nothing about much," he says, and he stands up angry-looking and he hits my bedroom wall with his fist and Mae jumps and begins to cry. I put the tip of my finger in her mouth and she begins to suck it. I look at her and think how she's the prettiest thing I ever seen.

Another day I wake up and he's holding her. He's on the rocker next to me but he isn't rocking. She's lying on his knees and he's bent down, looking into her face. I can see in that moment how it might have been if I was a different person, instead of myself. I can see the family we might have had. Anybody can see she ain't his, but still his face is full of tenderness. I shut my eyes and wish I'd never opened them in the first place.

It's summer, July, and the corn is knee high.

Usually people will come by when you have a baby and look at it and say how it's the sweetest thing they ever seen and isn't it just a little doll and doesn't it look just like so and so. They'll bring you flowers and presents, nightgowns for the baby and clothes you can't imagine the baby ever being big enough to fit, and they'll bring food. People are friendly around here, everybody says. Everybody pitches in to help out, they tell each other. But nobody brings Mae nightgowns or sends us casseroles or chocolate to eat. Only Sadie Pinshaw brings over a pecan pie she made and a card saying Congratulations!

One day I get a letter and it says *Nigger lover* and that's all. Which is not even accurate. I don't know if it's Jimbo or not. Could be almost anybody. It's a far cry from a casserole though. It's a far cry from baby clothes and flowers and chocolate candies. And one day I get a letter. *You don't belong here, bitch.* But it ain't Jimbo because all the spelling is correct and anyway he never was good at writing.

I think Mama and the girls are getting letters too but they don't say. Everyone is uneasy.

They keep the curtains pulled shut even though it's summer and the sun is out and all the flowers are blooming sweet and you want to let the smell in the house, usually. We've got honeysuckle planted by the living room window and the smell of it will come right in, if you let it. But they keep everything pulled. And when the phone rings they look at each other. Evaline is the one who always gets it and half the time she hangs right up and nobody says who was it or was it for me?

I don't belong here but it's the only place I ever been.

"The Bybees are coming tonight to meet with us," says Evaline one day, and she begins to walk back and forth in my room, wringing her hands together. I've never seen someone actually wring their hands and now I understand where the phrase comes from and it's not a figure of speech, like how you might imagine, but something real that people do. She wrings her hands and paces while I watch.

"They want to arrange a settlement with you."

She waits so I can ask her what kind but I don't ask.

"Sadie Pinshaw told me they've been talking to a lawyer over in Jacksonville."

The baby, hearing that, begins to whimper.

"Have you thought of what you want to do?" she asks. Which is Evaline's way of giving me a hint to start now, if I ain't already.

I never thought of myself as liking this place but lately it occurs to me that I do. I like the prairie how it stretches out flat and goes on forever so you think you can about see the whole world from one place. I like the smell of the dirt when Will Dunavan drives his tractor in long straight patient lines over it. I like the cottonwood trees and I especially like the Burr Oak that grows outside my window. I like all of those things. I like the river. I like the sound my feet make against the ground when I walk on it and the way the wind blows from the east over the flat ground and brings the smells from far away and the sounds, too. I like looking out and knowing everything I see. And I think maybe it's everyone else that doesn't fit here. It's the rest of them who don't belong and should think about going somewhere else, Chicago maybe or Jacksonville. Neeva Gertler she went up to Chicago to visit her sister, Fannie Lou, and she said the stores never closed and anybody could get a job.

"Mrs. Bybee has been talking to the preacher about adoption agencies," Evaline says, and her hands flutter in front of her.

I'm thinking of Chicago though and hardly hear what she's saying.

"She's not an orphan!" exclaims Evaline like this is an argument. "They say you aren't fit to be a mother —"

"That never stopped any of them," I say and I giggle.

Evaline looks at me, exasperated. "They're lining up everybody against you!"

I don't say they better not try to take credit for what I already done myself. Evaline is not in the joking mood.

Now she sits down on the bed next to me the way she does when I'm sick. "They can't have her living here in Palmyra, reminding everybody how she ain't theirs, when she should have been."

And we both look at Mae who's in my arms, sleeping now, and think of the Bybee babies, unhappy, red-haired things, crying from the minute they're born like they already know, without being told, what they're in for.

Evaline notices the sleeping pills on my nightstand and she slips them into her pocket, but I've stopped taking them already. And standing up, she goes to the window to look out. "I think you can get a settlement out of them anyway," Evaline says. "Just let me do the talking tonight. Let them say what they want and don't pay it any mind. You know how they are. Just let them talk. You hear me?"

That evening we wait for them in the living room. Mama has made a bed for me on the sofa and I'm sitting there in one corner with Mama and Flora and Evaline across from me.

Mama and Evaline are tense. They have dresses on and high-heeled shoes, like they're going to church. Mama is sitting in the rocking chair. She has her knitting out, but Evaline's hands are empty.

Flora sits beside them, with a piece of paper on her lap and she's making a wedding list, guests' names or refreshments to buy or maybe she's figuring out what to put on the invitation. Even though she don't care about my problems, it's still good to have a extra Fooshee around, to Mama's way of thinking.

Mae's on the floor on a blanket lying on her belly and she's sleeping, but she's making beautiful little noises, singing noises, that she makes without even trying to.

When we hear the car stop out front, Evaline looks at Mama and she looks back and neither of them says a word. I pull my blanket up around me even though it's not cold. It's a hot night but I pull it up anyway.

Mama has brought all the chairs out so everybody has a place to sit. The chairs are on one side of the room, in a half circle, and I'm across from them, on the sofa. The Bybee women come in and they don't even look down at

Mae, sleeping on the floor with her hands held up to the side of each ear, but they walk right by her, and everybody sits, Mrs. Bybee, Bitsy, Babs, Evaline, Flora, and my Mama. They sit and look at each other and they look away and they cross and uncross their legs and they smile and they frown and they cough behind their hands. Flora is the only calm one. She's got the wedding list on her lap, making checks next to some names, but crossing other ones out.

When Mrs. Bybee sees that nobody is talking, she remarks that it's time to see to things. This is a clue of some kind, but I can't make out what it means. See to things. That doesn't paint much of a picture.

They go back to looking away from each other, shifting their weight around in their seats, twisting fingers together. Nobody looks at me. Finally, Evaline gets up and walks to the kitchen and I can hear her in the refrigerator.

Soon as Evaline is gone, Bitsy breaks the ice by leaning forward to say, "Mother thinks she belongs in Jacksonville." Which means the nuthouse. Mama doesn't hear good and Bitsy says it again, louder.

"Jacksonville!" Mama exclaims, and Bitsy shrinks back. "Jacksonville!" Mama repeats, like she doesn't need any more argument than just that one word to make her case. Flora, next to her, looks up, frowning.

"Nobody's taking my daughter to Jacksonville," Mama says. I notice she doesn't get in a argument over whether I belong there or not.

"No girl in her right mind would do what she done!" says Babs.

I think to myself if I'm crazy then I wish it was the kind of craziness that would make me cross the room and pull her hair.

"They got doctors who can help girls like her," says Mrs. Bybee. "I been looking into it. They got procedures now."

I never heard of a procedure for someone who don't love her husband. I never heard of a procedure for somebody born into the wrong town or the wrong family or the wrong time. I never heard of a procedure to fix someone who has a nature at odds with the life she's been handed and if there is one, I'd like to know about it.

Evaline comes in now, with ice tea. She's got a lemon slice perched on the side of each glass. Evaline thinks you can always make things better if you've got the right refreshment and now she hands a glass of ice tea to each of us, smiling and pleased with herself to always come up with a solution.

"Nobody is putting you in a mental institute!" says Mama looking at me for the first time. I can see this is the first Evaline has heard tell of this idea because it's like Mama has thrown a hand grenade into the room. Evaline drops the empty tray and throws her hands in front of her face.

"Mental institute!" she exclaims.

"If she's sick, then that's where she belongs," says Mrs. Bybee.

"I ain't sick," I say to my mother-in-law. "Only sick thing is having to sit here and listen to you."

But Mrs. Bybee acts like she didn't hear me at all. "Whatever you decide to do with her, it's clear she can't care for a child. And it's clear we can't have a child such as this living among us."

That's two clear things, I think to myself.

"A child that isn't even white!" exclaims Babs.

Mama coughs. She takes a drink of tea and then sets the glass on the floor. Her knitting is sitting on her lap, forgotten. She's in the rocking chair but the rocking is getting slower and slower and then, finally, it creaks to a halt and that's all you can hear, how there's nothing making a sound anywhere. Can't even hear the clock anymore. Even the baby on the floor, little Mae, is silent. The only noise in the whole house is the noise of the blood beating in my ears.

Mrs. Bybee says, "I knew something like this was bound to happen. Didn't I tell you? Didn't I tell all of you?" She looks at her daughters now and they nod to say, you sure did. "I said, That girl will give him a heart attack, you wait and see! I told everybody she was nothing but trouble from the start. I watched her all her life. Millard Hogg's grandchild — what do you expect?"

But they're going too far, bringing in our ancestors, and Evaline says, "We cannot sit here and listen to you —"

But Mama's too worried about those of us alive now to care if they go and insult the dead ones. "That boy wouldn't leave her alone," she exclaims. "You know how pretty she is and you know he wasn't from around here, he wasn't like the boys from around here, and he just wouldn't let her alone for a minute."

"Mama, that's a lie!" I say, but Evaline makes a face to remind me to let her do the talking, which I'd gladly do if she was talking, which she ain't.

"He forced himself on her," says Mama, pulling the hem of her skirt down over her knees. "And now she's protecting him —"

"Oh, Mama, shut up!" I say and everyone freezes and looks at me. Nobody ever said shut up to their mother before or heard of anybody else who did either and nobody can believe it, even from the likes of me. But my Mama does shut up and that's good anyway.

"What do you want?" I say, looking at each of the Bybees in turn, Babs, Bitsy, and Mother. I ain't afraid to look at them. "What are you here for?"

Mrs. Bybee is never going to talk to me again. "I'm not talking to you," she says and then she turns away, to my Mama instead and to Evaline who's not nice either but is, at least, someone who can be counted on never to say shut up to her own mother. "There are agencies that find loving homes for children like this," says Mrs. Bybee. "They find parents who can afford to raise them." She pauses now and looks around our little house, to show us — see, you can't give her nothing. "The parents they wouldn't even know they had a child that wasn't white." Something about this notion seems to disturb Mrs. Bybee and she pauses, making a face, but then she goes on, "It could pass for Italian, if you didn't know better, or Greek."

And we all look at little Mae, on the floor, beautiful and innocent. I try to look at her the way they do, the way someone does who don't love her, but I can't. I bend down now and pick her up. She's sleeping and I lay her on my shoulder, her warm breath turned to my neck.

"We don't have no obligation to this child, but we've gone ahead and made inquiries with a nice Christian agency. If you care about her well-being —"

Evaline throws her hands in front of her face and begins to cry.

But Mrs. Bybee don't feel sorry for her. "Nothing like this ever happened in our family before," she says, but then she waves her hand. "I don't think they had a real marriage anyway," she says, and the sisters shake their heads to say they don't think so, neither.

"But there was the wedding," says Mama, like maybe they forgot that part.

"But was it a legal marriage?" asks Mrs. Bybee. "Was she of a sound mind? I think you have to be of a sound mind to be legally married. And if they were never legally married, then we don't owe her nothing," she says. "She's just out, you understand?"

And I think to myself that's a funny way to put it, out, like I swung the bat and missed.

Mama and Evaline both start talking at the same time, arguing and fussing, and even Flora has started to show some interest, now the subject of weddings has come up.

"Does Bob know what you're up to?" I say, talking loud to be heard over everybody else. "Just tell me that." Isn't it bad enough Bob's got me wanting to divorce him, without his whole family jumping on the bandwagon.

"Farmers are dependable, reasonable people," says Mrs. Bybee. "They're people who realize you got to put the seed in the ground for it to grow. All the wishing in the world won't make a crop grow if you don't plant it first. And then you got to put the herbicides on or the weeds will come up. You got to watch your crop and admit if something is going wrong and then you got to correct for it."

She says, "A farmer knows how to add two and two together and get the right answer. He knows how to cut his losses." After she finishes telling us these things, she's quiet, letting them sink in.

Like many people who live in town, we come from families that have, for one reason or another, lost or sold off their farms but I don't think she's talking about us.

"If that boy doesn't know how to cut his losses, then he isn't cut out to be a farmer," Mrs. Bybee tell us. "Mr. Bybee says the same thing."

It's quiet now. Me and Mama and Evaline and Flora are froze, staring at them Bybee bitches while they sit looking back, with their tight little mouths and their round hard eyes.

"You'd take his farm?" I say, finally.

"It ain't his farm yet," says Bitsy, quickly.

"It could just as easy go to one of us girls," adds Babs.

"Get out of here!" I shout, jumping up finally, and charging at them. "Get out! You bitches!" I say, and they gasp and turn white — shocked! when nothing else shocks them, taking my child, taking Bob's farm, they aren't shocked by those things, but they don't want nobody to call them a dirty name.

They stand up quick, grabbing their pocketbooks and running toward the door, skidding across Mama's polished floor in their little high-heeled shoes, followed by my voice, "Get out! Get out! Get out!"

The next day there's a cross standing burnt in our yard.

"This is what they do to niggers and we're not niggers," says Mama. She's standing at the front window, looking out. She's in her bathrobe and her hair is in rollers and her arms are crossed over her chest and her fingers are pinching her arms like she thinks she's asleep and she's pinching herself awake.

I go and stand beside her to look out. It's a big cross, maybe four feet high, and it has been burnt sometime in the night but we slept through that part.

"But we're nigger lovers," says Evaline.

"I'm not!" cries Flora.

"He was not a nigger," says Mama. "I wish everybody would get that straight!"

I never seen a burnt cross in someone's yard before but I heard of it. "What does it mean?" I say. "Is it a threat?"

"Oh, I wish your daddy was alive!" says Mama. Usually she says she's just glad he ain't alive to see what has become of me, but today she's thinking how he'd go right out and pull that cross up. It's the kind of thing a man would do, if a man was here.

So I go out myself. I'm still in my nightgown but I go out and pull it up. They got it stuck in the corner of an old flower bed that ain't been planted so the ground is soft and it's not hard to pull up. Evaline comes out onto the porch to watch but she doesn't help. She lets me do this myself. I pull it up and my hands get dirty with soot. I toss it on the ground and look up to see old Mrs. Hobbes watching me from her window but when she sees me looking back, she drops the curtain shut and disappears. I've known her since I was born. She used to make me butter and sugar sandwiches but now she hides behind her curtain when she sees me look.

A few hours later, just to prove beyond any doubt that we're white trash and nothing else, we are Hoggs and always will be, Aunt Janelle shows up, driving her old blue Cadillac into Mama's drive, with her two boys along-side her, Rusty and Dave, the famous Hogg boys, meanest boys in the county and bigger than anybody else, too.

Neither Mama nor Evaline seem surprised by this visit and, even more remarkable, they aren't distressed neither, but look at each other and smile and go hurrying down the front steps and into the yard to meet them.

The Hoggs get out of the car one at a time, squeezing through the door and out into our drive. The boys must weigh over three hundred pounds apiece. They're big mean boys with red faces and swollen knuckles and scabs and scars and bruises all over them. They got on old dirty tore-up blue jeans and boots with holes in the toes and Rusty has a shirt that's ripped at the bottom so you can see his white stomach.

Evaline is standing at the car window, hardly letting Aunt Janelle get out, she's so excited. She keeps asking Aunt Janelle something but Aunt Janelle is thinking too hard about struggling up out of the car to pay her any mind.

I ain't seen Aunt Janelle in two years and I'm not happy to see her now. She's a big, mean Hogg woman and she never did like me, but always doted on Evaline instead. I don't know whose idea this was but I think it means we must be pretty desperate now. She pulls herself out of the car finally and stands up, steadying herself for a moment.

Next to her boys Aunt Janelle looks almost normal but she's huge. She's a big block of a woman, muscular and square, the widow woman of my Mama's oldest brother, Uncle Roy the pigfarmer. She's got wild peppered hair, much too long for a woman her age, and it's all around her face like it has been whipped up by a wind, and the face itself is tan and deeply lined from being out in the sun and the wind too much, from working too hard and having too many things to worry about. She's got bad teeth, like all them Hoggs. Yellow and cracked. She has got a red dress on and she's carrying a big alligator pocketbook. She limps across the yard while the boys follow her, cracking their knuckles and making jokes to each other. Aunt Janelle stops in front of the cross which I left there, in spite of Mama who wants it hid out back like it's something we done ourselves and should be ashamed of.

"Uh huh," she says to the cross, like it's confirmed something she only suspected, and then she turns to her boys. "You ain't the ones done this to your own family, are you?" and she shakes that pocketbook of hers at them.

"No, ma'am!" they say, like they're shocked by the idea.

They all stand around the cross, looking down at it.

"You ever do anything like this and I'll tan your hides, you hear me?" she says to them.

And then she looks up at me, squinting a little with the sun in her eyes, "Let me see that baby you had," she calls, hobbling towards me. She has got something wrong with her knees. Water on the knees, Mama calls it. "Let me see the most famous bastard in the county!"

Evaline and the boys help her up the steps and Aunt Janelle comes straight to me and I hold Mae out a little so she can see her.

"So you're the one causing all this trouble," she says to Mae, in a soft voice. And she takes one of the baby fingers in her hand. "Aren't you," she says, like she's expecting Mae to answer. And then Aunt Janelle slings her bulging pocketbook over her shoulder and she takes Mae from me and walks inside making the little noises people do when they talk to babies and asking her questions and waiting like she expects for Mae to answer back and then saying things like aren't you something like Mae has just said some brilliant thing or oh, yes! you don't say! like Mae has just told her some surprising news.

"You boys stay out on the porch," she says. "You're too big to come inside." Like she's talking about a dog, a Great Dane or a Saint Bernard, you got to leave outside or it'll knock your table over and break the furniture. But this is too much for Mama, the idea of them Hogg boys sitting out front reminding the whole town how she was a Hogg herself and making everybody ask how it is the Winklejohns and the Bybees ever got mixed up with the likes of us. She herds them inside where they stand, uncomfortable, drinking ice tea, and shifting on their feet, back and forth.

Aunt Janelle sets her pocketbook on the floor and sits in the rocking chair. She knows how a baby wants to be held and what it wants to hear and she's ignoring the rest of us, even Evaline who keeps pressing on her and asking questions.

I can hear Flora in the bedroom bawling her eyes out because Rita Hanks has called to say that Mrs. Vera Winklejohn has told her beauty operator she don't see how her nephew Pete can marry into a family like the one Flora has got. We can hear her clear out to the living room. I think it's a sign of how bad things are that Mama is not concerned about this challenge to the upcoming wedding of her daughter into the Winklejohn family. But at least she got Rusty and Dave off the porch, I remind myself, so she ain't too far gone.

I open the window wide and sit down on the couch between Mama and Evaline. They're nervous and they're making me nervous, too. I don't know if Aunt Janelle is here because of the Bybee visit or because of the cross or because she wants Evaline to come back and help her process pigs or maybe she's come to town so the doctor can look at the water on her knees.

"Aunt Janelle —" Evaline keeps saying, but every time Aunt Janelle waves her hand at Evaline like Evaline ain't her favorite niece in the world but something irritating she wants to shoo away.

I sit back in the couch and try to calm down. I can smell the honeysuckle from outside the window. I haven't been with a man in over a year, I think, and I miss it. I set my hands in my lap and look at them there.

"Can you believe we all start out little and sweet like this?" says Aunt Janelle, looking from Mae to her own boys.

But Evaline says, "Really, Aunt Janelle!" like this is just too much and she will not wait another minute.

And then, Aunt Janelle picks up her fat alligator purse and pulls a big envelope out of it, waving it at me. Evaline shoots forward shouting, "Mama! Mama! She got it!" like Mama will know without being told what she's talking about. And Mama jumps up and grabs the envelope from her sister and I look at the boys and they're laughing and slapping each other on the back and it's like a big surprise party that everybody knows about but me.

"Your money! Your money!" Evaline cries.

And Mama has spilled the money onto the table and is counting it out, putting it in different piles and saying over and over again how she never seen this much money, never.

"Your divorce settlement," Aunt Janelle says.

I look from one of them to the other, "Settlement?"

Evaline is so excited she runs up to Rusty and throws her arms around him. "Oh, you boys!" she says, and then she does the same to Dave. "Oh, you boys!" like aren't they wonderful.

"I told them Bybees you've outgrown this town and the only reason you ain't left yet is you got no money. How can you leave town with no money? How can you leave with no car? You ain't even got your own car they told me." And Aunt Janelle struggles like she's going to stand up but then she thinks better of it. "Bob give you the clothes he bought you, they said, and I said, Well, ain't that generous. Now Bob won't have nothing to wear." I can see Rusty and Dave have been waiting for her to get to this part and they laugh and slap each other on the back.

When everyone is calmed down again, Aunt Janelle says, "I said you need a dependable car and the only dependable car there is, as far as I'm concerned, is a Cadillac."

"A Cadillac?" I say, and I go to the window and look out, but this here is the same Cadillac Aunt Janelle has drove for fifteen years.

"You know the Bybees got all them white cars," she says, and she shakes her head. "They show the dirt so bad. I said your favorite color is baby blue, and there's no reason you can't have a baby blue Cadillac to drive out of town."

"A baby blue Cadillac?" I say, and it's like someone has rung my doorbell and said you won a contest but it's a contest I never entered.

"You don't go and divorce a Hogg girl and then leave her with nothing," says Aunt Janelle. "I don't care if she is a whore!" Aunt Janelle's legs are too big to cross and now she squeezes her knees together and pulls the hem of her skirt over them.

"Them goddamn rich people think they can do anything they want if they want to," says Dave and Aunt Janelle says to him, "Mind your French now!" which means don't cuss.

"Maybe they own half the goddamn county, but they don't own us!" adds Rusty, forgetting his French, too.

"I told them we could get a lawyer like them and go to

court, if that's what they want," says Aunt Janelle. "I told them we don't mind getting our name drug through the dirt and mud. That's one thing about being trash, you ain't got your name to worry about."

"But they might not like it, she said," adds Rusty, who can't wait for her to tell the story but has to help her along.

"You said that?" asks Mama. "You called us trash?" Like she ain't heard it all her life. "You said that in front of them?" Mama sinks back in the seat. She has found a napkin somewhere and now she folds it over and over again into smaller and smaller pieces.

"I told them this ain't the first time a bull has jumped the fence!" Aunt Janelle laughs with her yellow cracked teeth and her bosom heaves up and down and Mama looks up in alarm and begins fanning herself, like maybe she'll have to go and faint now.

"I think we heard enough," she says.

"Which is exactly what Lyle said!" cries Aunt Janelle. And she lowers her voice like we're in a public place and she only wants us to hear her. "I told him we better talk alone, him and me and Rusty."

Evaline and I whirl our heads around now to look at our red-headed cousin.

Aunt Janelle leans towards us and we lean forward too, and the boys behind us and Mama, we all lean towards her and watch her face and we think of Aunt Janelle when she was young with her wild black hair and heaving breasts, "Lyle said that wouldn't be necessary," she whispers and she winks.

*Chapter 27*

Used to be that Babe's was the only place in town to eat but now there's a new Mexican restaurant, Bill's Big Taco Restaurant, down in the old part of town. Bill's Big Tacos has got booths, side by side, and the backs are so high you can't see who's sitting next to you. If you're at one booth, you don't know who's at the next one.

I'm there with the baby and she's laying in my lap, sleeping. I got the car parked outside, a baby blue Cadillac, almost new, everything clean and shiny. I'm going to Aunt Janelle's to help out. Aunt Janelle says it'll do me good to be useful for a change.

There are Mexicans in Bill's Big Taco Restaurant from Mexico and you can hear them talk in their soft Mexican voices and their language that's all vowels, sounds like, and the laughs that come from them make you think of hot places where people walk around at night with music playing and children running everywhere. People say Sadie Pinshaw quit the hardware store to work here but I only see Mexicans.

"Ain't Sadie Pinshaw working here?" I say to the

Mexican boy who's clearing tables and then he looks up from the table he's wiping down and calls out something to the kitchen. A fellow comes out from the swinging doors and says something very fast to the boy, looking at me suspiciously at first until he sees the baby in the booth with me. People think if you got a baby then you must be all right. He comes over to my booth. He's a Mexican and I never seen a Mexican this close before. He's muscular but compact, like he comes from a long line of people who didn't waste nothing. Everything extra fell off and everything that stayed got developed. He has an apron on, from working in the kitchen, and he has dark skin, darker than Billy Lee's was so you don't mistake him for a Greek or a white boy who works in the sun.

I say, "I'm a friend of Sadie's and I'm leaving town and I come to say good-bye to her."

He's only a couple years older than me but he isn't like the boys here who don't know how to stand next to you yet. He gets a pad of paper from the waitress and I spell my last name for him.

"F-O-O-S-H-E-E."

I order myself lunch. Mae is next to me in the booth, sleeping. She's laying on her little yellow blanket.

Mae, I named her, but with an 'e' and not a 'y'. I like it better with the 'y' so it's like the month, but that's the way they wrote it down when I said it. M-a-e. May is the month all this started and it's the reason I gave her that name. Gave her the name of when Billy Lee came because I couldn't give her the name of who he is. Or, it can mean yes. Like how you say to someone you may do such and such. So, it's a name like you're saying yes. Or the other thing is that it can mean might or maybe. Like it may happen or it may not.

The baby smiles while she sleeps. It's the funniest thing you ever saw, how she smiles. People said that all my misery would get into the baby, but that didn't happen. She's a cheerful little thing, smiles even while she sleeps. Gas, Mrs. Bybee said, but it isn't gas.

So we're at Bill's Big Tacos and I'm having three chicken tacos and the baby is smiling beside me. I'm having a cherry coke.

I'm thinking my own thoughts, you can see that, when I hear Rita Hanks and Mavel Runels, the one with the wedding dress that didn't turn out right, come in the door and sit at the booth behind me and they're talking about me to someone else, a stranger. Mavel's cousin from over to Jacksonville, it turns out. They're saying how this Indian man come to town and how I throwed myself at him.

"And her not married more than a week," says Mavel. Which is a big exaggeration. I was married two weeks by then, I beg your pardon.

And how he pretended to be interested in my old maid sister, but anybody could see it was me he was after. "I don't know why," says Rita Hanks.

"No, it was her that was after him," says Mavel.

"He was after her money," says Rita.

"Her husband's money, you mean."

"That's right. Them Fooshees, they don't have nothing of their own."

"Huh uh."

"And then what happened?" says this cousin of Mavel's.

They've been saving the best for last. Now they tell her how I had a baby by this Indian man and how this baby ain't even white, you can just look at her and tell that, and I hear Mavel's cousin say, "Oh, my God," like it's the worst thing she ever heard. And they say this part loud enough for the Mexicans to hear, "Ain't even white!" but they don't care.

And they go on eating their chicken tacos, letting this sink in.

Finally Rita says, "She's about the prettiest baby you ever seen," and I think anyway, that's the truth.

"Looks just like her father," says Mavel.

"A Indian?" says the cousin.

"Ought to be adopted, is what everybody says. So she could be raised in a good family."

"A real family, that could take care of her," adds Rita.

Mae's face starts to scrunch up then but I put the tip of my finger in her mouth, a little ways, and she begins to suck it, happy now.

"Lucy Fooshee said the baby belonged to her and she wasn't giving nothing that was hers away for free."

But then Rita corrected her, "Some things she give away for free, Mavel."

Like I should have charged.

And they all giggle.

Mavel says, "They say she offered to sell the child but she wanted five thousand dollars!"

"It was more than that!" exclaims Mavel. "Ten, at least."

"I declare!" says the cousin.

They're quiet now, thinking of it.

"For a baby that ain't even white," adds Mavel, so they don't forget that part.

"Her boyfriend run off and left her," says Mavel.

"Where'd he go to?" asks the cousin and I think to myself that's the million-dollar question, but Mavel she doesn't say how nobody knows. She doesn't say nothing. I wait, listening.

Mae stops sucking. She doesn't make a sound. She's listening, too. Mavel must have eaten the rest of her food and smoked a cigarette before she bothered to answer that question. Finally, she says, "Nobody knows."

And I sigh and the baby sighs too. I pick at what's left of my chicken tacos but I can't eat any more.

"He's in Bowling Green," Rita says, and I freeze, holding my breath. "Bowling Green, Missouri, working at the post office. Virgil got a call just yesterday from a mailman out there who mentioned it to him."

"I thought you had to be American to work at the post office," said the cousin.

"I thought he was out in California," says Rita, "but then I talked to Virgil and he told me himself how he got this phone call from a buddy who's a mailman and he works with Billy Lee who come through town here."

Missouri ain't but the next state over.

But Mavel thinks they're veering off the subject and she says, "Lucy Fooshee ruined just about everybody's life." And then Mavel starts to name everybody who had a life I ruined and she starts with Hammer Johnson. And she lists everybody in my family, including Jimbo, of all the nerve. And then she names everybody in Bob's family and it's such a long list you'd about think I ruined the whole town and then she winds up with Aunt Babe.

"She used to have the best little restaurant down by the highway and she had to shut it right down and leave town. She had the best pies you ever tasted." Rita lowers her voice, "Mr. Lyle Bybee called in her mortgage and she lost her business."

Then Rita says how the whole thing drove me insane

and Mavel says that's what happens, like she's a big authority on such things. "Now she lays in bed all day staring at the wall."

"Saying things that don't make sense."

"Like if she was talking in another language," says Rita.

"Something like Greek, is what I heard."

"Tongues, is what Maylene Quigg says."

Mavel says I wouldn't iron my own husband's shirts. "That's how bad it has got."

Rita says they're about ready to put me in Jacksonville, which means the nuthouse.

"Goodness!"

"What do you expect?" says Mavel. "You can't just go around all the time doing whatever you want."

I think to myself, I don't have to sit here all day and listen to this. I've got better things to do than that, I think. I take out my compact and look at the little round mirror and I look good, I'll tell you. I put on my lipstick.

I can hear them saying how I'm the same one who Hammer Johnson killed himself over.

I snap my compact shut. I only had the baby two and a half months ago, but I'm not fat.

I slide over in my booth. I stand up with the baby in my arms and they all three stop talking and stare at me with their mouths wide open. They're going back over all the things they said and it's as bad as it can be, they know that.

I look at each of them, one at a time. They're flung forward in their seats like when you slam on the brakes.

"You know it's funny," I say. "But none of you girls look like members of a superior race." And then I turn on my heel and go out the door, calling good-bye to the handsome Mexican that Sadie Pinshaw is sure to fall in love with someday, if she ain't already.

I walk out the door of Bill's Big Tacos and climb into my new baby blue Cadillac which is parked right in front of the big picture window where the girls are sitting. I can see the three of them, their round white faces turned to watch me and their little red mouths hanging open.

And each of them having the same thought. *It just ain't fair!*

I got a basket on the seat for Mae to lay in. The back seat is full of clothes. I turn the radio on and drive down the street. I got my windows rolled down and everybody who passes me looks because this is a new car in Palmyra and a Cadillac! and when they see who's driving it, they look again and see me wave.

When I get to the highway, I turn the radio up loud, and keep going. I don't look back. I just go. I pass by the cemetery where Mrs. Farrell planted the gingko trees for her husband, so long ago. I can see the tops of those trees from the highway. I can smell the river, from way over here.

People say all rivers run to the ocean, but I don't see how that can be true.

I think of the cemetery where the old pioneers are buried and the boys come in and tear down their markers and write bad words on them. And I try to think of that place the way I thought of it the first time I went there with Billy but I can't. I'm different now. And I take a hand from the steering wheel and hold it against my chest and feel my heart beating.

Aunt Janelle says it'll do me good to stay at her house. She says at her house she'll teach me hog processing like what she done with Evaline, so I can be useful, and Mama said that was a golden opportunity and I know she's thinking maybe then some good old boy will marry me after all, even with a child who ain't all the way white and a bad reputation, divorced and everything else. If you can process a hog, it counts for a lot. Aunt J's got extra room from when her boys lived there and the thought strikes me that now I've left the Fooshee side of the family and moved to the Hogg side but that don't bother me. I've been worse things.

Aunt Janelle lives in Whitehall but whether it's named after a hall that's painted white and it might have been called Greenhall or Bluehall just as easy, no one can tell me.

Billy said one time that every name has a clue in it. Now he's in Bowling Green and I wonder if it's bowling like the bowling alley and why you'd name a whole town after that.

There's a combine in the road in front of us and we're driving slow. The field next to us has horses in it. They've got their summer coats and their bodies shine in the sun like metal. They run along beside us, the sound of their hooves on the ground soft like drums, until they get to the end of their pasture and kick their heels out, whinny, veer off and race away.

The things we make up aren't nothing compared to what's really around us.

The turn off to Aunt Janelle's is up ahead but there's no question I won't be making that turn. I don't even have to wonder about it. Later I'll come to another turn and whether I take it or not, I'll just have to wait and see. I take off around the combine, waving to the farmer driving and him waving back.

I'm driving down Highway 100 along the Illinois

River which the Indians used to call the Big Blue Water, Billy said one time. He said the Illinois River goes all the way to St. Louis and then it joins up with the Mississippi River and goes on and on until the Gulf of Mexico. I never been to a gulf before, or a beach, and I never seen an ocean. Billy said that down south it's always warm except in summer and then it's hot. He said in New Orleans people walk around on the sidewalk at night, holding drinks in their hands and listening to music.

The baby starts to cry and I lean the bottle against her basket. She watches me while she sucks and then her eyes flutter and roll back in her head.

I pass the turn off to Beardstown and I remember Trudy Deere who got in an accident and wound up in the hospital bed next to me and how she had died for one whole minute and seen angels. Just a regular old farmwife from over to Beardstown and she got to see that. Those angels told Trudy Deere she wasn't living her life's purpose which surprised me, even if it didn't surprise old Trudy herself, the idea that someone like her would have a purpose that angels knew about and here they were, reminding her. Well, she forgot again, wouldn't you know.

I been on this same road a thousand times, but today it's different. It's just Highway 100, running from Hardin to St. Louis, I tell myself. It's not the road where I live anymore, but the road I'm leaving from. Someday I'll tell Mae about this place, where she's from. I'll tell her about the wide flat fields of corn and the gingko trees with leaves shaped like tiny fans. I'll tell her about the Dunavans' horses and the river and the birds there that fly up out the brush. I'll make a story out of it and tell her while she lays in bed.

I turn the radio up loud. Mae is asleep but she doesn't mind noise. It's Patsy Cline singing about walking in the moonlight. The words are sad but it's got a happy feel. I'm driving but I'm not driving fast. I look at each thing as we go, so I can remember it. I look at the green soybeans, low to the ground, and the rows of corn, tall and brown. Every now and then we pass a big white house and a barn. There's a pasture with cows and there's a dog, barking from a front porch. Each of those things is sharp, like it's been traced with a red pen and cut out with a pair of scissors. Above us the sky is a fierce blue and, on every side of us, the horizon goes on forever.

## Acknowledgments

Many days I sat at my computer wondering if I should be doing something else instead. Washing the windows maybe or mowing the lawn. Many people have encouraged my writing and I'd like to thank some of them here. Chuck, first of all, and our children, Charlotte and William (Sasha). Candice Fuhrman, my agent and friend, for her unrelenting support. My writer's group, Sara Backer, Dorothy Blackcrow Mack and John Ginn. Friends and readers, Carolyn Lochert, Karin Power, Steve Mainville, Maggie Pondolfino, Frank de Pirro, John Swanson, Bruce Holland Rogers, and my sister, Tamara Taylor. My mom, Mari Dunavan Clement, for checking facts with the ladies at the Rushville, Illinois Genealogy Center. Sue Hyde, who saw me through my own personal Palmyra. Thanks also to the people at MacAdam/Cage, especially my editor Pat Walsh, for cheering me on.